HE'D RATHER BE DEAD

AN INSPECTOR LITTLEJOHN MYSTERY

GEORGE BELLAIRS

AGORA BOOKS

ABOUT THE AUTHOR

George Bellairs was the pseudonym of Harold Blundell (1902—1982). He was, by day, a Manchester bank manager with close connections to the University of Manchester. He is often referred to as the English Simenon, as his detective stories combine wicked crimes and classic police procedurals set in quaint villages.

He was born in Lancashire and married Gladys Mabel Roberts in 1930. He was a devoted Francophile and travelled there frequently, writing for English newspapers and magazines and weaving French towns into his fiction.

Bellairs' first mystery, *Littlejohn on Leave* (1941), introduced his series detective, Detective Inspector Thomas Littlejohn. Full of scandal and intrigue, the series peeks inside small towns in the mid twentieth century, and Littlejohn is injected with humour, intelligence and compassion.

He died on the Isle of Man in April 1982 just before his eightieth birthday.

ALSO BY GEORGE BELLAIRS

Death Drops the Pilot

Death in High Provence

Death Sends for the Doctor

Corpse at the Carnival

Murder Makes Mistakes

Bones in the Wilderness

Toll the Bell for Murder

Corpses in Enderby

Death in the Fearful Night

Death in Despair

Death of a Tin God

The Body in the Dumb River

Death Before Breakfast

The Tormentors

Death in the Wasteland

Surfeit of Suspects

Death of a Shadow

Death Spins the Wheel

Intruder in the Dark

Strangers Among the Dead

Death in Desolation

Single Ticket to Death

Fatal Alibi

Murder Gone Mad

Tycoon's Deathbed

The Night They Killed Joss Varran

Pomeroy, Deceased

Murder Adrift

Devious Murder

Fear Round About

Close All Roads to Sospel

The Downhill Ride of Leeman Popple

An Old Man Dies

He'd
Rather Be
Dead

GEORGE BELLAIRS

"Tobacco, coffee, alcohol, hashish, prussic acid, strychnine are weak dilutions: the surest poison is time."

EMERSON

To Anne and Tom

1

THE MAN WHO ROSE FROM NOTHING

Perhaps someday a worthy biographer will write the life story of Sir Gideon Ware as a signpost to guide the young to success.

Here, however, we are mainly concerned with his death, which occurred at the height of his fame and fortune and shook the country from end to end.

Gideon Ware was born in Hull. We know nothing of his parents, for he never mentioned them in after life, except to tell how they threw him out at the age of twelve to earn his own living. At twenty he was a bricklayer. At twenty-three he left Hull for personal reasons and turned up at Westcombe. He was sixty when he was murdered at the banquet he was giving to celebrate his election as mayor of the place.

In its early days, Westcombe was a highly respectable, almost austere resort. Frequented by select little family parties, who boarded at very sedate establishments on the sea front and came year after year at exactly the same period. A small, rough promenade, a few bathing huts and very discreet Pierrots. Little else. By ten o'clock in the evening, the children were all in bed, their elders indoors preparing to retire, and the whole town peaceful and quiet.

Look at it now, as left by its benefactor, Sir Gideon Ware!

It has absorbed its neighbours one after another with insatiable appetite.

Miles of level, concrete promenade fronting an area five times that of the original borough. Acres of pleasure beach, embracing every kind of device for human entertainment and sensation. Huge hotels, cinemas, theatres, ballrooms, bars. Enormous restaurants and railway stations. During the season, the latter can hardly hold the vast throngs which come and go from and to every part of England.

Shouting, singing, brawling and dancing go on until the small hours of the morning.

Nothing remains of the original Westcombe but the quaint little harbour, which the mushroom town has thrust aside like a poor relation, down by the riverbank, where the fishermen take home their boats at night after days of pleasure tripping.

When first he arrived in Westcombe, where bricklayers were temporarily in demand, Ware called at a small beer-house and there, over a pot of ale, overheard two men arranging to buy land for development. Gideon left his beer and somehow contrived to secure an option before the pair of jerry-builders. He made two hundred pounds out of the deal; and that was the beginning. After that, Gideon Ware set about Westcombe with a will!

He might not, of course, have remained so firmly wedded to the place but for an accident. In 1913, Ware tried his luck elsewhere, overstepped the mark, and became bankrupt. By that time, he was a member of clubs in various parts of the country. When disgrace came his way, those august institutions, metaphorically speaking, passed by on the other side. Each of them accepted his resignation from membership before he had time to tender it.

All except the Westcombe Constitutional Club. Its committee were so busy cashing in on the building boom that they quite forgot to blackball Gideon. *He* never forgot it. He thought of the WCC as his friend indeed and when he re-made his fortunes and earned a knighthood in 1918 by building huts for the Government, he made straight for his old haunts, settled down there for good, and gave the WCC the finest headquarters that money could buy.

He then set out to put Westcombe on the map, and, by Jove, he did it with a vengeance! Look at the posters on every hoarding and the hundreds of thousands of guidebooks annually scattered nationwide!

Sir Gideon would not, however, join the town council until he had had enough of building and finance and decided to retire and become a gentleman. Then he put up and was elected. Two years later he became Mayor, long before his rightful turn.

And now, we take steps to be in at the death.

It is about noon on a sunny day in August. The awning is out over the door and approach of the Town Hall at Westcombe. The red official carpet has been unrolled on the steps and the corporation silver plate has been taken from the bank and laid on the tables of the banqueting hall. This is the day on which His Worship the Mayor gives his annual lunch to the Borough officials.

A number of holiday-making sightseers have gathered in knots on the pavement, and two policemen have arranged them in orderly and becoming lines. When, however, the audience discovers that the Prime Minister or, at least, the Regional Commissioner is not expected, but only the Mayor and retinue, they begin to melt away. They can see such palavering at home any day!

By old custom in Westcombe, the officials honour the Mayor by a dinner each November after his election. His Worship returns the compliment in August, when visitors are in full spate and are in the mood to gasp and gape and say how wonderful it all is.

This Year of Grace 1942, it is to be something special. For, whenever Sir Gideon Ware does anything, he beats the band. This time *No Expense Spared* and Black Markets shriek from the menu.

Hors d'oeuvres.
Barley Cream Soup or Clear Cold.
Fillets of Sole Mornay. Anchovy Sauce.
Lamb Cutlets and Peas. Fried Potatoes.
Cold Chicken and Tongue.
Cold Asparagus. Salads. Tomatoes.
Fruit Tart and Cream.
Charlotte Russe.
Bombe Gideon.
Cheese. Celery. Fruits. Coffee.

Canon Silvester Wallopp, incumbent of the largest church in Westcombe, could not resist it! An epicure of the first water, he had firmly decided to give the lunch a miss, but when he saw the menu (the chef, who was a member of his flock, let him have a peep) he gave in.

The Canon has been deeply offended by the Mayor. Hitherto, he has been Mayor's Chaplain, *ex officio*. Ware is a Roman Catholic, but instead of appointing the priest, Father Manfred, has picked the Rev Titus Gaukroger, head of the Beach Mission, if you please! "He's put religion on the map in Westcombe," said Sir Gideon. "Honour where honour's due, I always say." And it was so.

Canon Wallopp is by far the most imposing of the guests. Six feet and clad in fine raiment. A heavy, round red face with roving little eyes. Viewed through the golden glass of the vestibule where we first meet him, wondering where he's left his ticket of invitation and fuming inwardly because he can't enter without it, he looks like a dogfish in aspic. Some toady once told him he was the image of Cardinal Wolsey. Later, our friend Inspector Littlejohn is to notice in him a strong resemblance to a casual alcoholic tout who shouts loudly in front of a cheap-jack-auctioneer's shop on the promenade. The Canon is a bachelor, too, and very partial to innocuous dalliance with young ladies, like the warden of a seraglio, or as he himself expresses it, *in loco parentis.*

Now, the Canon walks eagerly into the dining hall, cutting dead on the way the Official Chaplain and Father Manfred, slips on the polished floor and measures his length. Fortunately, this accident in no way impairs his appetite, for he later gormandises his way steadily through all the courses, alternatives and all.

The great hall of the Municipal Buildings is fine and spacious, the embodiment of the prosperity of a community which derives its extensive revenues from its enterprises. The dining tables are dwarfed by their surroundings, Lilliputian, and are in the centre of the polished parquet on which Canon Wallopp has just come a cropper. Tall pillars of waxed sycamore, exquisitely grained, soar upwards to an arched roof, further enlarged by a great dome of transparent golden glass, which adds the tint of sunny wine to whatever kind of light penetrates through it.

On a dais at one end of the room, Sid Simmons and his Ten Hot Dogs play swing music. Sid is the permanent attraction at the Westcombe Winter Gardens (open from April until October only!) and has brought his "boys" and their hideous noises to honour the Mayor, free of charge. As the party enters, the maestro raises his silver trumpet to the heavens in ecstasy and, wringing his body in a series of awful convulsions, stamping his feet, and rolling his eyes, flings his own arrangement of Liszt's *Liebestraum* in a hundred cacophonous bits all over the place. Mr

Cuthbert Acron, Mus Bac, the town organist, takes Sid aside and reminds him that this is a solemn civic function, not a jungle wake or a Saturnalia. Thereafter, the maestro is in difficulties, for like certain cooks, he cannot concoct a straight dish, but specialises in garnishing existing stuff in odious or exotic trappings. He lays aside his trumpet sadly and for the rest of the time grimaces and waves his hands at the boys who distastefully and unsteadily plough through Strauss waltzes and polkas by Offenbach.

A congratulatory group gathers round the Mayor. They shake his hand and exchange pleasant or barbed greetings. Sir Gideon makes for the high table and takes his place. Like a flock of rooks alighting, the rest seem somehow to shake themselves into order in next to no time.

Sir Gideon is clad in his official garb. Purple robes trimmed with scarlet and ermine. Cocked hat and chain of office, the latter with a gold link, an inch long, for every Mayor since the creation of the borough — thirty-six of them. What it will be like at the centenary celebrations is a faint municipal nightmare already!

Ware is a stoutly built man of middle stature, with short arms and legs. Round, florid face, sandy moustache, dark mottled complexion and eyebrows like tufts of grey cotton wool. His nose is small, snub and thick at the roots. Low forehead, merging into a bald head with close-clipped white hair at the back. His eyes are grey, malicious and set in pouches of wrinkles. With a podgy hand he gestures to the head waiter to begin.

Mr Gaukroger looks outraged and disappointed. They are starting without saying grace!

Grace has been waived. So have many other things, including formal arrangement of seating in order of precedence. Sir Gideon has fixed that according to his own dictatorial tastes and sense of humour.

"No toasts either," he also said.

"Oh, just one, sir…or two. First 'The King.' One to you; and another to the guest of honour," deferentially suggested the Borough Treasurer and mayor's major-domo.

"All right, then. But no more. There's too many coming who like the sound of their own voices. If we get *them* going, we'll be here all night and I've work to do in the afternoon, if you other chaps haven't."

He was always hinting that the corporation officials were underworked and overpaid.

The high-table guests, who have been hanging round His Worship's chair and place, dissipate themselves to their proper seats as indicated in the plan by the door.

There, in his glory, sits Sir Gideon.

Then, to his right, the guest of honour, Mr Wilmott Saxby, chairman of the neighbouring Urban District Council of Hinster's Ferry. A square-set, little fellow, with a mop of white hair and a little white moustache. He looks surprised to find himself where he is.

Beyond Saxby, the Rev Titus Gaukroger, gaunt, bony, long faced and pale. With long, knobby fingers he clutches the water carafe specially placed before him, for he is fanatically TT. By his side at the extreme end of the table, Canon Wallopp cutting him dead and concentrating on the victuals.

At Sir Gideon's left hand is the Town Clerk, Mr Edgar Kingsley-Smith, a tall, lean, clever-looking solicitor and a member of an old Westcombe family. Next comes the Deputy-Mayor, plain Tom Hogg, one of three Socialists on the Council. A sturdy, forthright man is Tom, beloved of all the working classes, son of a fisherman and himself a carter until his trade union made him their secretary.

Lastly, Father Manfred. A long, cadaverous ascetic countenance, with burning eyes and no hair whatever on his head or face. This defect gives him a clean-swept, reptilian appearance.

A good friend and a terrible enemy, this Jesuit might be found any day chasing the alcoholic members of his flock from the pubs with a stick or walking along the promenade with six little boys and girls laughing on either hand. The sight of him in a street where Catholics are rioting brings an awful hush over the place, whilst children will rush from the houses yelling with joy and prattling to clutch the skirts of his cassock.

On the two arms which radiate from the high table are posted the lesser lights according to Sir Gideon's malicious sense of humour. Opposite Mr Oxendale, the bank manager, sits Mr Oliver, the Borough Treasurer, with whom he is always quarrelling about rates of interest and commission. Mrs Pettigrew, JP, Chairman of Magistrates and a member of the old aristocracy, faces Mr Pott-Wridley, Head of the Department of Dry Goods and Edible Oils, evacuated to Westcombe from London, and who has requisitioned Pettigrew Hall and forced Mrs Pettigrew to live over the stables. They cannot bear the sight of each other and glare ferociously through their transparent cold soup. The same applies to two other partners, Mr Harold Brown, the Magistrates' Clerk, who has been turned out of his spacious business premises by the Department of Poultry and Incubation, whose Principal is his *vis-a-vis*, Mr Ryder, OBE. Mr Boumphrey, the Chief Constable of Westcombe, alone is blessed by having no comrade in hate opposite him or by his side.

On the other arm of the tables, the Medical Officer of Health, McAndrew, frowns across at Liptrott, editor of the *Westcombe Gazette*, which has resisted his campaign against inadequate hospital accommodation in the Borough. Opposite Mr Openshaw, Borough Accountant, sits his implacable opponent on matters of expenditure, Mr Barcledyne, Chairman of the Westcombe Development Board. There follow Messrs Whyte, MA, and Budd, Headmaster of the Westcombe Grammar School and Chairman of the Pleasure Beach Proprietors' Alliance respectively, a pair like cat and dog — one very superior, the other grossly ignorant scholastically, and proud of it.

Beyond these, a medley of magisterial, municipal and administrative nonentities.

The only women present are officials of the town, and magistrates. Male diners are not accompanied by wives or other feminine counterparts. The women of Westcombe have taken this badly and are planning to boycott Lady Ware's "At Home" next Saturday, which means that they'll probably all turn up smiling.

A limited choice of wines has been brought to light from mysterious sources and circulates. The epicure is not impressed, for whilst the quality of some is good, they are served indiscriminately, without regard to the dish accompanying them.

Those at the high table drink from ceremonial silver goblets, the freak gift of a past mayor anxious to impress. That of Sir Gideon bears the Corporation's arms in fine enamel. It is the mayor's cup! The lesser lights lower down drink from glass vessels.

Oswald, the head waiter, has given the signal. His underlings begin to deploy and circulate like planets round the sun. They must be subject, like the orbs of heaven, to some law, but only Oswald seems to know it. They race hither and thither, sweating, running, serving with little jerky movements which convulse the whole of their bodies. At any time, one expects them to rise from the floor and fly over and around the guests like winged Mercuries, dropping the courses like manna on their plates.

Soup. Joint. Sweets. The tail-end of the repast. They all come and go. Canon Wallopp ploughs through them. Now he's busy at the asparagus, like a conjurer who has swallowed a hard-boiled egg and immediately afterwards tugs from his gullet the flags of all nations. Again, pecking at the celery, like a huge, corpulent parrot at a chunk of cuttlefish. Noisily, too. Clickety-chup. Clickety-chup. Gulp. Like those of a voracious earwig the great mandibles of the Canon chew their way through Sir Gideon's eatables.

The board is cleared. Coffee, and cigars for those who speak in time. Cigarettes for the rest.

The toast "The King" is drunk with enthusiasm.

Mr Kingsley-Smith is on his feet. The town clerk is a good speaker. Calm and polished. But he is not too comfortable at present. Sir Gideon is a difficult one to whom to hand bouquets or render thanks. Still, as head official, Mr Kingsley-Smith must rise to the occasion. He balances himself on his heels, slips a nonchalant hand in his pocket and beams around.

"Mr Mayor, ladies and gentlemen…"

And he goes on to look here, upon this picture, and on this. Westcombe before Ware; Westcombe after…and so on. Like an advertisement for a patent medicine.

All the time, Sir Gideon regards him with a twisted smile, mingling pride of achievement with scorn for the orator.

"…and raise your glasses with me in a toast to our Mayor, Sir Gideon Ware. His Worship the Mayor!"

There is a shuffling of feet and a scraping of chairs. The Canon just manages to raise himself by swinging on the table.

"HIS WORSHIP THE MAYOR!"

The crowd mutters it like a response in church.

The clatter subsides.

Sir Gideon rises. He doesn't look well. His face is pale, and he seems like one in the first stages of influenza. Whether he has taken a chill, too much wine, or the food's a bit "off", it is hard to say. However, he rallies.

Ware's diction is good. Not in vain has he spent a few hundred pounds and five years' study on courses in elocution and "the art of psychological speech." His private secretary, too, is a past-master of speech writing.

He renders formal thanks and then turns to his right-hand neighbour and proposes "Our Visitors."

Mr Wilmott Saxby gives Sir Gideon a sidelong, upward glance. He has not been brought here for nothing and well he knows it! Hinster's Ferry is the last UDC in the district to hold out against the encroachments of the new Westcombe. In the river Swaine, Hinster's Ferry has its "moat," its protection against the assaults of the sprawling, upstart resort. It is a small fishing village, with little or no promenade, but a certain type of visitors like it immensely, for it is quiet and unspoiled. A tiny harbour with a few yachts, an annual regatta, good fishing in the river and the Swaine Deep beyond, and little besides. The ferry-boat crosses every quarter-hour, taking visitors to and fro, and the last one goes at ten-thirty. After that a deep peace descends, broken only by the sea and the rustle of winds across the salt flats. Hitherto the river has acted as a sanitary cordon against the vulgarity of Westcombe.

Sir Gideon, unable to extend the promenade and absorb the tempting resort over the water, wants to build a bridge, and the Hinster's Ferry UDC, headed by Mr Wilmott Saxby, have resisted like mad, and with success.

But when Sir Gideon is intent on anything, he concentrates every power of his mind, wind, limb and purse on the task.

Wilmott Saxby is the bastion. For years he's held out. To yield would ruin Hinster's Ferry and all its charm. But lately, Ware has been gradually getting his yes-men on the UDC. In fact, Wilmott Saxby has now only a majority of one on his side against the amalgamation and the bridge.

Is Ware now going to announce publicly his final triumph?

"...of course, Mr Wilmott Saxby and I differ on minor matters. Who doesn't? For example, the joining of our two communities and the building of a bridge..." (loud laughter).

Sir Gideon pauses. What's the matter? He eases his collar,

mops his sweating brow, and wipes his lips. He clutches the table and, by a supreme effort of will, goes on.

"You all know I'm a man of progress. Progress. Progress. Progress or perish. As Pericles said, 'We do not copy our neighbours; we are an example to them.' Rather than stagnate…rather than stagnate…"

He is in great distress. The Town Clerk rises and fills a goblet with Mr Gaukroger's water. Ware waves it aside.

"Stagnate! I'd rather be dead!"

And with that, he collapses, slips down in his chair, sprawls there for a moment and slides to the floor beneath the table.

The assembly rises in great confusion. McAndrew, the Medical Officer, rushes to Sir Gideon's side and they move the Mayor behind his chair. Ware is convulsed. His body arches and becomes shockingly contorted. His breath comes and goes with great labour and in painful jerks.

"Is it a fit?" asks Wilmott Saxby.

Hastily, the doctor sends the first man he sees as he raises his head for the ambulance.

"We must get him to hospital right away…"

"What's the matter, McAndrew?" asks the Town Clerk with a trace of impatience.

But the MO is not committing himself. It is Father Manfred who breaks the tense silence.

"Looks like strychnine to me, doctor."

McAndrew purses his lips and nods. He has sent for his bag to his room in the building and this arrives just as the orderlies from the ambulance enter with their stretcher. Even as they bear out the wretched Ware, the doctor continues in his efforts to administer an emetic.

The Chief Constable, a heavy, officious man, takes charge of the situation.

"Close all the doors," he bawls. "Nobody's to leave unless I say so."

"Where are *you* going, Father Manfred? Nobody's to leave."

But the priest thrusts him aside.

"I am going where I'll be needed before Sir Gideon reaches his journey's end," he says and strides from the place with purposeful steps and enters the ambulance with the patient.

The good priest was right. On the way, Sir Gideon Ware died.

2

A BREATH OF EVIL

The Chief Constable of Westcombe County Borough was a huge man, with a face like a bulldog and a militant manner. The latter arose out of half-conscious feelings of inferiority, for he had risen from the ranks and possessed none of the inborn advantages of breeding and impudence which characterise some of the holders of sinecure headships.

Boumphrey, as Superintendent of Police in a distant seaside place, had recovered with remarkable speed a pearl necklace stolen from Lady Ware. When the former Chief Constable retired, full of years and honour, from Westcombe, Sir Gideon made up his mind that Boumphrey was the man for the job, focused all his powers on the end in view, and secured his election without even the compilation of a short-list.

That does not mean to say, however, that Boumphrey was pitchforked, inefficient, into a ready-made job. He was a competent, painstaking, conscientious and ambitious official. His force was as smart as any in the land and carried out its duties, often under difficult conditions, with the greatest skill and zeal.

The Chief Constable's main stumbling block lay in his education. He had to acquire polish and *savoir-faire* in the hard school of experience. Trial and error and plenty of hard knocks and false steps on the way. For example, the time when, mounted on a white hack hired from a livery stable, he rode at the head of his men in the Jubilee procession…

Boumphrey's blustering manner and loud voice concealed many doubts and misgivings.

He took over the situation following Sir Gideon Ware's suspicious collapse at once. He dived in at the deep end and, irrespective of the rank and prestige of the assembled guests, closed all the exits of the Town Hall. Nobody at all was allowed to leave, except the Medical Officer and Father Manfred.

"And now, ladies and gentlemen, I'm sorry to appear officious at this unfortunate juncture, but I shall have to ask you all to remain where you are until we take a list of those present," he said, mounting on the dais where Sid Simmons was still sitting with his pustular face looking like cold rice pudding. "After which, you'll all be able to go about your lawful occasions."

"But haven't you a list of the guests already, Chief Constable?" drawled the Town Clerk, ever adept at explaining the law, but very contemptuous of its executive machinery.

"I beg your pardon, sir, but you'll kindly leave me to handle this. There *is* a list, but there may be more or less in the way of guests here than it contains."

"Dear me!" replied Mr Kingsley-Smith, and drained a goblet of black market Vougeot, whilst his deputy could hardly restrain his joy at thus hearing his boss put in his place for perhaps the first time.

Mr Boumphrey issued loud and rapid orders to a small posse of his men who had appeared on the scene like genii of the lamp.

"You, Jacques and Williams, take the names of all the ladies and gentlemen present." Then, to the assembly, "Those concerned will be interviewed later."

"And you, Hibbert and Schofield, go to the kitchens and see

that all the pots, pans and dishes are left just as they are." Again to the waiting throng: "Nobody's to touch anything on the tables from now on, *if you please.*"

"Winrow and Faragher...you search the building for anybody hangin' round and not connected with the proceedings, takin' names and addresses..."

And so on. The Chief Constable deployed his troops like a general in action and many there gaped in silent admiration.

It was past tea-time when the army of officials presented their reports to their chief.

The tide had gone far out on Westcombe Sands, leaving a vast expanse of shining shore glittering under the setting sun. Children in hundreds fell-to with buckets and spades, erecting sandcastles and pies or grubbing among the seaweeds and in rock pools for treasure. Some caught crabs and shellfish, others poked at starfish or mussels on the rocks, and a few fell headlong into one or other of the hundred and one salt-water streams and were hustled off howling to their hired beds. Boumphrey stood at the window of his office in the Town Hall watching with unseeing eyes.

A breath of evil swept over Westcombe. A special edition of the *Gazette* bore an eye-witness's account of the tragedy. "DEATH STALKS IN WESTCOMBE!" Boumphrey had forgotten to place a seal on Liptrott's lips, and he was terribly annoyed with himself for his oversight.

The visitors to Westcombe waited eagerly for something to turn up. The Mayor had been done-in. What a sensation! Better than a side-show or an evening at the pictures! Perhaps it would be the Town Clerk next!

Sid Simmons and his Hot Dogs, who had enjoyed seats in the dress-circle for this shattering event, played as men possessed that night at the Winter Gardens, tearing apart Tchaikovsky, Chopin and César-Franck like savages on the warpath, to the exaltation of all the dancers present.

The multitude of diverse organs and loud-speakers on the pleasure beach continued their harsh, blaring accompaniments to sensations of bobbing-up and bobbing-down swinging, flying, gyrating and quaking eccentrically provided in plenty for all who came. The Corporation undertakings, consisting of the Winter Gardens, the two Pier Pavilions, the Botanical and Zoological Gardens, and the Municipal Restaurant, had not closed down, in spite of the decease of the civic head. Too dangerous to leave the teeming crowds of holiday makers with nowhere to go and nothing to keep them occupied. *Dolce far niente* might be all right in working hours, but on holidays would be an outrage and would certainly cause trouble for already harassed officials and probably bring in a crowd of embarrassing sightseers and amateur investigators to confuse the trails of the Ware murder case.

Boumphrey glanced through the reports on his desk and groaned.

All the washing-up done before His Worship collapsed! Or, at least, all the dishes were immersed in water and the pans scrubbed.

Wineglasses and goblets tested with negative results. Banqueting room meticulously searched for poison bottles or packets, in vain.

Portions of remaining food carefully analysed for poisons. Nothing.

Mr Kingsley-Smith, who combined a good memory with excellent powers of observation, had given precise details of the courses and wines taken by the Mayor.

Those dishes and the stub of Ware's cigar had been diligently gone through by the County Analyst and his staff. The dregs of the mayoral goblet, too. No good.

How had the poison been administered? Admitting, of course, that it *was* poison. May have been a fit, heart failure or apoplexy. But McAndrew had stuck to his provisional diagnosis and the police surgeon had concurred. The body of Sir Gideon was now in the mortuary awaiting their further attentions.

Boumphrey cursed under his breath. Why hadn't they heeded him when he applied for a proper laboratory and pathological department? Instead, Sir Gideon had been foremost in brushing him aside. Fantastic nonsense; better spend the money on advertising the town! Now, the viscera of the very man who'd opposed him would have to be shipped-off to the Home Office pathologist for examination whilst the grass grew under Boumphrey's feet.

Boumphrey picked up the list of guests at the luncheon and ran his eye over it. In imagination he saw them all again assembled in the great hall and as he read their names, little pigeon holes seemed to open and disgorge their unsavoury contents into his consciousness. Facts and incidents half-forgotten, but now grown tremendously important. A bright lot some of the guests and no mistake! Hate, fear, envy, jealousy stalked everywhere. Sir Gideon was truly surrounded by his enemies when he died!

The Chief Constable was a keen student of other Chief Constables and their methods, from the highlights of detective fiction to men like M Chiappe, deceased, and Herr Himmler, unfortunately still alive. In the room adjoining his own, Mr Boumphrey kept a vast system of card indexes, dossiers of all and sundry in Westcombe and district. Presided over by the best little rooter he'd ever met, Horace Powlett, a sort of minor replica of M Fulgence Tapir, of Anatole France's *Penguin Island*. Some of those files would now come in useful. Boumphrey licked his lips and stretched in his chair like a huge cat. There were few indiscretions committed by the bigwigs that he hadn't caught and imprisoned in Horace's steel cabinets. A breath of scandal confirmed by a little private investigation; a scrap of strange behaviour, added to another scrap or two like the pieces of a puzzle; a chance word dropped in a public house and overheard; a secret meeting after dark and mentioned jocularly by the constable on the beat. These and a lot more, recorded, pondered over by Boumphrey, a few notes or deductions added and then tucked away by Powlett for future use. Dangerous as dynamite and as unsavoury as a charnel house! But Boumphrey placed great store by these records. They might, in the future, save him a lot of trouble in more ways than one.

The Town Clerk's mistress in London...

The time when the Borough Treasurer was £1,200 short in his books, visited his wealthy aunt, and "found" the mistake the day after.

Father Manfred's fearful row with Sir Gideon about the appointment of Gaukroger as chaplain...threats of fire on his head, damnation, striking him down dead by thunderbolts from an angry God...

The Chief Constable rubbed his great red hands as though preparing publicly to wash a lot of dirty linen.

He paused and pondered. This wasn't to his taste at all. He'd forgotten that the one man who'd support him in his unholy investigations was now lying on the slab of the morgue. No Sir Gideon to back him now! Henceforth, he was alone. His manner of conducting this case would make or break him in West-combe. Without exception, every one of those in the list of interviews was a power in the land. And one of them *must* have killed Ware. How many corns was he going to stamp on before he reached the right one? If he ever did!

Boumphrey burst into a cold sweat, straining at an ebony ruler until the veins of his hands stood out like cords. Even if he put subordinates on the job, the repercussions would be on his own head.

How could you question impartially a lot like the Town Clerk, Mr Wilmott Saxby, Canon Wallopp, Mr Oxendale, Father Manfred, without causing offence and endangering your position?

"You owed Sir Gideon quite a lot in private loans, didn't you, Mr Kingsley-Smith? I saw a letter from him once on your desk. A snorter it was, too. Good grounds for quietly killing him, eh?"

Imagine the Town Clerk's reactions!

Or, "Hasn't Sir Gideon been threatening to get your Head Office to move you from Westcombe Branch to a smaller one for incompetence, Mr Oxendale? He's a big shareholder in your bank, you know. Only his death would prevent your disgrace... and you've only four years before your pension, too."

Mr Oxendale, who nervously prefaced almost every sentence with "It's all a case of this..." would start spluttering indignantly and go straight to his wife's brother, who was an MP and was sure to talk to the Home Secretary about Boumphrey.

Or Mr Oliver, the Borough treasurer, who, Oxendale fashion, constantly introduced a parrot phrase in his speech. "Fr'instance..."

"You're in Sir Gideon's bad books, eh, Mr Oliver? As likely as not he'll get you the push as soon as he finds a chance. You remember how, in righteous indignation, you stopped him from beating a setter-dog with a putter one day on the golf links before a large audience...?"

And Oliver would say, "Well, fr'instance..." and make things awkward through his uncle on the Watch Committee!

A vision of Oxendale and Oliver, once irreconcilables, now drawn together in relief, standing on the Town Hall steps after their release from the death chamber, came before Boumphrey's mind. Both of them, eased of great burdens, palavering almost jocularly about the case.

"It's all a case of this, Oliver..."

"Fr instance, Oxendale..."

Outside on the promenade, a group of young men and women on their way home to tea trooped by singing and wearing paper hats. A girl detached herself, flushed, from the throng and a man chased her. A nymph pursued by a battered faun! Or was it a centaur? The pair of them tore along the concrete, the woman regulating her pace so that the man eventually came up with her. He seized her in his arms, and they halted, stared stupidly into each other's eyes, panting from their exertions and strange emotions, gawked at each other, and didn't know how to pass it off...

Boumphrey turned away in disgust.

The beach had cleared for tea and a melancholy light was settling over the distant sea. Gulls squabbled and cried like lost souls. A few sailing boats bobbed over the water, heading for harbour in the old town. Fishermen were digging for sandworms on the tide line.

For once, Boumphrey wished he could take a long holiday and contemplate the sea in peace. Here in this mecca of holiday makers, he felt like one faced with a delectable feast of choicest food and wine yet who longs only for a crust of bread and a cup of spring water.

His hand groped for the telephone.

"Give me Whitehall 1212, please. And hurry," he said. "Yes, I want Scotland Yard."

3

"THE CHIEF CONSTABLE IS A TIME-SERVER"

L ittlejohn's instructions were brief and to the point.

Sir Gideon Ware, Mayor of Westcombe, has been poisoned. The Chief Constable's got the jitters and wants our help. You'd better go and look after him. The sea air will do you good.

It was raining when Littlejohn arrived at Westcombe. The glass had been removed from the roofs of the long station platforms and passengers, encumbered by their baggage, broke into ungainly running, to avoid the waterspouts streaming from the unglazed girders overhead. There were many travelling, although it was mid-week.

The Inspector buttoned his raincoat from top to bottom and turned up the collar. Then, he inverted the bowl of his pipe and, passing through the barriers, reached the open street.

Acres of black and white promenade swept clean of people and shining like a mirror in the rain. Shelters and the doorways of shops crowded with holiday makers in summer attire wondering what to do. Already some bolder spirits were beginning to brave the elements and forming bedraggled little family processions, intent on reaching hotels or boarding houses in time for lunch.

Footsteps pattered behind Littlejohn, who turned to face a medium-built man in a dripping waterproof and bowler hat who was hurrying after him.

"Inspector Littlejohn?" said the man, who had a round, tanned face and a small straight nose. He looked fed-up with more than the weather.

"Yes..."

"I recognised you from a photograph I once saw of you... My name's Hazard. I'm a Detective-Inspector here. I came to meet you off my own bat. Such a thing would never occur to our Chief Constable."

"That's good of you, Hazard. I've chosen a rotten day to begin."

They shook hands.

"Yes. Weather's generally good about this time of the year and needs to be. We get more visitors here than we can cope with indoors in the season. Look at them..."

With a compassionate wave of his hand, Hazard indicated further groups of half-drowned people, clad in flimsy summer wear which clung soaked to their bodies and with grim, even offended looks, as though condemning Westcombe and all in it for a dirty trick.

"Are you on the case then, Hazard?"

"Who? Me? Not likely, Inspector. I'm the Public Morals Squad. Betting, soliciting, touting, indecent behaviour. That's my little line. I also test the thrills of the pleasure beach to make sure they're safe for the holiday makers. But murder... Oh, dear, no. Nobody but the Chief himself takes charge of such enquiries."

Littlejohn felt in a dream. A four-hour train journey, and no dining car. He'd sworn to Letty that the train was marked with an "R" in the timetable, but she'd slipped a substantial packet of sandwiches in his bag all the same. He was as dry as a bone internally, however. Then, to be greeted by rain plastered down one's front by a howling gale. And lastly, a disgruntled detective to meet him, running down the Chief Constable for all he was worth.

Hazard seemed to divine Littlejohn's thoughts.

"Had any food, Inspector? I see there was no diner on the train."

"I brought some sandwiches...but I haven't had a drink. I could do with one..."

"Come on, then. We'll soon put that right."

Hazard piloted Littlejohn to a large new hotel built in red brick.

"Like to have it at the bar...or...?"

"Let's sit in the window there and take our ease for a bit, Hazard. Then you can tell me what this business is all about."

"I've no standing, you know, Inspector. I can only tell you what I've picked up. Hi, waiter! What'll yours be, Littlejohn? ... Two pints of lager, then..."

Their table was in a long sun lounge, looking straight across the deserted promenade to the sea. The windows could be opened in fine weather, making an open air café of the place. There were not many customers, for it was lunchtime and meals were not served there.

The sea was choppy and the colour of lead. On the horizon, trails of smoke marked the paths of passing coasters. A lighthouse built on metal piles looked like a Meccano model in the far distance. The tide was almost full.

"It'll probably clear up with the ebb..." said Hazard and buried his nose in his tankard.

A party of Salvationists, headed by a band and carrying a rain-soaked banner, marched past, bravely singing and playing.

When the roll is called up yonder,

I'll be there!

Their refrain mingled with that of a strident loud speaker advertising the wares of a music shop.

> *'Twas a night*
> *Of delight,*
> *When I first met you...*
> *When the roll is called up yonder,*
> *I'll be there!*

There was a wild contest of cacophony for a minute or two, until the waiter closed the one window remaining open and shut it out.

"To tell you the truth, I've given in my resignation here," Hazard was saying. "I've got a transfer to Manchester. You see, I've two little girls and I don't want to bring them up in a place like this. It's a moral sink... Nobody knows better than I do. And there's no proper life here, you know, except amusing and catering. The season now lasts from March until well in November, with another little spurt at Christmas. Nobody's any time for anything but the superficial. You get what I mean...?"

"Yes. I think I'd feel the same myself if I'd kids to bring up."

"Haven't got any of your own, then?"

"No. We'd a little girl, but she died..."

"I'm sorry... Waiter! ... Same again. And bring me a packet of cigarettes."

"Besides," went on Hazard, "Chief Constable's a snorter. A regular time-server, if you ask me. He's risen from the ranks. Got on the right side of Sir Gideon Ware...the murdered man... and once you did that you were made. Ware pushed his appointment through."

"A bit unusual, that."

"Everything's unusual in the running of this place. It's all

31

Ware, Ware, Ware. Sir Gideon's word was law... Well, perhaps now there'll be a change. I'm not saying that Boumphrey...that's the Chief...isn't efficient. He's damned good at organising. But he's had no education in anything but police routine. Well, just take your own case. Here you are, a big man from Scotland Yard. You arrive in the rain after Lord knows how many hours' train journey. And Boumphrey never thinks of meeting you or telling anybody else to do it. It isn't an intentional slight or rudeness. It's just that he's no *savoir-faire*. *He* wouldn't expect to be met and welcomed and just hasn't thought you'd want it."

"I must confess I was a bit surprised to find nobody there to tell me the way. But it doesn't matter, so long as we know, does it?"

"No. Not really. But I happened to hear something about your arrival and thought I'd pick you up. Make you feel welcome... WELCOME TO WESTCOMBE, as the posters say. I hope I get a bit warmer reception in Manchester when I go next month."

"I wish you the best of luck, Hazard. I started there..."

"Did you really, now? Well, there's hopes for me, then. I suppose you know why they've sent for The Yard in this case."

"I understand it's a bit involved, the Mayor murdered and all that."

"Yes, but there's more to it than that. The murder happened at the Mayor's banquet and all the big shots of the town were there. They've all got to be questioned. So far, the Chief's spent his time bullying waiters and town hall attendants. He's not made a start on the high hats. That's *your* job. You see, Boumphrey's likely to be skating on thin ice when he starts on the bigwigs. He's not got Ware to protect him anymore and he's not popular in certain quarters. So, if he keeps out of it — except when the thing's solved and there's kudos flying around, of course — any blame or recriminations will be your pigeon."

"Yes. I see... Shall we be getting along to the police station?

Probably the Chief's expecting me."

They drank up and went out into the rain again. The weather was already improving, as Hazard had prophesied.

The officers did not speak much on the way. Littlejohn felt sure that whatever topic he opened it would eventually be turned to a discussion of the Chief Constable with whom Hazard seemed thoroughly disgusted. In fact, the man was positively disloyal, even infringing the rules of discipline in his views on his chief. He must be almost at the end of his tether. Littlejohn wondered what exactly Boumphrey was like. He had not long to wait, for the police headquarters were just down a side street off the promenade and about two hundred yards from the hotel.

"Don't mention my meeting you to the Chief," said Hazard, as he left the Inspector at the enquiry desk. "He might suddenly realise that he's given an exhibition of bad manners and get peeved with me. I've another month still to go, and he might take it out of me... See you again!"

The Chief Constable rose with outstretched hand as Littlejohn was ushered into his presence.

"Glad to meet you, Inspector. Had a safe journey? I heard that Hazard had met you at the station... Always get to know these things, you know. Boumphrey's my name. Expect you've heard of me."

Boumphrey seemed to think that his name had spread with the fame of Westcombe, blazoned over thousands of hoardings all over the country!

"Yes, sir. Glad to meet *you*, too. A most awkward time for an affair like this; right in the middle of the season, eh?"

"Yes. A very awkward time. *And* a very awkward victim, too. Has Hazard told you all that happened?"

"No, sir. He was more concerned with finding me something to quench my thirst. There was nothing on the train in that line. Hazard and I weren't long together."

"Hm. He's leaving us at the end of the month. Doesn't like the seaside apparently. Seems to think Westcombe's a bit *common*. So he's going to Manchester. No accountin' for taste, eh? Well, you've not come here for the life story of Hazard. Let's get to business. Like another drink of somethin' before we start?
"

"No, thanks. I'd like the full story and then to get down to work right away."

"I ought to tell you first that we've fixed you up at the best hotel in the place. The Grand. At the Corporation's expense. A place like Westcombe knows how to treat its guests."

"Thanks very much... I'm sure I'll be quite comfortable there."

"Have anything you like, within reason. Now to business. You know the Mayor's been poisoned. We haven't a properly equipped pathological department here, so His Worship's innards have gone to the Home Office. Our official surgeons, however, provisionally report death from strychnine."

"Strychnine, eh? Nasty death!"

"Yes. He died during the annual lunch given by the Mayor to the Corporation officials. Collapsed right in the middle of a speech, proposing a toast to our guests. *And* he was surrounded more or less at the time by men who detested him and with whom, for the most part, he'd recently quarrelled."

"Was he a difficult man to get on with?"

"I'll *say* he was. He was self-made and ruthless. His big idea was to put Westcombe, *and* himself, properly on the map. Anyone who ran counter to his aim...well...he just rode over 'em roughshod, that's all. He'd some queer ideas...you might almost call it a malicious sense of humour, except that he wasn't a humourist. No... I'd say rather, that he did queer things just to show he was his own master, and nobody could push him around."

"I see."

"You *will* see when you get going with the case. That's where my difficulty comes in. As I've said, all those present at the luncheon were town officers, magistrates, Town Clerk, Borough Treasurer...you know what I mean. The ones who were closest to Sir Gideon, that's the late Mayor... Sir Gideon Ware...the ones who were nearest to him were the big shots of the place. And it's difficult for me to go bald-headed for any of them. I've my position here to think about after the crime's solved and done with and...well...it's a bit awkward."

"I understand."

"Now, don't get me wrong. I'm not a coward. I'll tackle any of 'em. But they're a queer crowd of cusses and need a tactful approach. The prestige of Scotland Yard and a man like yourself will make 'em open up better than to me. They've to live with me after this thing's blown over. You'll go back to London and be forgiven and forgotten. See?"

In other words, thought Littlejohn, I'm to pull your chestnuts out of the fire. Well, it won't be the first time.

"I'm at your service, sir."

"That's the stuff! Any help you want, count on me, of course. Well, to begin with, here's a list of the guests and I've had a plan drawn to show where they were all sitting when the tragedy happened."

He passed a sheet of drawing-paper across the table. It was a well-finished piece of work and gave a bird's-eye view of the scene of the crime.

"Thanks. That'll be very useful. As regards those involved. Have any of them been interviewed yet?"

"A few. Not the main characters, though. I'm leaving those to you, as I said. You'll bring a fresh mind to 'em. My men, of course, are after the source of the strychnine... The Home Office report should be here tomorrow or the day after. That will throw light on the whole problem. Meanwhile, we assume that somebody gave Ware poison. How, we don't know till we get a proper medical report. Might have been in the wine, or the food, or anything."

"Perhaps we'd better go through the likely suspects and consider their chances of poisoning the victim. What about the food and drink?"

"No good. Every dish eaten and everything drunk by the Mayor was in the common pot, so to speak. Other folk had similar portions and suffered no after-effects. So there was no question of doctoring a dish behind the scenes in the kitchens."

"Any chance of a waiter adding poison en route?"

"We've covered that. Now, the doctors say that if the food and early wines had been doped, Sir Gideon would have passed out long before he did. In other words, the poison would have taken effect before the speech-making. Sir Gideon didn't take coffee. He took wine for 'The King' from the same bottle as others. He didn't drink his own health, which was the next toast, and he hadn't got to the part of the speech he was making in honour of the visitors where he'd to drink from his goblet. So, we're just left with a cigar he was smoking."

"What *about* the cigar?"

"Taken out of a box into which half-a-dozen others dipped as well. So there couldn't have been any pre-meditation. The head waiter, however, took it from Sir Gideon's hand after he'd chosen it and cut it for him."

"Ah..."

"Yes. And the head waiter had a grievance against the Mayor. Oswald Tuckett, he's called. Used to be head waiter at the Winter Gardens restaurant. A good job in the season. Sir Gideon got him sacked earlier in the year. Said he was impudent. Tuckett has an invalid wife who must live by the sea, so he's had to subsist on casual work since. Mathieson, the Corporation's catering manager, thought Tuckett didn't get a square deal against Sir Gideon, so on the QT used to get him jobs.

There are plenty in the season. Tuckett never tired of saying how he'd get even with the Mayor..."

"You've questioned him, then?"

"Yes. The cigar-end and the ash have been tested, too, with negative results. I can't see how cutting the cigar could have allowed the introduction of poison, can you? Anyway, put Tuckett on your list for a further grilling. He'd no alibi, of course. All he could say was that it was ridiculous to think he'd had anything to do with the death."

"How about the poison...? Have enquiries been made from chemists and such as to sources of supply?"

"Yes. We've drawn a blank so far, locally. Chemists, corporation labs have been visited. Now, we're on with the doctors. The stuff might have been bought out of town... We've contacted the County Police to ask if they can help, too."

"And I'll ask Scotland Yard, although that's throwing the net a bit wide."

"Yes."

"And now, what about the other guests with a grievance, sir? Can you give me some details?"

"Oh, yes. But I've a better plan than spinning a long yarn. I've a card-index system here that covers such things. In a place like this you never know what you'll want. We've a lot of dossiers," — he pronounced it "doshers" — "with all sorts of information we've gathered about this and that pundit in the place. Now, while I've been waiting for your arrival, I've brought the files up to date. Dictated a few notes about each to my secretary and there we have them..."

Boumphrey pointed a large forefinger at a pile of folders standing formidably on a small table.

"They're all yours and more besides. There's a room next door where you can work, Littlejohn. Meanwhile, perhaps you'd like to see our filing department. I pride myself on it... I'm keen on such things. Nothing like system and nothing like putting down little bits of information when you get 'em. Surprising how they come in at a time like this."

Boumphrey opened a door leading from his room and ushered his colleague into a moderate sized office with filing cabinets round every wall.

In the middle of the room, standing to attention beside his desk, was Horace Powlett, the guardian of it all. A tall, thin man, with stooping shoulders, a shock of unruly sandy hair and straggling moustache to match, and pale face and short-sighted eyes behind powerful spectacles.

Powlett offered a clammy hand to Littlejohn and said he was pleased to meet him.

"Inspector Littlejohn's to have the run of this place while he's here," said Boumphrey.

Powlett blinked with myopic astonishment. A great boon indeed! The Chief guarded his information jealously and forbade entrance except by special and personal permission each time. Boumphrey, followed by Horace, pointed out his treasures, like a curator taking a party round a museum.

"Fingerprints, photographs, records of my own staff. Then here's the doshers I was telling you about. My word, someone'd be surprised if they knew what was in those. Things they've forgotten themselves or that they think only them and God knows about…"

Littlejohn didn't like the atmosphere of the place or the idea of collecting dirty linen at all. It reminded him of the Nazis' private files or of the scandalous collections of private papers involved in pre-war French government corruption. He made for the door as quickly as he could.

As he turned to nod goodbye to the zetetic Powlett, Littlejohn noticed that Horace was taking from a drawer a new card and entering something on it.

"He's got me on the list!" he thought and lit his pipe to create a more healthy atmosphere.

4

AT THE WINTER GARDENS

"I'm sorry, Littlejohn, that I can't cooperate fully with you on this case, but you'll appreciate my difficulties."

They were back in Boumphrey's private room and settling the routine details of the investigation.

"You see, my job is one of constant coming and going all day long during the season."

Littlejohn didn't see but didn't tell the Chief Constable so. What he needed to be coming and going about more than anyone else, was a mystery, but the Inspector took it that Boumphrey was trying to excuse himself from the intimate and awkward contacts which would be encountered as the case progressed.

"But I'll tell you what I *will* do. You seem to have taken a fancy to Hazard. I'll assign him to showing you round, generally making you comfortable, and helping you out in matters of irritating routine if you need him."

Littlejohn was not aware that he had expressed any particular liking for Hazard to the Chief Constable but had to admit to himself that the Inspector of the Public Morals Squad would be a much better and more straight-forward associate than his chief.

"That'll suit me very well, sir, and, if you don't mind, I'd like now to get my things down to the hotel ready for an early start in the morning."

"Fine! Fine!" said Boumphrey, clutching one hand with the other. If he had raised them above his head, he would have looked like a boxer acknowledging the plaudits of his followers as he enters the ring. "I'll just ring the bell for Hazard, and you can become even better acquainted."

Hazard seemed agreeably surprised when he arrived and discovered his new assignment.

"That'll be a pleasant change," he said, *sotto voce*, and Boumphrey scowled disapprovingly at him.

"Well," said the Westcombe Inspector, "We'll be getting along to the Grand Hotel."

"Don't forget these, Littlejohn," said the Chief Constable, and pointed to the dossiers which he had selected, still reposing on their table. "They're confidential, so I'll lend you this briefcase. Lock it up and put it in a safe spot among your luggage. If you take my advice, you'll give those papers the once-over before you start. They'll help you to understand the parties of the case. Here's the key. The lock's a patent one and they'll be safe enough."

"What's the old chap been giving you there?" asked Hazard, as they descended the Town Hall steps. He was carrying Littlejohn's suitcase and looking in every direction for a free taxi.

"Files about some of the principal citizens, for perusal."

"Good God! Is the Gestapo at it already! I thought your briefcase smelled of stinking fish. However, as the CC says, it'll throw light on some of the hierarchical activities of Westcombe."

A taxi drew-up at length and they climbed in. The driver seemed disgusted at the shortness of his journey, for they merely drove two hundred yards along the promenade and were deposited at the doors of a huge edifice of concrete and glass, built in the most modern style of architecture and advertised as containing two hundred bedrooms all with H&C, box-spring beds, and conditioned air. There were also one hundred bathrooms, three lifts, a commodious air-raid shelter and a system of silent signals for summoning the staff to the bedrooms.

"Always best to drive-up in a taxi," said Hazard, "even if you only pick it up round the corner. Creates a healthy respect from the start. I booked you a room, and after a lot of haggling got one with a bath and view of the sea on the second floor, which is out of the way of dining room smells."

"That's decent of you, Hazard."

"Don't mention it. I'm only currying favour," replied the cynical supervisor of seaside morals. "Put down *New Scotland Yard* when you check-in, too. That'll knock 'em cold!"

Littlejohn did as his colleague advised, whereas the desk clerk began to scutter around and chatter excitedly like a macaw, rang the bell twice and thereby produced two page boys, who relieved Littlejohn of all his portable property and almost carried him in triumph to the nearest lift.

The bedroom was sumptuous, with a purple carpet, and eiderdown and bedcover to match. In the spaciousness of it, the bed seemed lost, but the ensemble brought to Littlejohn's mind a theatrical setting of a highbrow little theatre presenting a tragedy in which the Borgias smother a victim in bed.

The place smelled stuffy and Hazard hastened to open a window and let in the sea breeze. The attendant page boys rushed in horror to close it.

"The air's conditioned, sir," said one of them. "It's washed clean and warmed in the basement, and if you open the windows, you'll dirty the air and put the system out of order."

"Good Lord! It's a plot to suffocate the police before they've got started!" replied Hazard as if to himself, and he opened two more windows. The page boys rushed away to their burrows like a pair of startled hares and without waiting for a tip.

"Now before you start on the Chief's dark secrets, I suggest you see the parties in the flesh. Tonight is gala night at the Winter Gardens and most of them will be there. The place is owned by the Municipality and the principal Corporation officers have free admission. They serve the best food and drink in town and, as likely as not, most of the possible murderers will be there. If you're not too tired, I'd like to take you. Local high life and all that."

"I'll be delighted."

"Right. I'll call back in half an hour. Give you time for a shave and a bath, if you want one. We'll have a bite of food there and then do the rounds. There's the long bar where all the lads foregather. A troupe of all-in wrestlers, if you're a sadist. Organ recitals by Acron, Mus Bac, and anything from the rumba to corn-pickin' to the strains of Sid Simmons and his Hot Dogs..."

An hour later they were eating a surprisingly good meal for wartime in the mirror-hall of the Winter Gardens.

"Hullo, there's Oswald back again already," muttered Hazard. "That's the waiter just across by the door. The catering manager and Sir Gideon had a row about that fellow. Ware insisted on his being sacked for cheek, just because he found the place full when he called with a party, and Oswald said, quite reasonably, that he was sorry he couldn't just tell somebody else to leave and vacate their seats. He's soon been reinstated. One of your suspects, by the way. He was engaged as a casual head waiter for the fatal banquet by the caterers who had charge of the affair. Probably Ware arranged it by way of recompense. He was that way."

A small party composed of two men and two women passed the detectives' table.

"That's the deputy-Mayor, now the civic head again, and his wife, son, and daughter-in-law. A good scout is Tom Hogg. A rough diamond, who sat next-but-one to Ware at the feast of death. He's general secretary of the local Carters' Union, a Socialist, and a sworn opponent of the victim. They were always scrapping. Ware didn't believe in trade unions and their rates of pay and was for ever in trouble with his men and their officials. Hogg's putting up as MP for some division at the next General Election and Ware was backing his opponent. Said he'd one or two cards up his sleeve that would cook Tom's goose. So there you have another possible."

Littlejohn demolished an excellent apple charlotte and looked round the dining room, ablaze with the lights of heavy chandeliers and teeming with pretty women and prosperous-looking men, as well as humbler holiday makers doing themselves well while the going was good.

"There's Kingsley-Smith, the Town Clerk," said Hazard, raising his hand in salute to a tall, well-groomed, middle-aged man, sitting with a mixed party of six at a round table in an alcove.

"Likes the pretty girls, does the TC. His wife's not among that lot. A funny thing, you know, but at a seaside place like this, with the holiday feeling always in the air, things get slack. It's quite the habit in a certain set for husbands and wives to go about separately. Mrs Kingsley-Smith's probably inspecting the ARP nurses — she's a big shot in the VAD — whilst the old man runs around with somebody else's wife. They don't seem to think there's anything wrong in it, provided there's a party of 'em together."

Hazard reeled off the names of one local celebrity after another in quick-fire succession. The Borough Accountant and his wife, the latter rudely staring out of countenance a number of elegantly dressed young ladies and gentlemen, her husband's underlings by day, who now greeted him and his lady with varying degrees of familiarity. Mr Oxendale, the principal bank manager of Westcombe, who with his wife was entertaining the

Principal of the Department of Dry Goods and Edible Oils. The banker was consulting the menu and choosing what he thought was a tasteful meal.

"It's all a case of this…" he told the waiter.

Mr Ryder, OBE, of the Poultry and Incubation Office, glared from a solitary table at his antagonist, Mr Brown, the solicitor, dining with his wife. At yet another table, Mr Oliver, the Borough Treasurer, was regaling his wealthy aunt, a perfect tartar of a woman who couldn't make up her mind what to eat.

"F'rinstance," Oliver was saying, and after each spasm the old aunt shook her head peevishly.

The Inspectors were glad to leave the hot room, heavy with the scent of women and table-d'hôte.

"Let's just pop in and see the big attractions and then we'll see the habituals in the long bar," suggested Hazard, and led his colleague into the thickly carpeted corridor.

Through a heavy glass door they saw a thin gathering listening to Acron's recital. The organist looked like a contortionist, clawing at his four manuals of keys, trampling the pedals, whipping the stops in and out… Beyond, the strains of more savage music seeped through another entrance.

"The dance hall. Better seen from the gallery, Littlejohn."

They ascended a staircase and found themselves in a square balcony high above the dance floor. Light drinks and refreshments could be obtained there, but Hazard waved aside the expectant waitress. He led his friend to the edge of the gallery. Below was a remarkable sight.

Soft music ascended. Sid Simmons and his men were resting for the time being, or rather, all except the pianist and drummer. The former was playing tinkling cascades, without rhythm, apparently the first thing that crossed his mind. The tempo was made by his colleague, who was operating on his drums with what looked like wire pan-brushes. Wearing a look of intense, leering concentration, this percussionist leaned over his instruments, tickling them softly with his scrubbers, for all the world like a doctor auscultating a patient's chest.

Meanwhile, those in the body of the hall danced. There seemed to be thousands of them. Littlejohn had never seen anything like it. From his viewpoint it looked as if you couldn't throw a penny between any pair. Shuffling languidly, many hardly moving, but just rolling and swaying, others with heads askew and buried deep in their shoulders and with hindquarters rhythmically rotating, this great amorphous mass looked like the contents of a drop of pond water viewed under a microscope. Twirling, wriggling, revolving or oozing dreamily. A shot from a René Clair camera, showing heads going round and round.

Suddenly, at a signal from Sid Simmons, the whole thing changed. The Hot Dogs were torn by a frenzy of harsh sounds. Sid himself blew rending blasts on his trumpet and his "boys" began a series of the wildest and noisiest contortions.

A great wave of passion seemed to possess the dancers. As though into the drop of water under the microscope someone had injected a dose of toxic fluid. They began to fling one another about in the most savage abandon, now the closest of clinches between partners; then hurling themselves apart as though spasms of distaste had seized them. Arms, legs, buttocks, bosoms, heaved and smote those of their opposite numbers. On each face a look of intense concentration and unflagging energy. Almost involuntarily, Littlejohn's hand, resting on the balustrade of the balcony, beat a tattoo and his foot gently rose and fell to the rhythm of the band.

"Well, I'll be..." said Littlejohn, lacking words.

"Oh, this goes on every night. Same people, too," said Hazard. And as Sid and his boys finally ceased abruptly, the astonishing thing was that the recent protagonists grinned calmly at each other, clapped and shouted vociferously for more, and then, when the Hot Dogs responded, set grimly about each other with redoubled intensity.

"What about a drink after that," suggested Hazard. The two men descended the stairs and made for the long bar. On the way, the Westcombe officer opened yet another door, disclosing two huge lumps of flesh writhing in a rope ring to the diabolical shouts of hundreds of spectators, a good half of them women.

"Choke him!"

"Break his bloody arm!"

"Chuck him over the ropes!!"

"Tear his hair out!!!"

And the mountain least in labour thereupon buried a hand like a ham in his opponent's crisp thatch and tore out a handful, whilst the victim yelled his head off and contorted his face like a baboon.

"I've seen that sort of stuff till I'm sick of it," said Littlejohn, who in his earlier days, had suffered spells of duty in a district which revelled in such sports and frequently rioted or tried to murder the referee.

As they made their way to the corridor, the man who had lost his hair threw both his opponent and the referee, indistinguishable from each other by this time, right over the ropes, greatly to the satisfaction of all the ladies present.

"You know, Littlejohn, that troupe have their own doctor and he told me recently he'd never had a serious injury, let alone a hospital case, all the time he'd been with 'em."

A wilder burst of demoniacal cheering than ever signified that the ejected parties had recovered and, in turn, had hurled their enemy into the audience. The last thing Littlejohn saw through the glass doors of the hall was the two wrestlers allied in the common cause of attacking the referee.

The long bar of the Westcombe Winter Gardens is the evening gathering place of most of the local men-about-town. Nine-thirty, after the BBC news bulletins, sees such of them as are free from nocturnal duties, drifting in for their symposium before closing-time. The belated equivalent of the French *heure de l'aperitif*

Littlejohn and Hazard could scarcely find a place in the vast extent of counter on which to rest their elbows.

Enquiring eyes overhauled the "chap from Scotland Yard," whose arrival had already been noised abroad. Some wondered if he were on somebody's trail already; others were surprised to see him in that place of relaxation and entertainment, for they were under the impression that an official detective, like a bloodhound, diligently follows the scent to the exclusion of all else until the job is done. This, to a certain extent was true of Littlejohn, but he had his own methods of working. He placed great reliance on gathering atmosphere in his cases.

It was obvious that Hazard was regarded with respect and treated with the reserve which arises from it. He was greeted, but never with familiarity or invitations to "have one" with this or that of the customers there. Nobody slapped him on the back or called him "old man," although there were many there in the bibulous condition when a man's the friend of all the world.

Four barmaids and a cocktail shaker, who was incessantly convulsed, had their work cut out in satisfying the clamouring crowd.

"This lot's on me!"

"What'll you have?"

"Cheers!"

"Here's to you, old man."

All the questions and answers of the toper's litany. Faces growing more and more excited, flushed, or melancholy, according to how the drink took them. Gestures less and less restrained. Alcoholic bonhomie rising like the tide across the promenade outside.

A tall, athletic youngster, going to seed physically, probably through relaxing training, entered and was greeted by his cronies.

"That's young Christopher Swift, Ware's private secretary. Cambridge blue. Smart chap," said Hazard, and buried his nose in his glass. "You might like a word with him on his way out. He won't be here for long, I'll bet, with the funeral hanging over him."

A knot of men gathered round Swift, but grown suddenly subdued, as when a funeral passes by, or as when the chattering crowds at a French church service become suddenly hushed at the Elevation.

"Do you think this is the place to introduce one's self?" asked Littlejohn.

"Preferable to calling at the house, until things settle down. Better not make a show of approaching him at the bar. Let's take our glasses to that free table by the door and stop him as he passes."

Hazard was right. Swift merely had his drink and spoke a few words to his pals. Then he bade them goodnight and made for the door. He paused to give a friendly greeting to Hazard, who introduced him to Littlejohn.

"Glad they've got you chaps on the job so soon. Boumphrey's quite incapable of tackling this himself. Too scared of giving offence."

A friendly young chap with an open, healthy countenance and fair complexion. He squinted slightly behind his glasses when he looked you in the eyes.

"Sorry about all this," replied Littlejohn. "You must be having a worrying time. How is Lady Ware?"

"Taking it badly, I'm afraid. Whoever else liked or disliked the chief, she was his best friend. A regular trooper, bless her!"

"I'd like to talk with her, but don't feel like bothering her with all this upset."

"I wouldn't, if I were you. Not yet. It'll distress her. Can I do anything?"

"Well...just one question, please. Did Sir Gideon call anywhere on his way to the lunch?"

"As far as I can remember his programme...he opened his letters first thing after breakfast. Talked over them with me and told me in general terms how to deal with them. Then, to the Town Hall for official letters and any other civic matters. He hadn't long to spare there, for he'd an appointment with his doctor at eleven. A cold cure inoculation. He was terribly troubled by coryza in the autumn and that treatment did him a lot of good. After that, he was due at the Town Hall for the lunch."

"Who is his doctor...or who *was*...?"

"Preedy. There he is, at the bar, taking a late one with Fenwick, the dentist, a pal of his, and Miss Latrobe, his dispenser."

Swift pointed to a group of three, drinking cocktails soberly. Or rather, two of them were. The dentist seemed to be satisfying his thirst with tonic water.

The doctor was tall, slim and dark, with a sleek, well-groomed look about him. A cold fish, apparently, and very efficient by the look of him.

Fenwick, his companion, was a small, thin shrimp of a fellow with a long sallow face, hooked nose and dark, roving eyes. His streaky black hair was brushed back from a large, globular forehead.

The girl was striking and bold looking, with auburn hair, a slim figure, and was dressed in a well-cut tailor-made. She was quite at ease with the two men and admiring eyes from all parts of the room followed her movements and glanced enviously at her escorts.

Conversation between the trio seemed desultory. They looked to be rounding-off a tiring day with a moment's relaxation before breaking up and making for home. They seemed a bit out of place among that revelling throng and nobody intruded on them. One and another simply greeted them and passed on.

"Preedy seems to be easing-up after hours. He's a busy man, making great strides in his profession. He's a local lad, too. Born here and returned to practice in his hometown. Rather unusual," Swift was saying. "Fenwick, his friend, is on the water-waggon. Says he's got a duodenal ulcer and has to take care... Well, I'll be off, if that's all I can do for you. See you again. I'll let you know as soon as Lady Ware feels fit to see you. Goodnight."

Swift made a hot-foot exit, as though suddenly remembering many things to be done.

"Good chap," said Hazard. "The source of the fine speeches Ware used to make..."

Preedy and his two friends paid for their drinks and left the bar.

Fenwick spotted Hazard and stopped cheekily before him.

"Evening, Hazard. How's tricks...? Have a drink?"

"No, thanks, Mr Fenwick. We're just off."

"This the man from Scotland Yard we've all heard about?" went on the dentist. "Wish you luck, sir. A difficult business."

"Yes, so it seems," said Littlejohn. "Thanks for your good wishes."

Preedy and the girl did not approach the two detectives but waited with a show of patience for Fenwick to return. He, with a wave of the hand, joined them and they departed.

"Good-looking girl, Miss Latrobe. No better than she should be, though, if you ask me," remarked Hazard, gloomily. "That's what I mean when I say this isn't the place to bring up young-sters in. Look at 'em all. That group of lads, there. All of 'em in their teens and drinking like seasoned vessels with girls of their own age. What are their parents thinking of? I'd put 'em across my knee and wallop 'em. So many thousands are always round them, though, holiday making, that they get infected with the mood themselves and can't settle down to any serious everyday business.

"Once, this was a small, hard-working fishing community. Look at the legacy Ware's bequeathed to it! Gimcrack pleasure palaces, shoddy concrete, the holiday feeling three hundred and sixty-five days and nights of the year, and the enervating, decadent state of always being on the loose."

Littlejohn was only half listening to Hazard as he rode his favourite hobbyhorse. He was wondering about Sir Gideon's last port of call before his death-feast. The doctor's surgery for a hypodermic injection.

5

THE TEN DOSSIERS

The perfect black-out of the Grand Hotel, so necessary because it faces the sea, enfolds it and seals in its busy contents like a parcel carefully wrapped in thick brown paper. From outside the place looks like a towering abode of the dead. Break through the double vestibule which serves as a light-trap, however, and beyond is a humming hive of comfort and pleasure.

Flunkeys rushing hither and thither, or rather they *did* rush before the Forces took the most energetic of them. Now, many elderly waiters and other servitors have emerged from retirement or from those lower rungs of the below-stairs ladder down which they are forced by the passing of time. At present, the great place and its clients must be satisfied with middle-aged senior attendants and a host of grey-headed or physically unfit underlings, who do their best with failing, tired bodies, plantigrade or flat feet and memories which can only sustain half an order.

The dining room is a shadow of its former lavishness. Yet, it does very well, for there are sources of supply still to those who are "in the know," and many a housewife who has spent a morning queueing for fish, flesh and confectionery, only at the end of it all to find the day's stocks sold out, has to thank the management of the Grand Hotel for being up in the small hours and on the spot with a pocket full of cash far exceeding that available either to her or the more belated man who supplies her. The cellars, too… You can still manage a bottle or two of Champagne if you can pay for it; or if less expensive, Graves, Beaune, Moulin-au-Vent, or even Moselle or Hock. The other week, a customer for a bet ordered Chianti and Asti Spumante and got them!

The place was waking up when Littlejohn entered after leaving Hazard to his wife and family. The cinemas and theatres had just turned out, the Winter Gardens had put up its shutters for the night, and "Time, gentlemen, please," had been very definitely called in a hundred and one other places of refreshment by exhausted proprietors and managers. The guests of the Grand Hotel therefore returned to its public rooms, where the fact that they were living-in entitled them to alcoholic service for as long as the worn-out servants could carry their trays. The lounge was full, the bars and cocktail rooms could hardly hold another drinker, the thirsty throng had overflowed into the entrance hall and were occupying the chairs and settees there, and it was only by locking the doors of the dining room, ghostly with its tables laid for breakfast and its napkins folded in shadowy shapes like bishops' mitres, that the suave manager prevented the clamant guests from invading it and reducing it to a shambles, mitres and all! The writing room alone was a haven of peace. Tea, coffee and cocoa only were served there, and were being sedately consumed by elderly, scholarly, or totally abstaining clients, who from conservatism or stubbornness persisted in patronising the Grand Hotel when all the time they were like fish out of water there.

Littlejohn found the writing room and ordered a cup of cocoa. He always had one last thing at home and the smell of it when it arrived reminded him so much of his wife, Letty, that before he drank it — it was served scalding at any rate and useless for all practical purposes for several minutes — he indulged in a long-distance call to Hampstead at the expense of Westcombe Corporation and bade his wife goodnight, and told her he was behaving himself. As he spoke, his love of home was further increased by the sound of the grandfather clock chiming half-past-eleven in the hall of his flat. On the other hand, Mrs Littlejohn asked him for an explanation of the background of noise at his end, and he had to reply that it was the Westcombe Lodge of the Ancient Order of Oddfishers, terminating their proceedings by singing a ritual hymn which sounded like a cross between a dirge and "Nellie Dean."

Back in the writing room, the Inspector's drink had cooled sufficiently, although he vowed to himself that Letty could give the Grand Hotel points in making it, in spite of the fact that it was costing the Municipality a shilling! Suddenly, Littlejohn remembered the parcel of dossiers which Boumphrey had pressed upon him. He felt like taking a cursory glance at them and debated with himself whether to do it in the quietness of the writing room or in his Borgia bedroom. He decided finally on the latter, so entered the lift and was hauled to his own floor. This quarter of the hotel must have been reserved for the respectable, early retiring section of the clientele, for outside almost every room was one or more pairs of shoes. He was specially baffled by some leather bedroom slippers shut out from one of the bedrooms and contented himself by a jocular deduction that probably their owner had arrived home drunk, put out the mysterious footwear, and gone to rest in his boots! Sherlock Holmes would certainly have had a field day along that corridor.

Littlejohn changed into his dressing gown and travelling slippers, thrust out his own shoes, lit his pipe, and opened the briefcase containing Boumphrey's files. On top of the bundle was the neat plan of the seating arrangements at the ill-starred luncheon. The Inspector observed that there was a folder for each of the guests who sat near Sir Gideon. He took a sheet of notepaper from the rack on his writing table and made a list.

Canon Silvester Wallopp
Father William Manfred
Rev Titus Gaukroger
Ralph Arthur Oliver
Edgar Kingsley-Smith
George Bertram Oxendale
Percy Wilmott Saxby
Dr Alastair McAndrew
Tom Hogg
Harold Brown

All of them with deep-rooted grievances against Ware, all of them seated in a malevolent cordon round him when he collapsed, each one a potential red herring on whom to waste a lot of time and energy.

Furthermore, there was no dossier for Sir Gideon himself. That would have been useful indeed. And perhaps so would one of Boumphrey. Littlejohn smiled. It must be the sea air or the atmosphere of frivolous revelry permeating the whole place. What did he want a file of the Chief Constable's secrets for? He opened the first folder. Like the rest, it contained a number of plain sheets, with a two-inch margin down the left side of each for the date. In date sequence, the various scraps of information gleaned by the Chief Constable or his agents were tabulated. The first sheet was headed with particulars such as name, age, date of arrival in Westcombe, place of birth, previous places of residence and the like. The fact that National Registration numbers were included, showed whence much of the routine information had been gathered.

Littlejohn commenced to read. Much of the matter was more like paltry gossip than anything else. Boumphrey or his underling was thorough to the point of pettiness. He could imagine Horace Powlett terrified lest he should miss the slightest detail and bring down the heavy wrath of Boumphrey on his head.

Canon Wallopp's grievance was chiefly centred in the unchristian sin of pride. This elderly and heavy cleric had, according to his record, just missed a bishopric and consoled himself by behaving like the bishop of Westcombe. The latter place was no see, of course, falling under that of Westchester, but Wallopp did his best. He lived in style in a large rectory, with two curates to do all his menial parochial offices and two manservants to dance attendance on him. He was unmarried and was given to mild flirtations with young ladies whilst giving them scriptural instruction. He had been known to fondle the assistant librarians, too, under cover of helping them to find erudite books on theology for him in remote corners of the library. This the faithful Powlett had gathered and entered, like the recording angel, on his files.

Canon Wallopp had quarrelled with Sir Gideon for the reason already given, that instead of allowing him to continue as Mayor's Chaplain, *ex officio*, Ware had decided in favour of one who, he stated, had done more for the town than the Canon. Mr Titus Gaukroger was one of the attractions of West-combe Beach and daily contributed to its popularity, whereas Wallopp looked down his nose at holiday makers. So, Gaukroger had been chosen and Wallopp left to grind his teeth. For months the Canon did not speak to the Mayor, who did not grieve about it, for he knew that as soon as good food was to be had, the clerical glutton would return to the fold.

After reading that the Canon had quarrelled with the Mayor about the lost appointment, Littlejohn dismissed him as a suspect. Wallopp was more likely to wait until the end of Sir

Gideon's term of office and then put in another claim. Here was no motive for killing.

The "bishop" would be visited along with the rest of outstanding guests and interviewed concerning his evidence and reactions.

Now, Gaukroger's was a funny case. It appeared that he had started his working life as a shipping clerk and had a degree in commerce! He had triumphed in becoming Mayor's Chaplain, but after his appointment, his conduct had suddenly become very strange. In fact, his public promotion had given him a great boldness. Like many another in similar positions, John Knox, Bishop Ridley, Thomas Becket, for example, he had tried to reform his master, even to the extent of preaching against him and his works. He had not, in his sermons, actually cited Sir Gideon by name, but Westcombe had come in for a good gruelling or two. The Rev Titus had even compared it to Sodom and Gomorrah and foretold its destruction like the cities of the plain, unless it repented. All of which was, of course, unfair. It wasn't as bad as all that! But Mr Gaukroger, as official chaplain of the place, was intent on cleaning it up. His first sermon after election was based on "Ho! Everyone that thirsteth," and attacked strong drink. Just before the banquet at which he died Sir Gideon threatened to sack him if he did not change his tune. People didn't want the seaside holiday they'd saved-up for a whole year to enjoy, to be described as a Belshazzar's Feast by the official chaplain of the place where they were spending it. And the Rev Titus had stood and defied his master! Nevertheless, the evangelist would hardly strike his tormentor dead for questioning his wisdom. Another one to be interviewed.

Father Manfred, too, had been passed-by when the official chaplain was elected. His was a different case altogether. He had quarrelled with Ware not from pride, but from conviction that by this public act of heresy the Mayor had not only insulted the Mother Church of which he was a member but damned his immortal soul. He was not likely, however, to precipitate Sir Gideon's taste of hell with the help of a dose of strychnine. Manfred was with Sir Gideon when he died. A visit to him was very necessary in case the Mayor had recovered sufficiently between the spasms of illness which eventually carried him off, to speak and express any opinion concerning his murderer.

Kingsley-Smith, the Town Clerk, owed Ware a considerable amount of money. This Boumphrey had gleaned from a letter which he had read on the Town Clerk's desk one day in the latter's absence. The file stated that Kingsley-Smith had been responsible for introducing Ware into the best local circles when first he arrived in Westcombe, where the Kingsley-Smith family had lived for generations. Constitutional Club, Yacht Club, Golf Club. Kingsley-Smith had proposed Ware for membership in them all. And Ware had lent him money. The letter the Chief Constable had not hesitated to read, was pressing for repayment. The money motive was quite a feasible one for murder. A further note on the file stated that Kingsley-Smith ran another establishment in London! One of Boumphrey's men had come across him dining with someone not his wife in a fashionable West End restaurant and, on making enquiries, had discovered that the Town Clerk of West-combe kept a mistress.

It was quite obvious to Littlejohn that all the information on Boumphrey's files had not been acquired fortuitously. The Chief Constable had evidently set out to dig himself in at Westcombe by learning as much as he could about the shady side of its principal citizens. He wondered where Ware's file might be.

Littlejohn grew tired of grovelling among the questionable doings of Westcombe, like the man with the muck-rake. There was the constant friction between Westcombe and Hinster's Ferry, personified by the struggle between Ware and Wilmott Saxby, the latter fighting for the very existence of his little

Urban District Council and almost at the last gasp when Ware died.

Tom Hogg, deputy-Mayor, ousted from the Mayoralty by Ware and his men because Gideon was anxious for local honours. In times past, the Mayor of Westcombe had always been asked to continue in office for a second period. In Tom's case, precedent was broken because Ware was champing at the bit for the cocked hat and robes and the golden chain. Besides, Hogg and Ware were like cat and dog about labour conditions. The eternal battle of master versus man, with Ware using the additional threat of queering Hogg's pitch in the constituency he proposed to contest as Labour candidate next election.

Oliver, the Borough Treasurer, suspected of being wrong in his books on one occasion and of borrowing money to put them right. Then, finding Sir Gideon beating a dog with a putter on the links one day, he stops him in a rush of righteous indignation. And later, discovers that Sir Gideon is calling for a thorough examination of his books just to try and catch him out for revenge! What if the defalcation comes to light? Boumphrey's record merely indicated that a chance remark by one of the Treasurer's staff about trying to find an error in the books, happened to coincide with Oliver's sudden visit to a wealthy aunt and a quick solution... The money motive again, with Ware sticking out his chin for the rap!

Oxendale, the bank manager, within a short time of retirement, being badgered by Ware for the sheer joy of showing his power. Ware, a large shareholder in Cotts' Bank, was threatening to have him moved to a smaller branch far distant from the place where Oxendale planned to settle down when he got his pension. After all, his friends were in Westcombe and he'd bought a nice little house there. Then, along comes Ware and upsets the applecart. You'd feel like murdering him if you got a chance!

The last two men in the ring round Ware when he died were

Dr Alastair McAndrew, Medical Officer of Health, and Harold Brown, Clerk to the Justices. According to the files, McAndrew had no bone to pick with Ware, except that they frequently quarrelled about the Mayor's opposition to Health Grants. Ware was all for advertising Westcombe. His financial interests were there, and he liked spending the town's money to their advantage. The doctor wanted better hospitals, better equipment, better research. Ware, in common with many of his kind, was overawed by science and hence treated it with a show of contempt.

As for Harold Brown, Ware, as Chief Magistrate, couldn't bear taking advice. He would have liked to administer the law after his own fashion, irrespective of what the acts and statutes, in which Brown was so well versed, had to say about it. In Court of Petty Sessions when Sir Gideon began to pontificate, the Clerk would turn in his little pen-like enclosure and in a stage whisper inform him that he just couldn't do it. And that if Sir Gideon persisted, he'd be finding himself publicly hauled over the coals by Quarter Sessions or by the King's Judges in High Court. Ware, tired of seeing the solicitors grinning at their table at the sight of the Clerk taking him down a peg or hearing the audience in the gallery whispering that Brown had scored again, was scouring about for some means of discrediting Harold Brown. Brown was very distressed about it. So much so, that it looked as if there *was* something which might come to light if Ware's lickspittles hunted hard enough!

Littlejohn yawned. This was the first case in which he'd been presented with such a lot of dirty dishes at the start. In Paris, his friend Luc of the Sûreté, had shown him the stacks of dossiers in the archives there dealing with the private lives of nearly everyone of note. But in England… The thing nauseated Littlejohn. As it was, this information hadn't interested him much. There was hardly a motive among the lot. Just a bit of background for the parties he would be visiting on the morrow.

There was a knock on the door of his room.

"Excushe me...this is my room..." stammered a small, porky little man with a white face and more drink than he could carry, when the Inspector opened the door.

"What's your number, sir?"

"Twenty-four...this is it."

"This is 124," said Littlejohn and gently closed the door in the face of his visitor.

On the wall of the bedroom some respectable, angry, long-in-bed guest beat a tattoo of protest.

Littlejohn looked at his watch. One o'clock!

He opened the window and let in the fresh air and the sound of the sea. The promenade was deserted, but somewhere in the distance somebody was singing a ribald song at the top of his voice. It seemed to go on and on and the singer never to flag or tire. He was still singing to the accompaniment of the incoming tide when the Inspector fell asleep in the bed which looked like a stage property for a Borgia murder.

The Inspector was aroused by the illegal sound of a motor-horn, apparently from the car of some petrol-wasting gadabout returning from an evening's pleasure. Littlejohn turned on the bed light and, although he seemed to have slept for many hours, he found that it was only two o'clock. He put out the light, lit a cigarette and drawing back the curtains leaned out of the window.

The last prowlers had turned into their rooms. The whole hotel was quiet. People who had rioted and shouted or who had quietly enjoyed another day of their holidays had returned to their lodgings and now lay levelled in sleep. The tide was on the ebb and far across the bay the siren of a coaster bellowed. All the tiny noises, obscured by the thunder of the day's activities, seemed magnified in the calmness of the night. The creaking and squealing of hanging signs swinging in the breeze; the seething of the tide on the shingle of the shore; engines and wagons hissing and clanking in the railway goods yards; stray taxis swishing along distant streets; the whine of an electric motor of some works or other on night shift.

The moon had risen and illuminated the promenade, the vast expanse of which looked like a tranquil sheet of water. Down below Littlejohn suddenly made out a solitary, foreshortened figure, wearing a coat and a slouch hat pulled well down over his face. There he stood, his back to the railing of the promenade, looking up at the hotel, too far away and his face too shadowed to be recognised. There was something intent in the attitude of this onlooker. He might have been a forlorn lover, trying to guess the window of the room behind which his beloved slept. Or…

Then, Littlejohn had the vague feeling that he was looking down on the murderer of Sir Gideon Ware. He reproached himself genially for imagining things in the small hours and flicked the stub of his cigarette out of the window. The tiny glow described an arc and fell like a shooting star at the feet of the watcher, who, with a start, lowered his head and moved rapidly away. Turning the corner, he was swallowed up by the maze of streets which compose the inner town.

6

A COOL CUSTOMER

It was barely 8.30 when Littlejohn, after a surprisingly
substantial breakfast at The Grand, stepped out and walked
briskly along the promenade to work. There seemed to be
something tonic in the early morning air of Westcombe, for,
although the Inspector had enjoyed a few hours' sleep, he felt
fine.

The rank and file of holiday makers were still in bed recovering from the previous day's heavy round of pleasures and last
night's revelry. A sprinkling of what Littlejohn told himself
were the cocoa-drinkers, the class who frequented such austere
retreats as the writing room of The Grand, or who put out their
shoes at their bedroom doors before eleven at night, were
taking their constitutionals. The feet of elderly men rang on the
concrete causeways as they picked them up vigorously and
smote them down briskly like ponies at exercise. Others strolled
along, admiring the calm sea and the fresh sunshine of early
morning. This was their only chance to take the air uncontami-
nated by the smells of beer, fish-and-chips, cabbage water, mass
cooking and all the other activities which are embraced by the
term "holiday catering." The vigorous old boys, the peaceful

flâneurs, the fire-watchers and air-raid wardens returning from duty and the natives hurrying to work all breathed deeply, held it, and then exhaled the ozone with conscientious ecstasy, extracting the last gasp of its goodness, like ducks who take water in their beaks, sift it of its useful and life-giving contents, and then spew it forth and forage for more.

Decrepit men and women rummaged on the tide line, sorting out the bits of wood, cork and more precious drift brought back from its dangerous depths by the sea and cast along the beach. Far out by the lighthouse, the dredger from the Swaine was depositing the mud which it had scooped from the channel, an Augean task, for the next tide would wash it all back, and so on, presumably until the end of shipping there or of time itself. One by one the fishing boats bobbed across the bay from the old harbour, their sails bellying in the fresh breeze, and lined up at a small jetty at the head of each pier, waiting for the day trippers to finish their breakfasts, which, judging from the white horses careering near the lighthouse, they would probably soon feed to the fishes.

From the end of each pier, which hung over deep water, enthusiastic fishermen were already casting their lines, for fish was scarce in Westcombe in spite of its proximity to the sources of supply, and the codling, plaice and sole which were hauled from between the girders of the pier were eagerly snapped-up by hotel keepers at fine prices.

Littlejohn turned in at the police station. Boumphrey was already at his desk. He looked anxiously at his visitor as the Inspector placed the briefcase with its contents on the nearby table.

"Mornin'!" said the Chief Constable morosely. "Find those things of much use?"

"Good morning, sir. Yes. And no. They gave me some background concerning the characters of the case, but hardly bear seriously on the matter in hand."

Boumphrey's Adam's apple rotated violently.

"Hardly bear seriously! … Why man, don't you realise that the killer's among those? I'd have thought they were of vast importance."

And he raised his hands as if to describe a towering edifice of clues and facts enough to sink a ship.

"You could hardly sort out a motive from the various items of personal and private squabbling and spite they record… Now could you, sir? And, by the way, I noticed you'd omitted the file of the Mayor himself. I'd like to see that if there is one."

Boumphrey threw his full weight back in his chair, raised his hands like a muezzin, and allowed them to fall back limply on the table.

"Well! I must have forgotten to get it out… I keep that under lock and key myself. It's not in the ordinary cabinets. Doesn't do to let even Powlett know too much. I'll get it."

The excuse sounded lame to Littlejohn.

Boumphrey rose, opened a small safe and extracted a folder from the top of a pile of other papers. He handed it to the Inspector, who thrust it in the inside pocket of his raincoat.

"You'll be careful with it, Littlejohn. Confidential, you know."

"Certainly," replied the Inspector, stooping to pick up a tiny scrap of paper which had fallen at his feet as he coaxed the folder to fit in the pocket. It was a small, white triangle with a little semi-circle punched in its base… In fact, a fragment of the top left-hand corner of one of the foolscap sheets of Boumphrey's files, detached by someone forcibly extracting a page of the record from the spiked fastener which held the lot together.

The eyes of Boumphrey and Littlejohn met.

"What you got there, Inspector?"

"Just a bit of paper. I've just been tearing up a dirty sheet from stock…"

"Yes? Well, I'll be getting along. Has the medical report arrived in yet?"

"No. I expect it any time. The inquest's tomorrow."

"Did you know that, as far as present reports go, Sir Gideon Ware's last call before the lunch was at his doctor's?"

"No. Who told you?"

"Swift, his secretary. Ware called for an injection of serum against cold in the head, to which he seems to have been a martyr. The medical report's sure to mention the needle wound arising out of the injection. I'm eager to see what the doctors say."

"Same here."

"Incidentally, have you any information concerning Dr Preedy, Ware's physician. I've been told he's a native of Westcombe."

"That's right. I'll get his file."

Boumphrey rang a bell and Horace, the filing expert, rushed into the room as if the place were on fire.

"Get me Dr Preedy's records."

"Yessir."

The folder was produced at great speed and Boumphrey opened and scanned its contents.

"Yes. I thought so. Preedy had every reason for bearing Ware a grudge. As I said, the doctor's a native of Westcombe. His father was a prominent builder here, but of the good old-fashioned type. Solid, substantial kind of houses, he built, and was at his best before the new development began. When Ware began his big schemes here after the last war, old Preedy was in the middle of a building estate in which he'd sunk all he had. Young Preedy had got through as a doctor but was in hospital practice. Ware set up in opposition to the old man, who was soon out of his depth. You see, he knew nothing of jerry-building technique, even if his principles allowed him such swindling, which they didn't. Ware whacked him out of the field, and he went bankrupt. They found his body on the shore. It was said he'd thrown himself off the pier at high water. Suicide, you see. But the verdict was death from misadventure…"

"Funny, Ware should have the son as his doctor."

"Oh, he was that way. Many a time, after impulsively doing a man a bad turn, he'd try to make it up to him in another way. He never apologised, but tried to ease his conscience by stealth, as you might say. Young Preedy's a cold fish. Never shows his emotions. So, it was never really found out how he took his father's death. At any rate, he came here just as the place was growing and started a practice from scratch. There were plenty of opportunities then."

Boumphrey scanned the file again.

"Oh, here we are. I thought I remembered it. At the last Roosters' Dinner…that's a bachelor club, here… Preedy remarked that Ware would eventually get what was coming to him. Now, if you ask me, we'd better keep an eye on Preedy, eh?"

"I'm just off to see him now, sir. He was one of the last to see Ware before the lunch."

Littlejohn had ascertained that the doctor's rooms were in Oxford Crescent, which is one of the last relics of old West-combe and lies some distance from the promenade. It reminds one of Bath, for it consists of stately old houses in terraces. These are occupied by doctors, dentists, masseurs and such, and by a number of nursing homes. It owes its survival to the outbreak of war, which, by holding up so-called development, prevented Ware and his kind from setting about it and replacing its graceful old property by blocks of flats.

As Littlejohn entered the crescent, he was met by a procession of men, walking in a ragged body, like a disorderly concourse of members of a lodge or a civic function without their regalia. For it was visiting day at a maternity home which had been evacuated to Westcombe from a vulnerable inland area. These were happy fathers, brought by special trains from their gathering grounds to visit their wives and new families, and one of such excursions had just disembogued in the nearby station. The Inspector found himself among this joyful throng, for Dr Preedy's surgery was next door to the lying-in hospital.

The bold, pretty girl whom Littlejohn had seen with the doctor on the previous night, answered the door. She was dressed in nurse's uniform and looked cool and efficient.

"Is the doctor in, nurse?"

"Yes. Have you an appointment?"

"No. But I think he'll see me. I'm a police officer and would like a word with him about his late patient, Sir Gideon Ware. Here's my card."

The girl's eyes opened wide and her lips formed themselves into a soundless whistle.

"He's busy, Inspector. It's his afternoon off today and he's several appointments this morning."

"Take my card in, nurse, please."

"Oh, very well..."

Miss Latrobe turned on her heel and flounced off, leaving Littlejohn in the dim hall, lighted only by a fanlight, to cool his heels. She was soon back.

"The doctor can spare a minute before his first patient. Come this way, please."

Dr Preedy was sitting at a large desk smoking a cigarette. The room was well furnished and it seemed that its owner had done very well since he arrived in Westcombe and started from scratch. He looked bright and alert and was just the one to inspire confidence in the ailing.

"Well, Inspector," said Preedy, holding Littlejohn's card in the fingers of one hand and flicking it with those of the other. "What do you want with me?"

"A little information, that's all, doctor. I won't keep you."

"Fire away, then."

"I have been informed that Sir Gideon Ware called here at eleven o'clock on the morning of his death, by appointment. Is that so?"

"Yes"

"Without violating professional secrets, can you tell me why he called?"

"I arranged to immunise him from the common cold. He came for a shot of serum, which I give him this time each year."

"You did that."

"Yes"

"How?"

"I injected the contents of an ampule of the serum. I get it in that way. Gave the injection in the left forearm. That was all."

"Nothing else injected?"

"My dear Inspector! What are you getting at?"

"Nothing. I'm merely seeking precise information."

"Well, I've given it. That's all I have to say."

The doctor maintained a phlegmatic good humour throughout. A good man to have about in an emergency and a damned difficult fellow to question. You simply couldn't get behind his guard.

"You didn't attend the luncheon at which Sir Gideon met his death, doctor?"

"No. Surely you know that already, Inspector."

"Yes, I do. Where were you at the time, doctor?"

"Ah! Now you seek an alibi, eh? Sorry, I can't oblige. I had lunch alone at about the time of the banquet. It was a cold one, made by the good woman who looks after these rooms. She was going out and left it laid for me. Miss Latrobe did me some coffee and then went off to her own lunch. Her rooms are just round the corner."

"Perhaps Miss Latrobe could come in and confirm that?"

"Sorry, Inspector. She's just gone out. The housekeeper's answering the door for me. You see, today's my half-day; and

Miss Latrobe's as well. We pack-off at twelve as a rule. We worked late last night, and I thought Miss Latrobe looked tired. So I told her to get off at eleven today. You'll see that it's past that already."

"So it is, doctor. Well, I'll confirm it with her later, then."

"Anything more? There are patients waiting for me."

"Just one more question, doctor. A personal one, but not asked out of idle curiosity, you'll understand that. Had you any particular reason for disliking Sir Gideon Ware?"

"Do *you* know of any?"

"I'm asking the questions, doctor."

"And I'm answering them! However, I suppose I'd better be candid with you. I did dislike the fellow. He was a patient, of course, and I treated him as a doctor should. After all, there's a code of ethics in medicine. But he wasn't my type... An opportunist, careerist, money-grabber. Wanted his own way all the time, and God help those who stood in his way..."

"Your own father, for example, doctor?"

"My own father."

Preedy was a cool customer and no mistake. He just said it as a matter of course, without heat and even without reproach.

"Yes. My own father suffered at his hands. They were in competition and my father was the loser."

"He died shortly after the crash, I understand, sir?"

"He did. Is there anything more? I suppose your theory is that I've long sought a means of avenging my father, and yesterday the chance came. I gave him a shot of strychnine instead of cold serum, eh? No, Inspector. I wouldn't have used the tools of my profession had I wanted to do that. I'd have just shot him out of hand."

Littlejohn was inclined to believe him, but knowing his man and his apparent resourcefulness, declined mentally to write him off.

"I think that's all, sir. Thank you for your help. I'll probably be round again as the case develops. Sir Gideon's medical adviser holds quite an important place in our field of investigation, I'd imagine."

"Yes? Well, here's to our meeting again, Inspector. Meantime, I wish you good morning. My patients are still waiting."

Preedy showed Littlejohn to the door himself, and when left alone on the doorstep, Littlejohn had the depressing feeling that he'd been put off with half a tale and that he would have to be content with it for the time being.

7

LAYMEN AT THE FEAST

Mr Edgar Kingsley-Smith had the most sumptuous office in the Town Hall and Littlejohn found him there, lounging in a padded chair, dictating letters to a typist who had one leg crossed above the knee of the other and looked fresh from the cover of a ladies' magazine.

"Right, Miss Travers. Better leave us. I'll ring when I want you again. Good morning, Inspector. Glad to meet you. What can I do to help?"

The Town Clerk shook hands with his visitor, giving him a hot, dry grip like that of a man with a fever. He was past his prime. His grey hair was thin and the skin-deep sunburn on his long, lined face might have concealed a bilious or even jaundiced hue. A man of the world, cultured and well-bred, yet whose natural indolence had carried him no farther than the Town Clerkship of his native town. He uncurled his long, slim body from his seat, stood with his back to the fireless grate, and waved Littlejohn to a chair.

"According to information, sir, you were sitting next to the Mayor when the tragedy occurred. I wondered if you saw or heard anything which might throw some light on how it happened."

Kingsley-Smith took a slim cigarette case from his pocket and offered it to Littlejohn, who, however, said he preferred his pipe and, filling it, began to smoke.

"To be candid, Inspector," said the Town Clerk, lighting his cigarette slowly, "in spite of my ringside seat, I saw no more than anyone else. The whole business is as much a mystery to me as to everybody else."

He drawled his speech. His self-possession was wonderful, and he showed not the least sign of regret or any other emotion.

"Sir Gideon was served from the same dishes as everyone else?"

"Yes. I've been asked that before and I presume you've already been told of it."

Littlejohn remembered that Kingsley-Smith was a solicitor and liked to show his acumen.

"Yes, sir, I have. But I'm trying to draw you out to tell me the story in your own words..."

"I don't see the use. I will say, though, that I've looked at the happenings from every angle and I can't for the life of me see how Ware could have been given poison that would kill him alone and not affect a dozen others at least."

"I agree with you, sir, from what I see of the affair. The only way of approaching it is to delete the impossibles from the list of names, and then go steadily through the probables until by elimination we get among the real suspects..."

"The animal, mineral, vegetable method?"

"Yes."

"And I'm among the probables, I gather?"

"Not quite that, as yet, sir. As chief officer of the Corporation and one in constant contact with the Mayor, can you tell me of any likely motives for murder?"

"Dear me, Inspector, what a question!" Kingsley-Smith puffed disgustedly at his cigarette and shook off the ash on the hearthrug. "You probably know by this, that Ware's arrogance and domineering ways made enemies for him wherever he went. *Nil nisi bonum*, and all that of the dead doesn't apply in this case. It's murder, so I must be frank. I don't think Sir Gideon had a single real friend among any of those present at the banquet. He also took a delight in setting off one official against another. If you could have seen the arrangement of the guests at the tables on that day, you'd have understood. Sworn antagonists sitting cheek-by-jowl... Ware's scheme and his idea of a joke!"

"Yes, but it needs a lot to make one man kill another in cold blood."

"I agree with you. I regarded Wilmott Saxby, the guest of honour, yes, the guest of honour, as the one with the greatest grievance and most motive for killing Ware. You see, Ware had just undermined Saxby's life work, by arranging for Westcombe to swallow up the little place where Saxby's the Chairman of the UDC. The poor fellow, a native of Hinster's Ferry...that's the place...has fought for years to prevent it. Yet, knowing Saxby, I say impossible. Not the type."

"I shall be seeing him later, I hope, and will judge for myself. How did *you* get along with Sir Gideon, sir?"

Kingsley-Smith shrugged his shoulders and flung away his cigarette end.

"No better than the rest. I had sharp words with him from time to time. I refused to tolerate any interference with my office by the Mayor or anyone else. Sir Gideon was a born meddler and, if I'd allowed him, would soon have been running this department for me, just as he'd have made the magistrates' court into a sort of Star Chamber if Brown, the Clerk, hadn't put his foot down."

"Is it true that when he settled down in Westcombe, Sir Gideon found in you a good friend?"

"Yes. He arrived as a prominent builder, and we met frequently. The Corporation owns a lot of the land here and all building ventures require proper consent, as you're no doubt aware, by the local authority. As principal legal adviser to the Council, I often met Ware. We got quite friendly and when he came to live in Westcombe, I introduced him to various people and clubs. He was much more reasonable then. Once he'd got settled down, however, he seemed to get the idea that he owned the place and grew somewhat obnoxious."

Littlejohn had already formed the impression that the Town Clerk had a strong personal dislike, bordering on enmity, for the dead Mayor. There was a deeper motive for this than mere departmental pin-pricking. He was seeking a way of broaching the matter of the Town Clerk's debts to Ware, when Kingsley-Smith surprised him by almost reading his thoughts.

"Unless I'm mistaken, Boumphrey's already told you that at one time, I owed Ware considerable sums of money..."

"Yes, sir, he has."

No use beating about the bush!

"I thought so. I once caught him reading private correspondence on the table of my room when I was called out. He thought I wasn't quick enough to spot him... A word of warning, Littlejohn. Don't believe all that Boumphrey tells you. Confirm it if you can. His appointment was practically forced through by Ware, who had a lot of influence in the right quarters. That's all I have to say on that matter. Meanwhile, I'm not evading the issue about owing Ware money. When he died, I was indebted to him to the tune of about two thousand pounds. I now owe it to his executors. He held a mortgage on my house in the town. He began to press for repayment recently. All I had to do was to shift the mortgage from Ware to the bank or a building society and pay him off. So, you see, Boumphrey only got half a tale. I had a series of large expenses many years ago — operation and such like — and Ware offered to lend me the money..."

Littlejohn rose. There wasn't much more to be gathered from the Town Clerk, who seemed more anxious to go one better than Boumphrey in laying bare his finances, than to give any objective background to the case.

"I'm very grateful for the information, sir, and I'll probably call again later in the investigation."

"Anything I can do to help, don't fail to let me know, Inspector. Goodbye."

The Town Clerk rang the bell for the blonde typist again and she eagerly resumed her place at his side, and again found that she could not firmly establish her notebook without showing an extraordinary extent of legs, knees and silken hose.

Meanwhile, Littlejohn was trying to hold a conversation with the Borough Treasurer.

Mr Ralph Arthur Oliver, custodian of finances of Westcombe, was a small, sandy, busy man of middle age, who had an extravagant and domineering wife and a wealthy, tight-fisted aunt. Between the two of them, he didn't know whether he was on his head or his heels.

Boumphrey's deductions concerning defalcations, put right by a loan from the wealthy maiden relative, were never confirmed but might have been quite true. Mrs Oliver wore expensive clothing and moved in the best circles; Miss Manciple, the aunt, never gave Ralph Arthur a stiver and was always hatching schemes for making *him* pay for *her*. The annual published accounts of Westcombe showed Oliver's salary at £1,000. How he made ends meet with two silly women sucking him dry, only he knew!

Oliver was on the defensive against Littlejohn from the start. He laboured under a disadvantage, too. On the day before, Mr

Oliver had had all his upper teeth extracted and, in his exalted position, being unable to put in an edentulous appearance at the office, he was wearing a temporary denture. This encumbrance left its moorings now and again during conversation with a choking, gnashing noise.

"Yes, I sat in full view of the Mayor, Inspector," said Oliver. "Or rather, side view. Fr'instance…"

And he demonstrated by means of a diagram on his blotting-pad, how he was seated on the inside of one of the arms of the subsidiary tables, at right angles to the high table, side-on to His Worship.

"You saw nothing unusual in the course of the luncheon, sir?"

Mr Oliver wrestled with his temporary teeth.

"Nothing," he gnashed. "Fr'instance, the band was playing, there was a hum of conversation, and the dishes were served as at any other function of that sort. I sat opposite Oxendale of Cotts' Bank. Now, he had a full view of Sir Gideon all the time. We've compared notes since and Oxendale says *he* saw nothing extraordinary…"

At the latter word, Mr Oliver's dentals refused to function further, and he had to adjust them for another spasm with the help of his handkerchief.

"Did you get on well with Sir Gideon yourself, Mr Oliver? "

The Borough Treasurer turned pale and his teeth chattered.

"What do you mean?" he asked.

"As civic chief, I hear he was difficult to satisfy. I have been told he meddled in municipal departments. For instance, were you troubled?"

Littlejohn made a note to guard against becoming infected with Oliver's catchword.

"No, we had no trouble," answered Oliver, too eagerly, Littlejohn thought. "He left my department alone, thank goodness."

"Yet you had a personal quarrel with him lately at the golf club, didn't you, Mr Oliver?"

The Treasurer had apparently hoped that the Inspector was ignorant of the episode and showed great alarm at this new development.

"It was nothing, Inspector, I assure you. Just a passing brush between us, but soon smoothed over."

"What was it all about, Mr Oliver? I'd better have a proper story, first-hand, in justice to you. Please be easy in your mind, however. I'm not suspecting you of the crime. Take it easy."

"A lot of silly stories have gone round about that incident," said Oliver, grinding his teeth to keep them steady. "Fr'instance, somebody said I'd actually struck Sir Gideon. What I did was, I held his arm until the dog he was beating got away."

"Tell me about it from the beginning, sir."

"It was at the eighth green. There was a setter running about there. One of the members' dogs — Fenwick's. Just as Sir Gideon played an approach shot, the dog picked up his ball and started scampering round with it. Ware was furious, rushed at the setter, got it by the collar and set about it with his putter. I'm very fond of dogs and I must have seen red, for, before I knew where I was, I had rushed from the ninth tee, where I was waiting to drive off, and snatched the putter away. That was all. But, as I'm usually even-tempered, this show of aggressiveness caused a bit of joking among the wags of the club. Ware was very annoyed with me and didn't speak to me for a fortnight. But it all blew over."

"How long since was that?"

"About six weeks ago."

"Did Sir Gideon threaten you, Mr Oliver?"

The Borough Treasurer turned pale again.

"No, no, Inspector," he managed to say sibilantly, and then his telephone rang. Littlejohn seized this opportunity to bid him goodbye.

Dr McAndrew, whose office was in the same building, was out in conference with Harris, the police surgeon, concerning the autopsy on Ware, so Littlejohn arranged to return after lunch for an interview. Meanwhile, he turned his attention to the Magistrates' Clerk, Harold Brown, who, since the seizure of his offices by an evacuated department of the civil service, had been housed over the Police Courts.

There was a hush in the court building when Littlejohn entered, for the magistrates were in session. An attendant policeman informed the Inspector that the last case was being tried — it was one of twenty for drunken and disorderly conduct — and that if he cared to wait, Mr Brown would soon be free.

The ante-room, a perfect *salle des pas perdus*, held a number of disgruntled witnesses, who had arrived early, bright and breezy, to give their testimonies and had been told that they would have to wait their turns, which had been put off until after lunch.

"Am I bloody mad!" confided a small man with the hanging chaps and loose-lidded eyes of a bloodhound, speaking in a reedy voice, which struggled for exit among his vocal cords. "Had to shut up my hoop-la stall to witness against two blokes who got tight and wrecked the next bloomin' pitch to mine, a pin table do. There's only me in my business, but there's two brothers on the pin table. One of 'em's here gettin' his revenge, while the other opens the stall and pinches all my customers and takin's. The ruddy perlice all over, that is. No mercy on the feller tryin' to earn an 'onest livin'... Not the perlice, are yer? You are? Well, why the 'ell didn't yer say so, 'stead of lettin' me go ramblin' on? Even if you *are* one, you know it's the truth an' I don't withdraw a ruddy word, see?"

Whereat the little bloodhound made his exit with the other disgusted witnesses.

At length, Mr Brown sent word that he was free. He was a

small, portly man, with solid flesh of apparently great specific gravity. His hooked nose looked like a misfit hastily assumed, his eyes bulged, and his curly hair was black and well pomaded. You could smell his hair-oil all over the room. He wore a perpetual, mirthless smile and when he was annoyed, he amplified it by baring his teeth.

"Well, well," smiled Mr Brown, "and what can I do for Scotland Yard?"

Littlejohn told him. The same story as before.

"No. Although I sat almost facing Sir Gideon, I didn't see a thing. I'd no idea what was going on until I noticed his colour go. Just like that..."

He snapped his fingers like a mesmerist reviving his victim.

"...then he seemed in distress, gathered himself together and finally collapsed."

"Everything seemed to be quite normal before that?"

"Absolutely."

"How did *you* find Sir Gideon, sir?"

Mr Brown's smiling lips parted to disclose two copious sets of teeth crowding upon one another like passengers for the last bus.

"Candidly, he was a thorn in my side. Always kicking against the legal pricks. A man for heavy sentences — outrageous ones — for those to whom he took a dislike. Only last week, he wanted to send a lad to prison or Borstal for breaking windows in the offices of Ware and Company. I'd to remind him that the boy was a first offender and merely called for a small fine and nominal damages. He didn't like being told and wouldn't stand corrected until I told him pretty plainly that there'd be an appeal to a higher court and a reversal with censure."

"I hear he was spiteful, Mr Brown. Did he try to get his own back on you for opposing him?"

Even more of Mr Brown's teeth showed themselves through his smile.

"You seem to know a lot, Inspector. Well, this constant friction in court puts me in a dilemma. It's as much as my job's worth to let Ware have his own way. *Fiat justitia*...and I'm answerable to others besides Ware. On the other hand, I'm not made of money."

"But surely, you weren't dependent on Ware that way, sir?"

"Yes and no. I may as well tell you everything, Inspector. To my dying day I'll regret putting myself in Ware's power. I have two sons, twins. Thanks to Ware, they're both now halfway through the university...becoming doctors."

Brown's smile suddenly vanished, and he looked Littlejohn proudly in the face.

"They're clever boys, both of them, and will go far. They did well at the local grammar school. Of course, I hadn't enough money to bring them both up as doctors and they were mad to take it up together. They got scholarships...the Gideon Ware Scholarships! I curse the day they ever got them. They won them in open competition, of course. No favours, and impartial examiners. But whereas any decent fellow endowing a scholarship would have placed down a lump sum to cover the course, Ware, just as always, had to be different. No. He'd foot the bill year by year. And whereas a real benefactor would have felt in honour bound to see the thing through, Ware, when he and I got at cross-purposes on the bench, started to talk about reducing his expenses, due to taxation. One day, after we'd had a passage of arms in court, he casually remarked, 'I'm thinking of cutting down my overheads, Brown. *Charities* first, too. If things go on like this, those lads of yours'll have to look somewhere else for their fees.' I could have killed him..."

Brown halted suddenly and his smile returned.

"I'd nothing to do with killing him, Inspector. You couldn't suspect me, now could you? That just slipped out. A figure of speech, so to speak."

"Quite so, Mr Brown," said Littlejohn and began to fill his

pipe. "I suppose, though, now that Ware is dead, his executors will honour his obligations."

"Ah. You're pinning a motive on me, eh? Well, you might as well know, that in his better days, Ware arranged for his executors to continue the fees. I made sure of that. But, naturally, in his lifetime, he could have annulled the trust…"

"You knew that, too."

Littlejohn rose and extended his hand to Brown, who took it gratefully.

"Don't worry, sir. I don't blame you looking after your boys. And I appreciate your candour. Now I must be getting along."

Harold Brown showed the detective to the door. He seemed too full for words and shook Littlejohn's hand again.

Ware seems to have left a bad smell behind him wherever he's been, thought Littlejohn, as he descended the stairs. If anyone deserved polishing-off, the late Mayor of Westcombe did!

The branch of Cotts' Bank in Westcombe occupies an imposing corner site and looks a veritable palace of wealth, for it is the largest of its kind in the town and the main accounts of the place are kept there, including those of the Mayor and Corporation.

Mr GB Oxendale, the manager, received Littlejohn in his office, a light and airy room, well-appointed and with expensive etchings on the walls. The manager himself was a medium-built, bald-headed man, with a small, brownish-grey moustache, thick lips, and a prominent nose and chin. His complexion was sun-baked, even to the back of his neck, and his blue eyes peered through his gold framed spectacles as though he might be looking for things on a distant horizon, which can be well understood when it is told that he spent his spare time in summer aboard his small yacht. He also had a little harmless weakness of posing as a scholar. He lectured to mutual improvement classes on literary subjects in the winter and gave profuse advice to his junior clerks on every subject under the sun. He was regularly to be seen knocking around with two or three large volumes under his arm. During a break in the interview, caused by his Accountant entering and bearing-off Mr. Oxendale for a minute or two on a technical matter, Littlejohn took a glance at the three current tomes. He found them to be consecutive library volumes of Romains's *Men of Good Will*, as though Oxendale might be trying to read them concurrently, like those mathematical prodigies who can, by glancing up a column of figures, add up the lot, £ s. and d., in one mental gulp.

Beneath his calm and dignified exterior, Mr. Oxendale was considerably scared by the Inspector's visit. Fundamentally nervous and imaginative, he had spent sleepless nights seeing himself under fire from the police, and whilst the appearance of his visitor was reassuring, Oxendale feared that certain spluttered remarks he'd made in public concerning Sir Gideon's character and what ought to be his fate, might be taken down and used in evidence against him.

"Although I was sitting right opposite the Mayor, I didn't see a thing unusual, Inspector," was his answer to Littlejohn's oft-repeated opening question.

"Everybody says the same, Mr Oxendale. Everyone seems to have fallen foul of Sir Gideon in some way or another, too. I really wonder if the crime might be a joint affair, concocted by all his enemies feasting with him on the day!"

"Surely not, Inspector. Nobody hated him so much as to go to the extent of killing him in such a horrible fashion."

"Had you any bone to pick with Ware, Mr Oxendale?" The bank manager braced himself for a clean breast of the affair.

"I disliked him intensely, Inspector. Intensely! But I couldn't have killed him. Not *that* way, anyhow. If I'd wanted to kill him, I'd have invited him for a sail in my yacht and pushed him off in the bay."

He was intensely serious about the whole business and looked owlishly at his visitor through his shining glasses.

"So, you did think about getting him out of the way, sir?" said Littlejohn, with a most disarming and whimsical smile.

"Well, no, not exactly. I thought of that method after the murder... He's caused me some loss of sleep and heart-burnings lately, though. Last half-year end, he accused me of charging him too much commission, on his business account and wouldn't listen to explanations. He's a director of our bank and told me that I was incompetent, and he'd recommend my transfer to a smaller inland branch..."

Oxendale shrugged his shoulders in a helpless gesture.

"I'm fifty-seven, Inspector. In three years, I'm due to retire and I'm getting ready for it. Panting for it, in fact, for I've planned with my wife to do so many things. We've bought a yacht and propose sailing all round the coast of Great Britain to start with..."

The manager grew quite excited and glowing at the prospect.

"We've bought a house here, too. We've always had our eye on it... You must call and see it one day before you return. Last year, it came up for sale and we got it at a reasonable figure. I was just beginning to look forward to a happy old age, as soon as the war's over. Then, this affair with Ware occurred..."

All Oxendale's enthusiasm died, as when a bucket of water is thrown over a fire of dry sticks.

"... He was quite capable of getting me moved. The house and yacht would be no use to us then and settling down at a new branch at my time of life, with a stigma attached to the move, would have broken me. Can you wonder at my relief when Ware died?"

Yet another! thought Littlejohn.

"Of course, Inspector, I'll admit I'm a possible suspect with a burning resentment like that I was nursing. But I wouldn't have killed him. Life's still good. I've got my wife and a son in North Africa to live for. Better to cut my losses, than kill and be hanged for it."

He looked searchingly at his visitor, questioning whether or not his sincerity was in doubt.

Littlejohn played his next card with considerable finesse.

"I didn't call to accuse you, Mr Oxendale. Nor yet to try to trick you into incriminating yourself. I don't for a minute suspect you. I even appreciate your relief at the turn of events…"

Oxendale beamed and relaxed like one who had shed a heavy load.

"…but I'd like your confidential help, sir," continued Littlejohn, somewhat apprehensive lest the banker's professional caution should intervene before his sense of relief was exhausted.

"Yes?"

"Can you tell me anything about the financial position of Mr Kingsley-Smith, the Town Clerk?"

"It's all a case of this," answered Oxendale rather dubiously. "If asked by another bank whether or not he were good for his engagements, I'd say, 'A highly respectable man, but fully committed financially, and should not undertake further liabilities.' That's as far as I can go, without breaking faith, Inspector. It's all a case of banker and customer and secrecy. You understand?"

"Yes, I do, sir. I'll keep it confidential. Does he borrow from you?"

Mr Oxendale began to wrestle with his feelings. Ingrained caution and duty against gratitude and genuine liking for his questioner. He decided to compromise.

"Well, yes. Again, in the strictest confidence. Please don't ask me to say more, Inspector. I don't want to appear fussy or punctilious, especially to you, but duty is duty."

"Certainly, sir. Just one small point, though, which I will keep strictly to myself. Does the Town Clerk deposit security and if so, is it his private dwelling-house?"

"As you seem to know, Inspector, yes. It's all a case of living beyond one's means, I think."

"He doesn't own any other houses in the town?"

"Not to my knowledge, and if he did, I'm sure I'd be aware of it."

"I'm very much obliged, sir, and I'll take up no more of your valuable time."

"Oh, that's all right. Only too glad to help. And I must confess that I feel greatly relieved at the confession I've made. You will keep the banking information dark, won't you?"

"I promise you that. Well, good day and thanks again, Mr Oxendale."

"Good day, Inspector, and don't forget, call to see my place if ever you're that way. It's right on the Hinster's Ferry Road. Anyone will direct you."

Outside the bank, Littlejohn paused deep in thought. Streams of visitors were winding from the beach and promenade to their lodgings for lunch, many of the children howling dismally at having to abandon a full morning's architectural activities on the sands. The Salvationist Band passed on its way home.

> The hill of Zion yields
> A thousand sacred sweets,
> Before we reach the heavenly fields,
> Or walk the golden streets.

"Penny for 'em," said a voice at Littlejohn's elbow.

It was Hazard.

"What about a spot of lunch, Inspector?"

"Gladly, Hazard."

"I've just finished a very edifying morning's work, Little-john. Somebody's complained that *The Human Spider* on the pleasure beach is indecent. A young lady with limbs like a jellyfish in a side-show, you know. I had to insinuate myself in the audience and then make a written report for the Watch Committee. I even interviewed the human octopus, and found her to be a hard-working, decent young lady, and very much annoyed that there should be any investigations or aspersions. The performance was a bit revolting. Contortions in a green light, like an aquarium. But nothing obscene, as the lady complainant said. And the girl was dressed in a costume which, compared with some we see displayed on the beach, was positively Victorian... What you been doing with yourself?"

"Discovering things. A lying, philandering Town Clerk. A shifty and impecunious Borough Treasurer scared to death of any light being thrown on his affairs. A browbeaten Magistrate's Clerk, fighting for justice and his two kids against Ware. And a pathetically terrified bank manager, afraid of his scheme for a happy retirement being utterly confounded by his late Worship the Mayor, and ready to drown, if not poison him as a result. So far, I've not picked up the trail of the murderer. But I will do... *I hope.*"

"And what's the next step?"

"I've still to see the three clergymen who were present at the banquet. And the guest of honour. Wilmott Saxby, was he called?"

"Yes. You'll have to cross the ferry for that. Quite a pleasant little excursion. See the parsons first, whilst I get my report done. Then, perhaps we could meet and go to Hinster's Ferry together."

"Right. But I'll not have to be long about it. I'm due to see McAndrew about the autopsy before he leaves his office today."

"We'll manage to get it in. And now, what about that lunch?

The hungry wolves are pouring into The Grand, and there'll be nothing left if we don't get at it."

Through the windows of the great building, they could see crowds of hungry diners falling-to with gusto, and with genuine apprehension in their hearts, the detectives hastened to the revolving doors, which, like the feeding apparatus of some great machine, gathered them up and passed them into the interior for digestion.

8

CLERGY AT THE FEAST

The vicarage of St Michael and All Angels was a huge, rambling building, with a dozen or more bedrooms, built in the days when badly paid clergymen were expected, as a matter of course, to multiply and replenish into double figures, trusting in Providence to provide. The last incumbent had done his best at eight. Canon Wallopp, however, had remained blessedly single. Perhaps the thought of all those spare rooms terrified that clerical sybarite.

Hanging over the whole neighbourhood was the great square tower of the church, from the belfry of which numbers of jackdaws incessantly flew with wild cries, as if shaken from the stones by an unseen hand, and then allowed to settle again momentarily, only to be agitated once more and launched into air from their high perching-places.

Littlejohn was ushered into a small, dingy room by a soft-footed manservant and asked to wait. The situation reminded him vaguely of Whistler's portrait of Carlyle, not that the detective fancied himself as either physically or mentally resembling the sage of Chelsea, but the chair he was offered was only comfortable on its extreme edge and he sat there, his raincoat over his arm and his hat balanced on his knees, like a suppliant in the antechamber of a Pope.

After a brief spell, the Inspector was asked to follow the flunkey again, this time to a larger room, also unoccupied. A pleasant, book-lined study, with a large desk, comfortable chairs and a huge window which overlooked a well-kept, walled garden. A screen obscured the main door, which was at the far end and soon a shuffling noise emanating from that direction, announced the Canon's approach. Then his reverence's face itself appeared over the top of the screen. It brought to Littlejohn's mind the man in the moon, peering over the dial of a grandfather clock to denote the current lunar phase.

Wallopp was walking stiffly with the help of a stick, for the after-effects of the toss he had taken at the banquet had manifest themselves only after the feasting had ended.

The Canon had a face almost identical with that of the deadly sin of gluttony materialised, along with his six companions, on a plaster plaque which Mrs Littlejohn had bought in St Malo years before

"Good day to you, Inspector Littlejohn," said the clergyman, refreshing his memory by a glance at the detective's card and moistening his heavy lips by drawing first the upper, then the lower one into his mouth. "To what do I owe this unexpected call?"

"As a guest at the Mayor's luncheon the other day, I thought you could perhaps give me some information which might help me and my colleagues in investigating his murder, sir."

"A shocking affair! Shocking! … But be seated, Inspector, be seated," said Wallopp and himself dropped heavily and with a groan into a large chair. "Drrreadful! But I'm afraid I know very little that will help you. Very little. Who could have wanted to do such a thing?"

"Many of those present that day were no friends of Sir Gideon, sir. I'm sure you know that as well as I do. The late

Mayor seemed to have a faculty for antagonising everyone with whom he came in contact."

"How right you are, Inspector. How right," sighed the Canon folding his large, well-kept hands beneath his pectoral cross. "I must confess that I myself have nourished the most uncharitable feelings towards Sir Gideon. You'll have heard of *our* little difference, won't you?"

And Wallopp looked anxiously at his visitor, as though anticipating his snapping the gyves on his wrists and hauling him off as a suspect.

"Yes. I've heard something of it, sir. About the office of Mayor's Chaplain, which I hear was filled this year with considerable lack of tact and not a little rudeness by Ware."

"Very true, Inspector. Very true. I grant that Ware was a member of the Roman Catholic community and had he politely intimated to me that in such circumstances, he preferred the services of Father Manfred during his term, no one...no one, I say, would have been more pleased than I to give place. But the thing was announced coarsely at a cocktail party — at which I wasn't present, of course — given to celebrate Ware's election. He announced that Gaukroger, of the Beach Mission, an un-denominational fellow, and formerly a commercial clerk, whom I question has ever been ordained... However, I mustn't waste your time with my little grievances..."

"I'm surprised you attended the banquet after such treatment, sir."

The Canon raised benedictive fingers.

"I'm not one to bear ill-will, Inspector. I regarded the invitation as one to bury the hatchet as well as to...ahem...feast and I acted as I felt right in accepting it. But as for throwing any light on *how* or *why* the crime was committed, I must confess I saw nothing unusual, and like many others, am baffled by the whole business."

"May I ask you, in confidence, sir, if in your opinion, there is much corruption in municipal affairs here?"

The Canon's eyes grew wide, and the whole of the front of his bald head seemed to slide forward, creating heavy, puzzled wrinkles on his brow.

"Corruption...? Certainly not! Or, at least, not that I'm aware of."

Littlejohn might have guessed that the mountain of flesh before him had no finger for the spiritual pulse of Westcombe. He rose to depart.

"Excuse my not rising to see you out, Inspector Littlejohn," said Wallopp. "I had a fall the other day which shook me badly and left my limbs so stiff."

He rang a small handbell on his desk, like a medieval bishop indicating that the audience was over, and the meek manservant entered.

"So sorry to have been of little help, but I'll give the matter more thought. I'll concentrate on what happened at the unhappy gathering, and if I recollect anything, I'll telephone you, Inspector."

He looked ready to add his blessing to the interview but changed his mind and offered his hand to the detective.

Gaukroger had just finished a late lunch when Littlejohn rang his doorbell. He lived in a small, detached villa near the large mission church which he had built from the proceeds of his own vigorous labours in the Westcombe vineyard. He was known to holiday makers from Land's End to John o' Groats. Everybody who spent a holiday in Westcombe knew Gaukroger and talked about him as a good chap on reaching home. He was, in fact, part of the entertainment of the place. He knew how to draw and keep crowds interested. His preaching was a form of religious delirium and nobody seeing him in repose out of the pulpit or off the rostrum or soapbox, could believe him to be such a spellbinder.

Titus Gaukroger had once been a missionary in the Hopeful Islands, among the most savage heathen. He treated his beach congregations just as he had treated his islanders in the old days, and his technique was a success.

Mrs Gaukroger, a cheery, chubby woman answered Littlejohn's ring.

"You'll have to be quick," she replied. "Mr Gaukroger's just going down to the beach."

As if to confirm this statement, the pastor himself emerged from the gloom of the interior, clad in black and white, wearing a black straw boater (which came and went with the swallows), and holding an umbrella clutched in the middle and waist-high like a bishop's crosier. He was like a frostbitten replica of the French comedian Fernandel, and he had three children who looked just like him and another on the way which Mrs Gaukroger prayed might be different.

"Oh, come in, Inspector. I can spare you a minute or two," said the parson, and he led the way into a large room, furnished in the old-fashioned style with odd chairs, tables, pictures and floor mats jumbled together.

"Excuse the state of the room, Inspector," said Gaukroger, whose grey eyes began to twinkle at the sight of it. "This is *my* den... I keep it tidy myself. Nobody but myself is allowed to touch a thing here. I like to find things where I leave them. And now, you want to see me?"

"Yes. About the luncheon at which the Mayor met his death. Did you notice anything unusual at the affair, sir? Anything which might throw light on the motive or the identity of the murderer?"

"Dear me, Inspector. There were motives in plenty. Everybody there had some grievance or other against Ware. He even upset the Christian spirit of the clergy. Canon Wallopp, who sat next to me, refused to recognise my existence at all, and Father Manfred, the Roman Catholic priest, seemed to think that by undertaking the purely nominal and sinecure office of Mayor's Chaplain, I'd aided and abetted the process of consigning Sir Gideon's soul to the pit. Really, I can't offer a single helpful suggestion to you, Mr Littlejohn. I can't begin to think how the murder was committed. Whether *you* know, is another thing, but to the layman it seems impossible for one man out of thirty or more eating from the common pot, to be poisoned without some of the rest being affected, too."

"We're waiting for expert opinion from the Home Office on that point. Then, maybe, we'll see more daylight. Meanwhile, I must explore every avenue. You were in the front line, so to speak. One of those nearest to the Mayor when the thing was done."

"The first I knew of it was when Ware fell under the table. Then, I thought he was drunk... I was very much against introducing alcohol on the occasion, but, as I expected, I was overruled."

"What do you think of the rumours that municipal affairs here are corrupt, sir?"

Gaukroger's eyes glowed with a fanatical light. He looked for a moment to be about to fall into one of his spiritual deliriums again, but it died down.

"I know nothing about the money side of affairs. But graft, unfair preference, bullying, toadying, bribery...to get office, power or profit, are rife. I accepted the office of Chaplain — although it was offered in a very unworthy and undignified fashion — in the hope that I might get to Ware's ear and thereby to his conscience. I took it on for no other purpose, for, since he arrived in Westcombe, things have gone from bad to worse in public life. The whole inside of the vessel wants cleansing."

Gaukroger was warming up again and Littlejohn thought that no useful purpose would be served by remaining longer.

"I won't keep you from your duties, Mr Gaukroger," he said. "Thanks for the friendly reception and the information."

"Sorry, I can't help at all, Inspector," replied the pastor, coming down to earth again. "I hope your efforts are crowned with success and thereby much good is done to this town."

He then accompanied Littlejohn to the end of the street, put him safely on his way to the Roman Catholic Church, and departed with his jaunty step, his straw boater and his crosier-like umbrella, to spellbind on the beach and to compete vocally with Professor Howie, a herbalist, who had the next pitch to his own, but who, in spite of his rivalry and inexhaustible stock of vulgar, physiological jokes, was his very good friend and supporter.

Littlejohn found Father Manfred in the church, where he was superintending some work on the fabric. The day was hot, and the priest was wearing an alpaca frock coat of an out of date cut and carrying a black straw panama in his hand. His eyes sparkled shrewdly behind his lozenge-shaped spectacles when Littlejohn told him the purpose of his visit.

"We can't talk here, Inspector. Come into the presbytery. But first let me show you some of the late Mayor's benefactions to the church."

Whereat, Father Manfred took his visitor by the arm and conducted him round the building. It was a spacious modern place, smelling faintly of incense and reminding one in style of a small replica of Westminster Cathedral. An amethyst light illuminated the nave and entered through magnificent stained-glass windows; the gift of Sir Gideon and Lady Ware, said the priest. The interior was being gradually decorated in the most exquisite mosaic.

"Ware brought Italian workmen from London to do the mosaic work, which, you see, isn't yet completed. It is very costly, I can assure you, for this type of decoration is hand-set piece by piece. Fortunately, the work will still go on, in spite of the unhappy end of the donor, for all the materials are here, and I have managed to find a refugee monk from Austria who's an expert at the art, and he will replace the Italians, who come every day from an alien camp near here, but whose wages cannot now be paid. It will take years to finish, however."

Ware had been lavish in his gifts. Stations of the Cross in the most expensive enamel work. Sacred vessels in gold. A number of rather showy images specially imported from Italy.

"And he quarrelled with me because I refused to allow him to erect a tablet enumerating the gifts as coming from himself," said Manfred. "This church has been built from the savings of hundreds of humble people, many of whom couldn't afford the money they gave. Not one of their names is publicly advertised. Neither shall I allow anyone else's to be."

And he snapped his thin lips together belligerently.

The room they entered in the presbytery was furnished in pitch-pine and as clean as a new pin. It seemed to be a kind of office where the priest transacted his public business.

Manfred flung his old hat on a chair and signalled Littlejohn to take a seat. A little, withered old lady, smiling all over her face, entered with a cup of tea for each of them, and after a lot of hovering round her master and his guest to make quite sure that the drinks were satisfactory, departed content and with a quaint little curtsey for each.

Father Manfred crossed his long, thin shanks and sipped his tea.

"Smoke, if you want, Littlejohn."

When they got down to business, his genial manner slipped from the priest like a garment. He was certainly very annoyed with Ware, and very concerned about what was going to happen to his soul now that somebody had forcibly released it from his body.

"I cannot understand it. All his life he has been a member of our Church. Yet, because I refused to allow him to advertise himself in my nave, he cut himself adrift for so long, and publicly and — I say it with regret — jestingly, attached himself to a heretic and one whose religion he knows nothing whatever about. To insult the Holy Church in such a manner was intolerable! Nay, it was damning to himself..."

The gaunt, hairless Jesuit was furious at the thought of the past. He looked ready to call down fire from heaven to avenge the indignity. Then, his face softened, and his old charm returned.

"... But he was received back at the end. In the ambulance on the way to the Infirmary, he had a calm spell in the midst of the most frightful spasms caused by whatever was killing him. He confessed and received absolution... That was a good thing."

"Did you give him the Viaticum, father?" asked Littlejohn.

"No. Why?"

Littlejohn hesitated. The priest's shrewd eyes sought his own and at once seemed to gather his meaning.

"You are thinking that I was the only one who, besides the doctor, might have given him anything on the way to the Infirmary. Yes, and I too suggested strychnine as the cause of the collapse at the luncheon table. Suppose the attack were some kind of fit and in the ambulance, I gave him a dose of something... You are thinking that?"

Littlejohn looked steadily into the bowl of his pipe and then back at Manfred.

"It crossed my mind," he replied candidly. "You know as well as I do, that such thoughts do come and go. Perhaps like bubbles of nasty gas rising from a stagnant pool..."

"Now, now, now. Don't use such a metaphor about what I'm sure is a perfectly healthy mind... You know I didn't murder Ware, don't you? I was concerned with other things than his convulsed and dying body when I forced my way in the ambulance."

"I know that, father."

"I can't help you at all in this investigation, Littlejohn. I'm sorry. It's public property that Ware made more enemies in

Westcombe than all the other notables put together. The banqueting hall was full of his enemies when death took hold of him. Who was responsible for the crime, I can't even guess. I'll tell you what his last words were, however. It will be breaking no confidences. He said, 'My son! My son!' That was all."

"I heard he had a son, father, but he's in Canada, training with the RAF, isn't he?"

"Yes. I cabled him the bad news and he has replied in kind with comfort to his mother. So, you see, he's still there. I think Ware must have been thinking of his son as he died and just uttered his name in his distress."

"I wonder, father. Well, I'll be on my travels again. I've still a long way to go, even for an idea of who might have done it and how."

"Do the best you can, Inspector. None of us can do more. If I can help at a later stage, don't forget to call on me."

Outside, Hazard met Littlejohn as arranged. He seemed to be bursting with some important news, for before he asked the results of Littlejohn's latest endeavours, he blurted it out.

"I say, Littlejohn, here's a stunner for you! The police have been round checking up poison books for the missing strychnine. Just after lunch, they went to Dr Preedy's. He's four grains short in his stock!"

9

TURNING POINT

"I'd intended calling on the deputy-Mayor and crossing the ferry to see Wilmott Saxby as my next jobs. However, it looks as though we'd better get down to headquarters again in view of your news," said Littlejohn to Hazard.

They retraced their steps to the Town Hall.

McAndrew was in his office as they passed along the corridor and they called in.

The MOH of Westcombe was a gaunt Scot with keen grey eyes, a rugged, clean-shaven face and an unruly shock of grey hair on which he had long since abandoned as a bad job, the use of so-called controlling agents.

"So we meet at last, Inspector," said the doctor as they shook hands. "Ah'm sorry ah've been so elusive, but I've other things to do as well as probing in the corpse of our late Mayor. It's about him you've called here, no doubt."

"Yes, doctor. The Chief Constable told me yesterday afternoon that your report was, as then, merely provisional, showing death from strychnine and that certain organs had been sent to the Home Office for further expert examination."

"Did Boumphrey show you my written report, Inspector?"

"No. He hadn't got one at the time I saw him."

"Aye, but he had it this morning. Didn't he let you have a peep at it then?"

"No. Never mentioned it."

"That's funny."

"I agree with you, doctor. I must be asking for explanations."

"Did he tell you what I told him last night when our post-mortem was finished?"

"No. Perhaps you'll tell me now."

"Certainly. Poison wasn't administered in food or drink. There was, as far as we could say, none in the stomach. In other words, it was found in the blood and had been injected hypo-dermically."

"But why wasn't I told this when you reported?"

"Well, ah naturally thought the Chief Constable would have told ye. Otherwise, I'd have made a point o' ringing ye up myself."

The doctor lit a large foul pipe and puffed phlegmatically.

"What are ye going to do about it, Inspector?"

"I'm going to see Boumphrey, and if I don't get a satisfactory story, I'm reporting the thing right away to the Assistant Commissioner. It looks to me like a deliberate suppression of evidence."

"But what good could it do Boumphrey? In the witness box tomorrow morning, Dr Harris and I'll make the whole thing public. He can't keep a thing like that to himself."

"Mind if I butt-in?" said Hazard.

Littlejohn and the doctor had forgotten the man from the Morals Squad in their preoccupation.

"Of course we don't," said Littlejohn warmly.

"Say nothing about it to Boumphrey. Behave as though you'd known it all the time, Littlejohn."

"But whatever for?"

"Listen. There's more than meets the eye in that omission.

I've told you before, this place is rotten with graft, wheels within wheels, corruption... I'm right, doctor?"

"Aye, you're right, man."

"Very well. This looks to me like some more of it. Boumphrey's conveniently forgotten a vital point in the medical evidence to give himself time to think. He couldn't withhold it for long, but he might have kept you from the right track just long enough to warn someone or confuse the trails..."

Littlejohn puffed his pipe disconsolately. This was a new experience indeed!

Hazard's face grew pinched with earnestness.

"I beg you, Littlejohn, don't quarrel with the Chief Constable about this. Carry on with the investigation and keep your eyes open. This is the very opportunity we've been waiting for to clean up this town once and for all, isn't it, doctor?"

McAndrew's long upper lip grew tight and he shook his head.

"This is your business, gentlemen; not mine. I'm just a plain scientist in charge of the pheesical welfare of this community. But this ah will say; when plagues and infections threaten the community, it's war for me. When the like attack the moral or social organism, it should be the same for you. Ye have my promise of silence and my moral support. More I cannot do."

"Ware's gone," continued Hazard. "Now's the chance to get rid of a lot more, from the Town Clerk with his fancy women, Boumphrey with his files and his Gestapo... Dammit, it's like it was in Germany, Spain and France before the war! You don't know who's honest and who isn't. Bench, police, town council... damned if you know who to trust! But get rid of Boumphrey now that Ware's gone, and we might see some changes..."

Littlejohn didn't say anything.

"I can guess what you're thinking, Littlejohn. You're thinking I've a grievance and want to take it out of Boumphrey. I assure you; my only grievance is that I refuse to serve in a corrupt police force, and that's what it is under that time-server. Now's your chance to prove what I say. Will you try?"

Hazard was so convincing and the doctor so obviously in agreement, although cannily sparing in speech, that the Inspector at length made up his mind to follow his colleague's advice.

They bade the doctor goodbye and hastened to Boumphrey's quarters.

The Chief Constable was very pleased with himself. He was animatedly making arrangements with a subordinate concerning the morrow's inquest and rubbing his great hands together with relish.

"Come in, come in, Littlejohn," he bellowed. "I suppose Hazard's told you the news. We've traced the strychnine to Dr Preedy. He's four grains short in his stock and can't...or rather won't, explain it away. Unfortunately, his dispenser's having her afternoon off and we can't get hold of her. He says she'll be able to account for it. I doubt it..."

"Are you suspecting Preedy of the crime, then, sir?" asked Littlejohn.

"Certainly. Almost looks as though we've brought you here for nothing, doesn't it?"

The Chief Constable was obviously relieved at not having to disturb the bigwigs of the town in the course of the investigation and at seeing the end of it without much fuss.

"But how does Preedy fit in with the murder, sir?"

"Well, this is how I figure it out, gentlemen. We know that Ware ruined Preedy's father. Now, why did Preedy come back to his native town to practise, when everything in it reminded him of the unhappy decline in his family fortunes and the loss of his father? He either came back to show the people that he didn't care a tinker's cuss for any of them, or else for revenge on Ware. My idea is the latter."

Boumphrey was thinking himself no end of a clever fellow in his theorising and exposition. He leaned back in his chair, gesticulating in a fashion which successively reminded Littlejohn of windmills, a diabolo player, and a performer on a concertina.

"... Now, gentlemen. Who was the last man Ware called on before the lunch? Why, Preedy, of course! And how was Ware murdered? Why, strychnine, of course! And what did Ware visit Preedy for? An injection, didn't he? And the poison was *injected*, not given through the mouth."

At this point the Chief Constable eyed Littlejohn shiftily like a small boy who has stolen the jam and wonders if the fact has been discovered.

Littlejohn met Boumphrey's eye and stared him out of countenance but didn't utter a word.

Boumphrey broke into a fit of coughing, cleared his throat and thumped the desk to restore his morale.

"Now, gentlemen. If that isn't a watertight case, I'd like to know what is..."

"But why didn't the poison act until more than an hour after the injection, if what you say is correct?" interjected the Scotland Yard man at length.

Boumphrey gave him a pitying glance.

"Good Lord!" he said. "There's no mystery in that! There must be lots of drugs'll slow down the action of poisons. Anyway, I'm going thoroughly into it, you can bet your bottom dollar on that. I'm not going to arrest Preedy right away. I'm going to watch him. Or rather, I want you and Hazard to do it. Sooner or later, he'll betray himself, and then we'll pounce on him and collar him."

Littlejohn caught his breath. The fellow had a nerve and no mistake!

"Very good, sir. So far, all you know is that Preedy's short in his stock of strychnine. The rest is theory."

"Sound theory, Littlejohn, I reckon. We *do* know, don't we, about Ware's visit to him and that he had an injection?"

Here Boumphrey coughed again. He was anxious to know just how much Littlejohn knew about the medical evidence and how he was feeling about the deliberate omission of vital facts from the verbal report he'd been given.

Littlejohn, however, was calmly filling his pipe as if he hadn't a care in the world.

"So, caution's the motto for the present, Littlejohn," continued the Chief Constable. "Preedy was just going out when my man called to check his poison-book. It's his afternoon off, and he was going golfing on the Hinster's Ferry course. The man found the discrepancy almost at once, and said Preedy seemed candidly surprised, and said he'd speak to Miss Latrobe, his dispenser, about it when she came in. With that, he asked if he could get going. Well, my man rang me up from a call-box about it. I didn't quite know what to do. We couldn't arrest him at that, and we didn't want to scare him by showing him we were shadowing him. So I said, right, let him go for his golf. If he bolts it'll be evidence of guilt and we'll soon pick him up. I told the constable just to keep an eye on him and see that he went in the right direction to Hinster's Ferry. He was in his car and drove off on the road that takes you over the toll-bridge some three miles up-river…"

"What puzzles me, though, is why should Preedy so obviously poison him, if he's guilty of doing it," said Littlejohn. "Why?! He might just as well have shot him in the middle of the promenade as fuss about injecting delayed-action poison. He might have guessed the first person you'd be after would be him…"

Boumphrey was just opening his mouth to reply when the telephone bell rang.

"Yes. Chief Constable…speaking, man, speaking. Get on with it!"

His face grew blacker and blacker, and his mouth opened slowly as the tale was told by the distant voice.

At length Boumphrey hung up the receiver and sitting back in his chair gasped for breath like a fish out of water.

"Miss Latrobe's been murdered on the pleasure beach!!" he whispered at length.

MURDER IN THE HOUSE OF NONSENSE

Grace Latrobe tidied up the dispensary, changed into outdoor clothes and, after wishing Dr Preedy a good afternoon's golf, left the house. She felt jaded from over-work and worried about the events which had shaken the town, and which intimately concerned the doctor as Sir Gideon's medical adviser. As she crossed Oxford Crescent to the flat she shared with a friend in a nearby block, the habitual idlers, who occupied the benches under a clump of trees in the middle of the crescent, noted that her comely face was without its customary smile. They watched her trim figure vanish round the corner and then began to chatter about her.

"Why don't you have a real afternoon on the razzle," said her friend, Phoebe Watson, noticing that Grace looked down in the mouth. "Do the round of the pleasure beach. Mix with the revellers. They'll take you out of yourself."

Phoebe was a big, well-built blonde, whose head was a mass of long, cylindrical curls set with consummate art, and she made the old rips on the promenade twirl their moustaches and the young bloods try to catch her eye when she passed. She worked in the Town Clerk's Office. Mr Kingsley-Smith was famous for the bevy of beauties in his department.

"I think I will. It's some time since I had a ride on the round-abouts. It'll blow the cobwebs away. That's a good idea!"

"Well, I'll see you on your way, then," replied Phoebe, pulling her lips into a frightful shape to make quite sure that they were evenly plastered with the lipstick she skilfully applied. "If I leave you here, you look ready for a good mope and you'll probably not turn out at all."

They parted at the door of the Town Hall, and Miss Latrobe strolled along the promenade to the amusement park. Crowds surged everywhere, enjoying the hot sunshine and the festive atmosphere. The beach was thick with people, sprawling, sitting, lolling in every kind of garb from the blatantly indecent to the formal attire, winged collar and spats of a man who suffered from a phobia and was afraid he'd lose his paternal dignity and look a fool if he loosed-up and wore flannels and a sports coat.

A motley crowd of humans and animals was actively engaged on the tide line. Donkeys running with shouting children on their backs, belabouring them for more speed. Dogs prancing about, barking and snapping at the waves. Youngsters paddling happily, with their elders gingerly following suit, holding their garments desperately and hobbling over the sea-washed pebbles as though they were hot coals.

Far along the promenade, the loftier amusements of the pleasure beach could be seen hard at it. The Figure Eight or Velvet Coaster, with its little cars whizzing and winding along its tortuous and precipitous tracks. Swing-boats almost, but not quite, describing a complete circle in their rhythmic plunging. The helter-skelter, built like a lighthouse with a Union Jack flying from the top and a long succession of screaming clients flying from the bottom at the end of a performance not unlike inverted skiing. Along the breeze as it waxed and waned, rose and fell the strains of a score of mechanical organs mingled with the screams of those enjoying the many sensations provided. The same light wind passed over the town, gathering in its embrace the smells of boiling cooking fats, cabbage water and stale fish and gently bathing the occupants of the sands and promenade in this aroma before it wafted over the sea and was finally swamped by ozone.

"It's a land breeze today," said the weather wise. "Not so good for the health, you know."

Miss Latrobe, avoiding the ocular invitations of scores of amorous and prowling males on the way, joined the stream of pleasure-seekers pouring through the three-ply portals of Westcombe's Coney Island. Gradually the huge crowd absorbed her, she forgot her own troubles and surrendered herself to the mass emotions of physical pleasure, dare-devilment and worship of the great god Luck.

Three-quarters of an hour after she had entered the throng, a very different Grace Latrobe was thoroughly enjoying herself. Her pretty face was flushed, her eyes sparkled and her auburn hair escaping from the band, which was supposed to keep it under control, fell about her face most becomingly. The crowd jostled her good-naturedly, hot, struggling bodies pressed her on every side, and voices cheered her efforts at various games of skill or luck. She won fourpence on a dartboard, a woollen doll on the Hoop-la stall, three packets of Woodbines at a shooting-range where pop-guns were used instead of rifles, and received the condolences of the crowd when she just failed to coax an automatic monkey up a stick in time to carry off a gloriously decorated plant pot.

A young man in an open-necked shirt and grey flannel trousers attached himself to Grace as she joined the queue for the Figure Eight. She accepted him as her escort over the track, clutched his arm and screamed like the rest as the cars made their spectacular descents at shattering speeds, and then deliberately lost him in the crowd at the exit, for she did not want any entanglements on that trip.

At length, she arrived at the House of Nonsense, which judging from the shouts, screams and hysterical laughter coming from within, was living up to its reputation. It was a two-storied wooden structure, large in size, with an ornate portal and cash desk. At the latter stood Harry Wragg, the proprietor, taking the sixpences for admission.

"Roll-up, roll-up, ladies and gents," bawled Mr Wragg. "A real tonic waitin' fer yer all inside... Split yer sides and get scared at the same time. Blow the cobwebs away. Roll-up... Continuous show."

Wragg was a little, fat man, always in a sweat, with a habitually loud husky voice, developed into a mighty organ through encouraging passers-by to hand over their money. He wore pebbled glasses over small button eyes, like those of teddy bears or rag dolls. His spectacles were large and like great pools of light, reminding one of the reflecting apparatus worn by opticians on their brows when they inspect the insides of patients' eyes.

Above Mr Wragg's head was displayed a small portion of what was going on within the side-show. It consisted of a small balcony across which tripped contorted customers, their limbs quaking as they fought to maintain their balance on an undulating floor and keep their clothing decent and in order against a strong current of air which blew around their legs. Their faces, as they suddenly found themselves in the open before a gaping, howling crowd of onlookers, were comic and registered surprise, horror, shame or delight according to temperament.

A revolving door ultimately emitted the victims, who shot down a long smooth chute and ended on a coconut mat in every conceivable posture, to be assisted to their feet and directed to the exit by Mrs Wragg, an enormous and strangely serious woman, who seemed to disapprove of the crudeness of her husband's inventions, yet tolerated them as a sound investment.

Now and then, Alfred Whatmough, the man in charge of the machinery which kept up the tremendous agitation, emerged from the dark depths of the interior through a side door, breathed the fresh air deeply, wiped his dirty face on an oily rag and retired again to continue the nonsense.

Grace Latrobe by this time was drunk with the exhilaration of her round of pleasures and sensations. She paid her sixpence to Mr Wragg and entered his show.

As soon as the new victim passed the main entrance, she was taken in hand by a moving floor, like an object of mass-production being passed from process to process and, after making the surprised transit of a corridor ornamented with gargoyles under green lights, found herself in a room illuminated in ruby-red, from the roof of which dangled skeletons and models of hideous marine objects, like squids, dogfish and herring-sharks. She felt quite unmoved so far and wondered whether or not she had paid her money for a mere childish entertainment of coloured lamps and synthetic horrors.

As if to dispel disappointment the next surprise of the tour was a passage through a wind-tunnel which almost blasted the clothes from one's body. This place was well illuminated, and the sound of the air currents was totally drowned by the shouts and screams of the suffering holiday makers. The men were too busy with their own jackets and trousers to notice that the skirts of their lady friends were whisked from their knees to their waists! The exit was in the form of a cakewalk, two steps forward, one step back, through the door in the balcony and into full view of the spectators outside.

Inside again, Miss Latrobe found herself in the Hall of Mirrors. Mirrors concave and mirrors convex, reflecting the onlooker as a dwarf, tortured, contorted, obese, leering, ghastly. Then, stretched out like a piece of chewing-gum, every grimace mournfully magnified. Other parties entered and stood quaking with mirth, awestricken, or shamefaced before their distorted reflections and then the lot passed on to the relief of the Mirror Maze, a nightmare of real and unreal scenes, false images and fantastic tracks, somewhere in the midst of which lay the right way to the next sensation. By keeping her attention on the floor and thus discovering where the mirrors were set, Grace Latrobe soon made her way through the labyrinth into the dark corridor outside. Here, in spite of the concentrated horrors and nonsense, lovers were cuddling in dark corners.

The end was near. Miss Latrobe passed through a primitive kind of revolving door into a room dimly lighted by dark-green lamps in imitation of torches. This place was intended to give you the creeps before you reached the open air and sanity again. From the roof dangled rubber trailers like the tentacles of an octopus, cold, slimy and revolting, caressing your head, face and neck as you traversed the chamber. Couples were fighting their way, squealing and laughing, through this childish device, which nevertheless, judging from the noises it provoked, was effective in many cases. Miss Latrobe thought it utter nonsense, but after all, she had paid her sixpence for nonsense, so couldn't complain. She rather impatiently brushed aside the obscene trailers which wrapped themselves round her hair and throat...

Almost at the last of the show, she struggled to free herself from one of the clinging objects, which seemed more persistent than the rest. It wound itself completely round her neck and she tried to brush it aside with a strained giggle. The giggle changed to a note of terror, for the grip tightened. A new bit of Wragg's nonsense? She screamed. But the hysterical yelling of other tortured customers of Mr Wragg's House drowned her cries or, synchronising them with their own shouts, caused no alarm...

Through the trap door and down the chute to the well-padded end of the adventure swept Miss Latrobe, but she remained prone on her face instead of struggling to rise. Mrs Wragg hurried to assist and turned Grace over...

The crowd screamed like one man and Mrs Wragg fainted on the spot, subsiding on the coconut matting with a loud thud.

Miss Latrobe was no longer pretty. Her tongue peeped horribly from between her livid lips and was gripped between her teeth; a rope bit cruelly into her shapely throat; her eyes protruded, staring in glassy horror.

The crowd stood petrified for a brief second, unbelieving. Then two more women fainted, another four went off into screaming hysterics, and utter pandemonium broke loose, spreading to and convulsing every part of the pleasure beach.

With monotonous regularity the final trap door continued to click and eject the remaining occupants of the House of Nonsense. There was no one to ease their fall at the end of the chute. Instead, they found themselves physically entangled in the uttermost horror. The whole building was empty by the time the police arrived. Every one of the fellow-revellers of the dead woman had melted into the crowd and gone. There only remained Mr Wragg and Alfred Whatmough. The one was weeping at the condition of his wife and tearing his hair at the ruin of his business which the murder would probably bring. The other was still somewhere in the heart of the nonsense, for he had not been notified of the tragedy and was busy keeping alive the commotion for no one at all.

INQUEST

The tragic death of Grace Latrobe caused a great sensation in Westcombe.

At first, there was some doubt as to whether or not the whole amusement park ought to close down for a period of mourning, if not for the victim, then for itself as the sufferer from a startling and uncertain blow to its light-heartedness. After a meeting between the Amusement Caterers' Alliance and the Watch Committee, however, it was decided that the entertainers should not be prevented from making hay while the sun shone, so, after an hour or two of confused wrangling and police investigation, the roundabouts began to rotate again, and the swings to plunge to and fro, and the hundred and one other diversions to pursue their usual courses.

Thereafter, the pleasure grounds were crowded. At first, sightseers flocked there out of morbid curiosity to inspect the gruesome scene and seek details of the horrible deed. They were thereupon drawn into the vortex of sensation and excitement and surrendered themselves to the search for pleasure whilst life was theirs. The caterers thus saw the genesis of a season of phenomenal profit which made them long for a murder every day. The House of Nonsense, after sustaining a terrified taboo for two or three days, burst forth into a frenzy of renewed activities. Mr Wragg's inventions then began to enjoy a period of exceptional popularity, which stimulated him to add two more items to his repertoire of nonsense, one being a haunted room and the other The Dance of Death performed by skeletons to the strains of *Dance Macabre* and *Orpheus in the Underworld*.

The police drew a complete blank in their investigations on the Luna Park of Westcombe. None of the usual methods could be applied, albeit the officers attempted to adhere to them. To talk of fingerprints, alibis, witnesses, was greater nonsense than that retailed by Harry Wragg, who alone from the hundreds of onlookers at the time of the crime, was identified and questioned. Of the multisonant clamour raised when the corpse was thrown to the public after the murder, Wragg was left to testify alone. True, in response to a broadcast appeal later, a flock of would-be assistants arrived at the Town Hall to give particulars of what they saw and what they did on the terrible occasion, but nothing of any use remained as a residue after fatiguing sifting of information. The case was considerably confused by the sudden decision of Boumphrey half way through it to conduct it himself. Taking it over from his underlings, he converted order into chaos, arriving like a man who suddenly leaps from a fast-moving bus and is compelled to run like mad along the pavement to keep his balance. He thus caused a great commotion, for even the smallest remark of an onlooker was treated with a maximum of officiousness quite out of keeping with the extent or importance of it.

There was one obvious point of contact between the deaths of Ware and Miss Latrobe. Preedy was the common denominator!

Littlejohn sought out the doctor again as soon as possible after the second murder. He found him in a state of great distress and confusion. The interview differed vastly from the previous one, in that Preedy's cold cynicism had given place to rage and despair.

"I may as well tell you, Inspector, that Miss Latrobe and I planned to get married as soon as conditions permitted," he said almost at once.

"Indeed!" replied the surprised detective. "I'm very sorry, doctor, and assure you of my sympathy. But what do you mean by conditions?"

The doctor sighed and flung out his arms in hopeless abandon.

"You might as well know everything. It's bound to come out now. Miss Latrobe was already married to a damned swine of the name of Faber. He left her—he was an actor—and ran away with his leading lady in a touring company. Grace sued for divorce and the decree would have been made absolute in about a month. Now, what's the use?"

"Are you in touch with this Faber?"

"Yes. The petition wasn't defended. He's still touring. We kept track of him for our own purposes. This week he's at Wimbledon. We didn't tell anyone of the engagement ... King's Proctor and all that, you understand."

"I see. I'm truly sorry about it. I must make enquiries about Faber's whereabouts at the time of the crime."

"You don't mean to say ..."

"No. Just routine, doctor. Now, do you mind telling me where *you* were at 3.30 today?"

"I'm afraid I've a poor tale to tell, Inspector. It was my afternoon off. Miss Latrobe and I weren't knocking about together alone until after the decree. You follow, don't you? She went off early on her own; I went to play golf at Hinster's Ferry."

"Did you have an appointment with anyone?"

"No. I can't as a rule make hard-and-fast arrangements. Anything might happen to upset things in our job. I just have to take potluck."

"You got to the club early then?"

"No, I didn't. My car's a Hardern — rather an old model — and the make-and-break springs in the magnetos of that type are very brittle and give a lot of trouble. Too highly tempered and tend to snap now and then. As a rule, I carry a spare, but today, I didn't. The thing went west right in the middle of Fettlewick Marsh. Three miles from the nearest garage, and as isolated a spot as you can find round here."

"But the road's busy, isn't it, doctor? Surely somebody saw you..."

"I know it all sounds daft, but what I'm telling you is the truth. At 3 o'clock I broke down. I was there trying to patch it up myself until 3.30. I think four cars and a lorry passed me meantime. I wouldn't know them from Adam again. Then I got a bit fed-up and flagged the next car. I was going to ask him to stop at the garage near the toll-bridge and send out a tow for me. Luckily, the chap happened to be a motor mechanic himself, and with the help of an old brake-clip, patched up the job."

"You didn't know him?"

"Never seen the fellow in my life before. And the funny thing is I didn't even get his name or the number of his car. All I know is that it was an Osborne 12. And there are thousands of those about. By that time it was 4.30. I went on to the club, had tea and played a round with Dr Vincent. When I got home, this was waiting for me."

Preedy crushed out the cigarette he had only just lighted and slumped down in his chair in despair.

"I suppose we can confirm the account of the damage by inspecting your car, doctor?"

"Well, I drove it to the Ferry Garage later and had a proper job done. They'd confirm, of course."

"Very good. And would your good Samaritan be crossing the toll-bridge?"

"Couldn't do anything else on that stretch of road." Preedy's face cleared suddenly. "Why, yes. The toll-keeper might remember the man."

"We'll look into that, then, doctor. And now, had Miss Latrobe any enemies?"

"None that I can think of. Of course, being such a good-looking girl, she'd a number of persistent admirers pestering her to marry them. But none of them knew she'd promised herself to me, so why bear her a grudge? In any case, murder was out of the question."

"Hm. Another point: reverting to the murder of Ware. You were four grains of strychnine short in the routine check of poisons, doctor. How do you account for it?"

"I'm stumped, Inspector. There. Miss Latrobe might have been able to help, but she was out when the police called, and now..."

He passed his hand over his eyes as if to wipe out unhappy thoughts.

"Sure you've no idea?"

"Certainly. I'm as baffled as you are."

"I must say things are looking a bit serious for you, sir. I think I ought to warn you that you mustn't leave town and you must hold yourself at our disposal until this thing's settled."

"You mean, I'm a suspect...?"

The doctor rose wildly to his feet, apparently ready to make a scene.

"Sit down, doctor. Your statements will be verified. You'll agree that is very essential. Where were you when Ware died?"

"That too! Well, I wasn't at his blasted party, if that's what you mean. I've told you all this before. I had cold lunch here. By God! Grace was my only alibi! The housekeeper left the food ready and went off to see her sister who's sick. Miss Latrobe made coffee... I say, do you think somebody's trying to pin both murders on me and has gone so far as to kill Miss Latrobe because she could clear me?"

"If your accounts of your movements are true, doctor, it looks very much like it. To return to our case... Sir Gideon was here at 11.00 on the morning of his death and left at 11.30?"

"I've told you that before. I gave him an injection for a common cold."

"How do you know he left at 11.30?"

"I'd another patient due at that time and commented to her as I let Ware out and admitted her, that she was dead punctual."

"I understand that Ware didn't arrive at the Town Hall until 12.15. Where was he in the interim? It only takes five minutes from here to there, doesn't it?"

"Yes. Why ask me where he went, though? He didn't say anything to me about it. All he did was to complain about his colds, how busy he was and how before the season was out, he'd have Hinster's Ferry in with Westcombe ... Oh, yes, and he mentioned the luncheon and wanted assuring that the injection wouldn't spoil his fun."

"You see the position, doctor! You're short in your stock of strychnine. Four grains is a lethal dose, isn't it?"

"Yes, indeed!"

"Ware's last call was on you and you gave him an injection. The cause of his death was from an *injection* of strychnine!"

"Good God!"

"Yes. So far, the only puncture on the body is reported to be in the left forearm, doctor. *Your* spot. Further, if someone had plunged a syringe into Sir Gideon during the lunch, he'd have kicked-up a deuce of a rumpus. He was irascible, self-assertive and liked attracting attention to himself. The only way, therefore, as far as I see it, was for somebody to give him a delayed-action dose of poison. That's possible, even by hypodermic, isn't it?"

"Quite. Plenty of ways of doing it."

"Such as, doctor?"

"Adrenalin. In simple terms, that drug will seal off a portion of the blood vessels from the main bloodstream for a period. An injection of it, followed by another drug, would, by retarding the latter's entrance into the blood, delay its action..."

"So you see, doctor, I'm not being unreasonable when I ask you to remain in town until the investigation's finished. In fact, I'd be justified in arresting you on suspicion."

"Why don't you, then? You know I've a motive, too! My father...you've heard about him. Ware ruined him and I believe drove him to suicide. Go the whole hog, Inspector! Haul me off to chokey."

"That's my business, doctor. Don't get excited about it. I'll leave it at that... A warning and a request, or rather, an instruction."

To tell the truth, that intuition which had so often served Littlejohn in the past, again sounded the warning bell in his mind. He couldn't persuade himself that Preedy was his man, however black things looked.

Boumphrey was of a different opinion, however, when Littlejohn returned to report progress. He was all for arresting Preedy on the nail. Only the Inspector's strong protest prevented the Chief Constable from taking immediate action. As it was, he put a plainclothes officer on keeping an eye on the doctor. This "shadow" was a man who considered himself well versed in the art of unobtrusive watching. With an air of what he thought was nonchalance, he strolled about the crescent, his hands in his pockets, his mouth pursed in a soundless whistle, keeping the doctor's door in sight, like a cat at a mouse hole. Or else, to relieve matters, he would, now and then, gaze at the sky with a preoccupied air, as though suspecting the weather or, having witnessed the Indian rope-trick, expecting at any time the dismembered body of the boy who had vanished in air, to fall at his feet.

Littlejohn, who borrowed another constable for the purpose,

was able before he returned to his dinner, to confirm Preedy's story of that afternoon's activities.

The Ferry Garage agreed that they had removed and replaced the patched-up spring in the ignition of the doctor's car. He had called at 7 o'clock on his way home from golf and the job had only taken ten minutes.

Furthermore, the keeper of the toll-bridge remembered the Osborne 12 car and knew its owner in the bargain. He was one Johnson, of the Premier Garage, Fettlewick. Johnson, in reply to a telephone call, said that he was the hitherto anonymous good Samaritan and checked the time of the incident, too, in a reliable fashion, for he knew when he started and when he arrived at his destination and estimated the hour when he met Preedy with precision.

Dr Vincent confirmed the round of golf at Hinster's Ferry links.

"Yes, yes, yes," said Boumphrey, "but the whole thing might be a cleverly faked alibi. Preedy could have gone to the pleasure beach in his car, killed Miss Latrobe and hared off to Fettlewick Marsh, bust up his car and come along with a perfectly legitimate tale and a gang of men to confirm it in good faith. Now couldn't he, Littlejohn?"

"Yes, I admit it, sir. All the same, it would be rash to arrest the doctor until the case is cast-iron. Things look black for him, I know, but, to me, his tale rings true."

"It doesn't to me, anyhow. Still, the responsibility's yours, Inspector. Handle it your own way."

"Besides, Chief Constable, Preedy's a prominent local man. There might be hell to pay if he's wrongly arrested."

"I'm willing to back my own judgment, Littlejohn, but we'll give you another day or two to prove your views, if you can," said Boumphrey patronisingly. And he left it at that.

After dinner Hazard called for Littlejohn again.

"I've been going through the House of Nonsense at

Boumphrey's request, to see if it might have been an accident after all!" he said and slumped down at the table where Little-john was sitting finishing his coffee.

"I feel like a change of air and scene after the day's efforts," said the Scotland Yard man. "My brain's tired out and I can't think properly. What do you suggest?"

"What about the pictures?" grinned Hazard.

"There's a good crime film at the Astoria! Humphrey Bogart, I think. It'll be a change!"

They went.

As they returned to the Grand Hotel, the streets were still thronged with people. Residents taking their dogs for a final airing. Lovers clinging to each other in the darkness of corners and shop doorways, or, in the case of the more intrepid ones, anywhere where they felt like it. Visitors hanging round the vestibules of cheaper boarding houses, enjoying the last of the evening, loath to go indoors and thus bring to a close one more day of the holidays.

The moon had not yet risen. People were groping home in the dark. Torches stabbed the black-out. Drunken men hung about lamp posts. One of them was being violently sick in noisy crescendos of retching. There were bursts of singing all over the place combined with the shouts of men and the squeals of women.

"So I said to him, mind your own bloody business... Just like that, I said it..." somebody was boasting in an alcoholic, aggres-sive tone.

The lamps of the side-streets were dimly illuminated by burners which were obscured by objects like small inverted straw-boaters, only made of metal. By the light of one of these, Littlejohn made out a skulking figure, like the one he had seen the previous night from his bedroom window. As he approached, the man scuttered down an alley and vanished.

"See that, Hazard?"

"Yes. What of it? Just another drunk."

"I wonder…"

* * *

THE FOLLOWING DAY, open verdicts were returned on Miss Latrobe and on Sir Gideon Ware.

Dr Preedy created a sensation by his answers to the Coroner. Injection for a cold cure and his having made the only hypodermic puncture in the body. The missing strychnine and no accounting for its disappearance. Death due to an injection of the same poison. Then, the death of Miss Latrobe, his dispenser. There was a lot of betting in bars later, concerning the number of days before Preedy's arrest. The jury might have brought a verdict of murder against Preedy on both counts had not the Coroner been masterful and thoroughly known his business.

The Home Office expert's report confirmed that of the local men. Death by an injection of strychnine, and the puncture in the left forearm was emphasised. It was stated to be possible to use drugs to delay or defer the action of poisons administered as in the case under review. These deferents were sometimes difficult to trace in the blood. Adrenalin, for example, was a product of the human body itself and the small quantities found in the blood of the deceased might have been self-generated by rage or fright.

Miss Latrobe had died from strangulation.

It was a great morning's entertainment for the holiday makers. It gave them lots of things to talk about among themselves and when they got home. The Coroner's court was packed to the very doors, and had payment for admission been imposed, would still have been as crowded.

The enquiry, apart from apparently incriminating Preedy, raised one paramount question. If what Preedy said was true, *where was Ware between 11.30 and 12.15,* when he arrived at the Town Hall?

On the morrow, a civic funeral was planned for the unfortunate Mayor, and visitors to Westcombe as well as the natives, looked forward to yet another high spot in a very full week.

THE SORROWS OF A PUB CRAWLER

The inquest of Sir Gideon Ware was followed by an outburst of further revelry, such as men indulge in after doing their duty by the dead. The thoughts of coffins, corpses and cerements are dispelled of food, drink and good cheer.

Nowhere was this mood more acutely manifest than in the Jolly Sailor, an up to date Olde Englyshe hostelry on the Old Quay at Westcombe. This hotel was once a tavern frequented by sailors and fishermen, but falling into the hands of a speculator who saw its possibilities, it speedily changed its style and its customers. Two adjoining properties were acquired with the inn and the whole converted into a restaurant, cocktail bar, night club and many other things. Before the war, the red neon signs of the Jolly Sailor illuminated the whole of the river-front, giving it the atmosphere of a pantomime Hell or of one of those strange haunts of the Red Death from the imagination of Edgar Allan Poe.

At the main bar of this establishment congregate many of the holiday visitors, as well as strange characters permanently resident in Westcombe. The landlord is unscrupulous in a battle with the Ministry of Food, and strange dishes, in addition to copious quantities of ordinary food and drink, may be had for the paying.

The bar has as many lady customers as men and some of the regulars bring their wives. These ladies, the permanent members of a certain set in Westcombe, vie with each other in attire and their presence creates a type of social ladder, from the rungs of which hang the various notables of the town, patronising those below and keeping them firmly in their places, smiling upwards and envying or admiring those above. The men are unwillingly swept into the toils of this snobbery and intrigue created by their womenfolk. Bonhomie and good will are banished and a spurious heartiness takes their place.

Many of the women drink whisky with the ease and capacity of the men. In many cases, the latter squabble among themselves concerning who's to pay.

"This round on me, old man."

"Well, mine's the next…"

"Same again, Gus, and this is mine."

And so on, in fierce conflict, as in the other spheres of animal life, where the males become ornamental, aggressive, or noisy whenever the female of the species appears on the scene, except that unlike the realms of fur and feather, man enjoys no closed season.

Hazard had suggested a visit to this place of local colour and Littlejohn soon found himself plunged in the heart of its activities. Gus, the bartender and cocktail-mixer, was solemnly presiding over a noisy gathering, his attendant barmaids hovering round like acolytes as he performed his rites. A vast congregation, the customers surged round Gus, crying for his attention and services. Women smoking, screwing up their eyes and wagging their cigarettes between their lips as they conversed, with practised ease and bad manners, emptied glasses of double whisky and gin with the recklessness and abandon of their male escorts... The place was thick with tobacco smoke and the noise of chatter was deafening.

Suddenly, into this bedlam entered Dashwood, the auctioneer. On his arrival, there was a pungent pause in the conversation, then a united roar of laughter, for one side of the newcomer's fat face was swollen to a great size, as though he were inflating a toy balloon with one cheek only. At the best of times, Dashwood was the ugliest man in Westcombe. Now, his head looked like a grotesque contorted mask, such as were worn by performers in the carnivals of southern France in happier, more carefree days.

Hazard had just been showing Littlejohn over the place. On their way through the dining room, they observed Fenwick, the dentist they had met the other night with Preedy and Miss Latrobe at the Winter Gardens. He was eating a substantial meal in which lobster mayonnaise seemed to predominate.

"Evenin', Mr Fenwick," said Hazard as they passed the dentist's table, and then aside to Littlejohn, "By gad, that mess should tickle-up old Fenwick's duodenum. He's always shouting about his ulcers..."

They entered the main bar just behind Dashwood, and it was as well they did.

'Slap Happy' Dashwood was a pub-crawling auctioneer and shark. He earned his living by selling 'bargains' in faked silver-plate to inexpert holiday makers with more money than they knew how to handle. Now, he was dressed in a shabby double-breasted flannel suit, with black stockings and brown shoes with white cloth uppers on his feet. Huge, gross and fat, he bore a certain resemblance to Hermann Göring, which had earned him a nickname he didn't seem to mind.

He was accompanied by Oscar, an ex-jockey, small, wiry and clad in riding breeches and a horsey jacket and neckwear. Oscar spoke with a stammer at the best of times, but in company, his defect always grew worse and he became like a Demosthenes overcoming his infirmity, not with a solitary pebble from the beach, but with a whole mouthful.

"Good Lord! What's the matter with your face, Dashwood?" said a man at the bar, when the laughter had subsided.

Slap Happy and his companion, already the worse for drink, tacked their way to the counter.

"You might well ask…" answered the cheapjack thickly but in loud tones for all to hear. "Here, Gus. This round's on me. What'll it be, chums?"

Those who wanted to drink with Slap Happy gave their orders. Others left his orbit and re-joined their own parties.

"Just one, Mr Dashwood," replied Gus. "You've had enough already, you know…"

"Who's drunk?" asked Dashwood. Oscar looked round as though prepared to take on anyone who challenged his pal. Joe, the chucker-out, at a sign from Gus, edged nearer the bar.

"A bloody dentist did this," complained Slap Happy, lowering a double whisky with ease, in spite of his infirmity. "I ought to 'ave rammed his tackle down his blasted throat. I would 'ave done, too, if I hadn't been under gas…"

"What happened, Dash?" someone asked.

"Got a bit o' toothache, so went round to Fenwick…the ruddy, half-baked molar-puller, that's wot 'e is… Went round to 'im to pull it out. When I gets there, he looks as if he's seen a ghost. The very sight o' me seemed to put the ruddy wind up him. I know I wasn't a bloody oil-painting, my cheek bein' swollen up, though not as much as this by a long chalk. He was terrified at the size of me, that's wot it was. Thinkin' I'd got teeth in comparison and if he hurt me, I'd ram 'is blasted forceps down 'is throat."

Here, having been refused another drink by Gus, Slap Happy in the heat of his narrative swallowed that of another customer without apologising.

"'Gimme a shot o' dope first,' I says. Cocaine, or such stuff.'

At that his nibs nearly 'as a fit. 'No, no,' sez he. 'Better 'ave gas.' So I agrees thinking he knows best. Well, he gives me gas, and I don't go properly under or something, because I can feel every pull he gives on that tooth. But somehow, I was like somebody paralysed. Couldn't get up and defend myself, until, at last, making a desperate effort, I raised myself and pushed him off. 'Is it out?' I says, like walking in my sleep. 'No. I broke it in. Have to try agen. But come tomorrow. I can't do it now.' 'Not ruddy likely,' I says and beats it. Lucky for him I was stupefied with his gas…"

Dashwood looked round for another stray glass and finding none grew melancholy.

"No wonder Sir Gideon Ware kicked the bucket," he said. "After visitin' a chap like Fenwick. As I went in, Ware was comin' out looking like thunder. Then, off he goes to his banquet and drops down dead. If he hadn't been murdered, I'd have said it was from shock being treated by that ruddy 'oaxer Fenwick."

Hazard looked at Littlejohn. They had been sitting in an alcove drinking beer and listening to the conversation with divided interest. Now they were very much alive.

Hazard made his way through the crowd and took Dashwood by the elbow.

"Hullo, Mr Dashwood. Whatever's been happening? Come and have a drink with me and tell me all about it."

"Evenin', Inspector. Oh, it's not a case for the police. No good you interferin'. I'll settle with that ruddy little runt when I lay me hands on him. I'll pull his teeth out one by one. But I'll have a drink with you. Double whisky, Gus."

Hazard gave Gus a nod and the pair of them joined Littlejohn in their corner.

The two Inspectors listened again to Slap Happy's tale of woe.

Then, "Did you say you met Ware leaving the surgery as you arrived?" said Hazard.

"Yes. If he hadn't been murdered, I'd have said he died from shock. I'd have done the same, but for my constitution. Here's to your very good health, gentlemen both."

"What time would that be, Mr Dashwood? "

"Twelve noon, exactly. The Town Hall clock struck as I went in Fenwick's house."

"And Ware was leaving then?"

"That's it."

"You'd be prepared to testify to that if necessary? We want to get as much information as we can about Ware's movements before his death," said Littlejohn.

"Sure, I've said so, haven't I? Jerry Dashwood doesn't say things he doesn't mean."

"Right, then. We'd better have another talk later."

"Yes. And I hope it puts Fenwick on the spot, what I've just said. I'll get even with him for the mess he's made of me. Him and his fancy ways. 'I don't touch it,' says he as he lowers me in the chair and smells my breath. I'd apologised for breathing whisky on him, but with a tooth like mine, aching like hell, I'd to take something to keep it quiet, hadn't I?"

"Sure, Mr Dashwood."

"But his pal can drink with the best of them on occasion."

"Who's that?" asked Littlejohn.

"Dr Preedy. Not often you see him drunk. But when he *is* drunk, he's drunk good and proper. I remember the last club do we had. The annual dinner, you know. Fenwick drinking his seltzers or something such — tonic muck — and Preedy his whiskies. I saw Fenwick taking the doctor home. Old sawbones couldn't stand."

"When was that?"

"August the fourth. Red-letter night that. Never had so many men drunk at a club dinner before. They'd been saving supplies at the club for that night and, by gad, we let ourselves go. Well, s'long. Oscar's waitin' for me. See you again."

"Fenwick tomorrow?" said Hazard as they left the bar.

"Yes. The sooner the better. I'm delighted with that bit of news," replied Littlejohn.

But they did not need to wait until the morrow to see the dentist.

He ambled up to them as they stood in the porch ready for leaving.

"How's things going?" he said, addressing them both with an air of familiarity, and before they could reply, "I've been looking for you since I heard about the inquest this morning. It seems they were wanting to know where the Mayor was between 11.30 and 12.15 on the morning of his death. Well, he was in my surgery from 11.30 to twelve. I filled a tooth for him..."

"It's getting late now, Mr Fenwick," said Littlejohn. "Thanks for the information, which is very useful. I'll be round to see you about it first thing in the morning, then. Goodnight."

And to Hazard's surprise, the Inspector took him by the arm and led him off.

"That fellow heard Dashwood talking, I'll bet," said Littlejohn. "Otherwise, he'd have said nothing. Now what does that mean? Anyway, it'll do him no harm to stew overnight. We've waited long enough for him. Now he must wait for us."

THE NIGHT OF AUGUST 4TH

Fenwick's house in Oxford Crescent was more tumble-down than its aristocratic neighbours, a sort of Cinderella of a place, pretty, but neglected. The stucco on the front had been patched up and the new material gave the façade a camou-flaged appearance, or as though a rash had broken out over its jaded face. The door had been painted a bright red, giving the whole exterior a raddled aspect, as when a harridan tries to rejuvenate herself by rouging her lips.

Littlejohn raised the chromium-plated knocker and brought it down again smartly. The noise reverberated throughout the building.

A shrivelled, suspicious-looking little woman shuffled down the passage and opened the door.

"Mr Fenwick in?"

"You got an appointment?"

"He'll see me. Tell him it's Inspector Littlejohn."

The woman almost whimpered.

"Oh dear! The police. Oh dear! Is it the dog again?"

"No. Please take my card in, will you?"

"Come in. There's a patient in the surgery, but you can wait. I'll tell 'im."

The old woman's erstwhile shuffling feet seemed suddenly to take a new lease of life, and she hustled Littlejohn into a waiting room, bade him be seated and scuttered off, not to be seen again.

There was a square table in the middle of the room with dog-eared copies of periodicals scattered across it. On a bamboo stand under the window flourished a number of geraniums and aspidistras. By the side of it a highly polished, out of date dentist's cuspidor, relic of a bygone age, and probably retained as an ornament. Pictures of cattle and deer adorned the walls. The remaining furniture consisted of a cheap suite, leather upholstered. Four dining-chairs, a carving-chair and two "easies." In one corner stood a bookcase. Littlejohn strolled idly across and examined its contents.

The shelves were about half-filled. Books on dentistry, anatomy, physiology, and kindred subjects. Thrust untidily here and there were professional pamphlets and leaflets advertising proprietary preparations. On the bottom shelf, a number of dental journals and, sandwiched between them, a large, dark-red volume. Littlejohn bent to read the title. *Forensic Medicine and Toxicology. Professor J Dixon Mann, MD.*

The Inspector tried the door of the bookcase. It was locked, but the bolt of one of the double glass doors had not been shot home, and with a bit of persuasion, Littlejohn opened it. He took out the book on Toxicology. It was an old edition, dated 1893, and had been well used. It did not, therefore, fall open at any suspicious page in the detective's hands. He tested it, but after finding "Placing Habitual Drunkards Under Restraint" and "Preternatural Combustibility" he gave it up. There was a bookplate stuck on the flyleaf. The name of Francis Merrivale had been scored out in ink and that of Alan Fenwick written above it. Obviously second-hand. Littlejohn had just time to replace it and adjust the doors of the bookcase to their original position before Fenwick entered.

"Good morning, Inspector," said the dentist. "You've called about Sir Gideon Ware's recent visit here, I presume. Afraid I can't tell you any more than I did last night."

Fenwick was dressed in a white jacket, which accentuated the pallor of his features.

"You're not looking well, Mr Fenwick," said Littlejohn.

"The death of Miss Latrobe's upset me, Inspector. She was a good friend of mine. Dr Preedy, of course, is one of my best friends, and working for him as she did, we met quite often."

"It must have been a shock to both of you."

"And on top of that, Preedy's now unpleasantly involved in the case, isn't he? I thought the questions the coroner asked him were a bit thick, you know... He's not the sort to commit a crime of that kind."

"You were at the inquest, then?"

"No..." Fenwick licked his lips. "Preedy told me afterwards. He was very upset about it."

"Well, to come to the point, Mr Fenwick. Ware was here just before the luncheon. In fact, this seems to have been his last port of call before the Town Hall. What did he call for?"

"I had a filling to finish. He'd called before with a broken tooth, which I cleaned up and in which I inserted a temporary dressing. Then, on the day he was...he died...he called, and I finished the job."

"Hm. Did you use a local anaesthetic, Mr Fenwick?"

Fenwick threw a sharp glance at the Inspector.

"Yes. On the first day. He was very jumpy and irritable if I caused him the least twinge. So I gave him a shot of dope."

"With a hypodermic, I suppose."

"Yes," Fenwick answered boldly, almost truculently. "Naturally."

"What did you inject?"

"A proprietary compound I buy ready mixed. Adrenalin and cocaine. Come in the surgery, I'll show it you. I only gave him a small dose…just one puncture. The second visit, he didn't need it, of course."

They went in the surgery to the discomfiture of a man seated in the operating chair, and Fenwick produced a bottle of a well-known mixture for Littlejohn's inspection. They returned to the ante-room.

"Where was the injection made, Mr Fenwick?"

"Behind the left canine. Why?"

Littlejohn ignored the question.

"Did Ware make any comments which you think might be useful for me to hear?"

"No. He was in a hurry as he always was. Mentioned the lunch and told me to get a move on. He couldn't very well talk with a towel and a cotton-wool pad in his mouth and me poking among his teeth, could he?"

"Did you know him well?"

"Tolerably. He was a member of the same golf club as I am. I never played with him, but we met in the clubhouse and at other gatherings."

"I heard about his beating your dog the other week. Did you have a row about that?"

"Now, now, Inspector. I hope you're not trying to pin some-thing on me. It's bad enough with Preedy under suspicion…"

"Please answer the question, Mr Fenwick."

"No. We didn't quarrel. Another member of the club was there when it happened. You see, although I took the dog with me to the links, she was roaming around when she fell afoul of Ware and I didn't see the incident. When I heard of it, the row was finished, so I said no more about it. I didn't want to get at cross-purposes with Ware. He's vindictive and can do a lot of harm."

"Right. That will be all for the time being. Probably I'll call again if there are any fresh developments on which you might be able to throw light, Mr Fenwick."

"Such as?"

Littlejohn again ignored the question.

"I think, however, you might have come forward with your information a bit earlier, Mr Fenwick. It would have saved us a lot of trouble if we'd known where Ware was just before the luncheon. Good morning."

"Just in time," said Littlejohn to Dr McAndrew later. "While the corpse is above ground, just have another look and see if you can find a needle puncture behind the left canine tooth, doctor."

"Great Heavens, mon!" gasped McAndrew. "Ye've saved my bacon. If we'd had to apply for an exhumation order, it would just about have finished me."

Whereat the worthy MOH slammed on his hat and rushed off to the undertakers who had been given charge of the body.

Littlejohn, too, had urgent business in many quarters.

He strolled back to Oxford Crescent, his pipe going and his hands thrust deep into the pockets of his jacket. It was a pleasant morning and crowds were on their way to the beach and promenade. The distant organs of the pleasure beach in full blast announced that fun and games were hotly in progress even at that early hour, for it was not then eleven.

On a bench under the trees which skirted the garden in the middle of the crescent, four old age pensioners who habitually gathered there in a little exclusive forum and jealously regarded this special seat, were sitting, smoking their pipes and turning over the morning's news. Littlejohn approached them. At first, they received him in hostile silence, returning his greeting curtly, for they thought he was seeking a place among them.

"There's no more room here," said the spokesman, a very smartly dressed old chap with a goatee beard and resembling a veteran of the American Civil War.

"I've no time to stay, sir," replied Littlejohn. "I'm just after a piece of information."

The heads of the four pensioners reared in curiosity and relief.

"Can you tell me if there's a second-hand bookseller's near here?"

They were all about to speak at once and then paused with respectful looks at their spokesman, the veteran.

"Yes. Just round that corner, there, sir," he said. "Name of Mottershead. Locally known as 'Old Mot,' and he don't like it much."

There was a quartet of shrill cackling.

"Thanks very much. I'll be off then and find him."

"You after some book or other?" continued the spokesman. "I'm a reader myself. Perhaps I'd know if he'd got it."

"*Twenty-five Years of Detective Life*, by Caminada," said the Inspector, naming the first title that came into his head.

"Never heard of it," said the old fellow, in peevish tones, for he felt his prestige before his comrades had suffered.

The remaining three pensioners looked at Littlejohn as though he were an ignoramus, quoting titles unknown to their chief.

"Been having sensational happenings in these quarters of late," said the Inspector, passing his pouch to his temporary friends, who set about its contents with frenzied good will and emptied it.

"We have that," said the captain of the gang. "We've our own opinion about those goings-on..."

"Indeed!"

"Aye. And we know who you are, too, so you needn't try to spoof us. You're the Scotland Yard fellow after the murderers..."

The pensioners nodded their heads and said "aye" like unanimous shareholders at a company meeting.

"... But you're wasting your time. Ware killed himself. Took a dose o' pizen, that's what he did. Financial worries. That's what it was. Too much money druv 'im mad."

"That's very interesting, sir. And what about the young lady who was killed on the pleasure beach?"

"No better than she should be, that one wasn't. One o' the fellows she led astray with her wiles, done fer 'er," added the veteran, handing back a limp pouch to the detective.

"You'd see her quite a lot here, wouldn't you?"

"Oh, aye, we did that. Didn't we?"

"Aye," echoed the chorus.

"Did you see her the day she was murdered?"

"We did, sir. Came out of the doctor's about eleven or thereabouts. It was her half-day. She was a bit earlier than usual."

These old gentlemen with nothing to do but watch and talk were apparently the historians of the crescent!

"Did she go straight home?"

"No. She went in the dentist's!"

"What! Fenwick's?"

"Yep. She did, didn't she?"

The chorus confirmed it.

"And stopped there until after we went off to our dinners at noon."

There was a trio of chattering concurrences by the other ancients of days.

"Very interesting, sir," said Littlejohn. "Well, I must be about my business, so I'll wish you good day."

"Good day to you, sir. And thanks for the baccy," said the spokesman solemnly, and the rest echoed him through a smoke-screen of Littlejohn's favourite mixture.

"Old Mot" proved to be a shrivelled man, as dusty as his own old books. Dressed in a green frock coat and wearing a tie like a string, he approached his visitor rubbing together two dirty hands with nails like talons. The shop was like a pigsty, but the owner apparently knew the exact spot where reposed every item of his stock.

"Medical books," he lisped in answer to Littlejohn's question. "Yes. I get 'em now and then. What were you wanting?"

"*Forensic Medicine*, by Dixon Mann."

"Pity. Had one in stock the other week. Got it from the late Doctor Merrivale's widow. Sold it cheap, too, to a young dentist chap. I could get you one, perhaps."

"When did you sell it, Mr Mottershead?"

"About a fortnight since. No use your trying to get Fenwick — that's the dentist who bought it — to sell. He was very keen on having it…"

"Thanks very much, Mr Mottershead. I'll try to get one elsewhere. I'm a visitor here, you see, and won't be able to call again, even if you manage to find one."

"Good morning, then," said Old Mot, and plunged once more into a pile of old books, like a diver hunting for pearls.

Littlejohn was soon using the knocker of Fenwick's house again.

The aged housekeeper almost fainted at the sight of him but made no delay in announcing him this time.

Fenwick was so agitated at this second visit that in his eagerness to find out what was wanted of him he left a patient in the chair with a half-explored cavity.

Littlejohn came straight to the point.

"Was Miss Latrobe here on the day she died, Mr Fenwick?"

The dentist's face lost every vestige of colour, he licked his dry lips and passed his hand over his large, bulbous forehead to wipe away the sweat.

"Yes. She called between eleven and twelve," he said with a show of boldness. "She'd an aching tooth."

"Funny thing, two of them got toothache before they died," murmured the detective as though expressing his thoughts aloud.

Fenwick smiled a sickly smile.

"I can't help that, can I, Inspector? I just did my job. I'd nothing to do with their deaths. Why should I want to kill them?"

"I'm not suggesting any such thing. But I wish you'd told me of their appointments here, without my needing to wring the information from you. Why didn't you tell me when I was here before?"

Fenwick looked pained.

"You asked no questions about Miss Latrobe. To tell you the truth, I quite forgot her visit when you were here. I was so interested in your investigation of the Ware case. I hope you'll excuse me. I wasn't trying to withhold vital facts. I want to be helpful if I can. I'm sure I wish you luck in finding out who did these abominable murders. Miss Latrobe was a friend of mine..."

"What did you do for her when she called?"

"A filling."

"Where?"

Fenwick fumbled with a small, steel card-index and consulted a record card.

"Top right molar."

"Had she an appointment?"

"No. It was a sudden pain, and she called. Quite a small job."

"Very well, sir. Now, I'll be off again. Good morning, Mr Fenwick."

"Good morning, Inspector. Best of luck and, again, apologies."

Littlejohn with sudden afterthought turned to Fenwick.

"Just as a matter of routine, sir. Where were you at about three in the afternoon of Miss Latrobe's death, two days ago?"

"At the golf club; The Royal Westcombe. Why? You don't suspect me of having anything to do with the murder, do you?"

"Who did you play with, Mr Fenwick?"

"I played by myself. My game's a bit off, so I did a practice round against bogey. I passed Thompson and Barwick about 3.30, because I asked them the time. My watch had stopped. I'd played eight holes then."

"Very good, Mr Fenwick, thanks. That'll be all for the present."

"For the present? Is there likely to be much more of this? "

"One never knows until the case is finished. Good morning, Mr Fenwick. I'll let myself out."

Littlejohn made straight for Miss Latrobe's rooms, where he hoped to catch her companion before she went back to work from lunch. He was lucky. Miss Watson had just arrived home.

"I'm awfully put-out about what's happened to Grace," said the big blonde girl, with great feeling. "If I could find the skunk who did this, I'd kill him myself..."

"Suppose you help me to find him, Miss Watson. That's a better idea."

"Gladly, Inspector."

As a rule, Phoebe Watson made great play with her charms in the presence of men, but this time she was in deadly earnest.

"... But what can *I* do? I've not the slightest idea who might want to do a dirty trick on Grace. I've tried to think until my head aches, but it's just got me beat."

"I don't want you to produce a cut-and-dried solution out of a hat, Miss Watson. My job is to collect facts and make them into a whole which will point right at the criminal. Now. Do you remember August 4th?"

"Good heavens! What a question to begin with. Of course, I remember it on the calendar, but I'd need to do a bit of hard thinking to recollect what I, or Grace, for that matter, did on that day."

"It's the evening I'm thinking of."

"As far as Grace is concerned, that's easy. She worked every night of the first ten days in August, except Saturday and

Sunday, getting out the doctor's accounts for the June quarter. Dr Preedy is a bit slapdash about money, and he's always late in making up his fees. When he does it at last, Grace gets…or got, I should say — at the job of sending out the bills right away. This quarter, it was as late as August before he did his stuff, and, as the bank were reminding him that his account had gone overdrawn, Grace had to get busy. She worked every night for about a week until eleven o'clock."

"You're sure of that?"

"Dead sure. She used to tell me most things and I told her quite frankly that she was overdoing it and would soon be a patient of her own boss if she went on as she was. Then, she told me why and said it wouldn't last long."

"Has she seemed in any great trouble of late?"

"Not really, until the death of Ware. And even then, she wasn't upset until things began to look bad for Dr Preedy…"

"You can speak about Miss Latrobe's engagement to the doctor; he's already told me."

"That makes it easier, then. She'd had a raw deal in her first marriage, poor kid. She and Preedy were properly in love, and it looked as though he was going to make it all up to her for past troubles. Then, she got to know that he was suspected in connection with Ware's death. She was in a frightful state about that."

"Did she say anything to you about it?"

"Only generalities. Nothing else."

"She was friendly with Fenwick, too, I hear."

"Yes. I can't bear that fellow, although she seemed to put up with him. She never said anything, but I'm sure he was in love with her, too. Fenwick's a lonely sort of fellow and got friendly with Preedy some way. They went about a bit together and, now and then, Grace went with the pair of them. Fenwick was then their unwitting chaperone, for, until the divorce came through properly, they'd no intention of taking any risks."

"Well, I think that's all for the present, Miss Watson. If you think of anything else that might prove useful, let me know, won't you? Ring up the police station. If I'm not there, Hazard will be. You can tell him."

"Right-oh, Inspector, and good luck. I'm not particular whether you get Ware's killer or not. He'd got it coming to him in any case. But Grace was different…"

They shook hands and parted.

After lunch, Littlejohn and Hazard made their way to the pleasure beach and the local detective conducted his colleague round the House of Nonsense. They had no time for relaxation, but, for the sake of realism, staggered, fumbled, cakewalked and groped their way through the various departments. Instead of being finally ejected through the trap door and down the chute, however, they were piloted by the proprietor, who was more than grateful for their kindness in not stopping the whole works whilst they investigated, to a private exit, used by the staff in coming and going in a more dignified manner than their clients. In the room of mirrors, one of the convex glasses proved to be a door as well, and thence a passage led to the back of the building and into the open air.

"Is this door always kept locked, Mr Wragg?" asked Littlejohn, as they stood by this private entrance, which gave on to a stretch of barren sandhills behind the amusement park.

"No, Inspector. Some of the staff's always bobbin' in and out for a breather. The knob just turns and you're in, except when we lock-up for the night."

The detectives crossed the dunes to the nearest road.

"What's that place?" asked Littlejohn, pointing to a large building set among the sandhills and flying the Union Jack.

"Clubhouse of the Royal Westcombe, Littlejohn. Like to cross and see the place and have a drink?"

"I certainly would, Hazard. Do you know anyone there of the name of Thompson or Barwick?"

"Sure. Thompson's a retired ironmonger, who almost lives on the links. Barwick's the paid adjutant of the local Home Guard. He plays quite a lot, too. You're sure to find Thompson at the clubhouse, that is, if he's not having a round with someone."

Again they were lucky, for Thompson, a lean Scotsman with a figure like a bundle of springs, was waiting for a pal to keep an appointment. Littlejohn first looked at the plan of the links, hanging in a frame in the hall of the clubhouse. Then he nodded to his colleague, who introduced him to Thompson. They all adjourned to the lounge and ordered drinks.

"Alarming epidemic of murders, eh what?" said Thompson, as if to draw out Littlejohn.

"Yes. It's kept the pair of us busy since I arrived, sir."

"Any ideas yet?"

"One or two threads we're following up, but it looks like being a tough job. By the way, we've been checking alibis in the cases of those who saw the victims just before their deaths, and you can help us in one case."

"Indeed! And who might that be?"

"Fenwick, the dentist. At 3.30 on the afternoon of Miss Latrobe's death, he says he passed you on the course and that he asked you the time."

"That's right, he did. He was playing alone."

"On the eighth hole, I gather."

"Yes. Said he'd played eight holes."

"That's the hole nearest the pleasure beach, isn't it, sir?"

"Yes."

"And what would you say was the nearest way from that part to the fairground?"

"The road runs parallel with the fairway. Just get over the fence, take the road for a couple of hundred yards, and then strike across the sandhills for fifty yards and you're there. Why, you don't think…"

"No. I'm just gauging distances. That's all, sir."

"Incidentally," went on Littlejohn, "were Ware and Fenwick recently concerned in an affair about a dog?"

"No. That was Oliver, the Borough Treasurer. But it was Fenwick's dog that Oliver and Ware almost got to blows about. Fenwick used to bring her — she was a setter — from time to time, and on the day we're talking about, she picked up Ware's ball from the fairway. He got her by the collar and set about her with the shaft of a putter. Oliver interfered. The funny thing was, however, that Fenwick didn't say a word when they told him later. He just let it drop."

"Has he still got the dog?"

"No. Oliver stopped Ware's antics with her. Almost hit him, in fact, and gave him a piece of his mind. The bitch broke away during the row and hared off like hell in the direction of the road, terrified. Ran right into a passing car and was killed outright."

"Where was Fenwick whilst all this was going on?"

"Playing on the sixth; and he didn't say a word. Simply gathered up his clubs, left the course, and went off with the chap who knocked down the dog. They picked it up and took it away in the car with them."

"He didn't even go back to Ware about it?"

"Nope. Scared, I guess."

On the way home the two detectives resumed their discussion about distances.

"Are you suspicious of Fenwick?" asked Hazard.

"He's a possible, isn't he? It seems strange that he was so near the pleasure beach when the girl was killed. Has he a car?"

"He had. But he had to give it up on account of the petrol restrictions. He rides a bike now."

"On a bike, it would take about five minutes from the beach to the eighth tee, wouldn't it?"

"That's about it."

They walked on in silence for some distance.

"Have you got a theory brewing?" quizzed Hazard, who seemed to be expecting something.

"I've a vague one at the back of my mind. I don't want to say anything just yet, though. I've a few points I want clearing up first. To give you a half-baked account will only confuse the issue."

"Righto. What do we do next?"

"A phone message to Scotland Yard for some background on one or two people…"

"Fore!!!" came in a voice of thunder from behind them and a fast-flying ball missed them by inches.

Hazard turned angrily in the direction whence the shot had been played. There stood Slap Happy Dashwood, his damaged face contorted in a ghastly leer.

"Let's get out of this, before there's another murder," said Hazard, and they hurried for the road.

14

PREEDY SHOWS HIS TEETH

D octor Preedy had just finished his tea and was preparing to attend to his evening surgery when Littlejohn was again announced to him. The doctor was by no means pleased to see the detective and told him so quite candidly.

"What! Again!" he said without any greeting, and Littlejohn nodded his head with jovial good nature.

"Well, it's time you either arrested me or stopped your pestering. Some way or other, it seems to have got about that I'm concerned in the murder of the Mayor and my patients are falling off alarmingly. No wonder! They don't want a doctor who's a reputation for poisoning."

"Now, now, sir. That kind of talk won't help. The best way to clear the air is to cooperate with the police, not to go off at the deep end whenever you see them."

"See them! They're never off the doorstep! No wonder rumours get around."

Preedy was showing his teeth with a vengeance. His usual air of collected calm had left him. He looked ready to commit murder with his visitor as the victim.

"Well, what do you want? I suppose the quickest way of

being rid of you is to answer your questions… 'and I must warn you that same will be taken down in writing and used in evidence against you.' You needn't say it."

"Not *against* you, sir. That's all wrong technically," replied the Inspector, patiently waiting for the doctor's mood to change, and imperturbably good-humoured as ever.

At last, Preedy gave way. His face even relaxed into a grin.

"I'm sorry, Littlejohn. But really, do you blame me? I've lost my girl and my reputation in a couple of days. I'm suspect number one in the Ware murder, and probably in that of Miss Latrobe as well. On top of that, you fellows are never off my doorstep. I'm at my wits' end, and all I've worked for seems to have gone up in smoke. Might just as well throw myself off the end of the pier."

All the doctor's professional dignity had gone. Littlejohn felt heartily sorry for him.

"As far as Miss Latrobe goes, I'm sorry that nothing we can do can bring her back, doctor. You know you've got my sympathy… But as regards her murderer and that of Ware, well… hat's another matter. Once we lay our hands on him, you'll be cleared. It's up to you to help us all you can."

"You needn't worry, Inspector. Anything I can do, you know, I will do, in spite of my petulance. What do you want this time?"

"First, where were you on the night of August 4th?" Preedy thought a moment and then looked sheepish.

"Do *you* know, Littlejohn?" he asked with an awkward grin and a sidelong glance.

"Yes."

"Then, why ask me?"

"Please let me ask the questions, doctor. I want your account of events."

"Very well. I was at the club dinner. I suppose you know I got tight and was brought home."

"Yes, sir. I do."

"Don't rub it in. You look like a schoolmaster... However, I'd been working hard and hadn't had much relaxation. This was an annual affair and is usually a good one. When Fenwick suggested we went, I fell in with the idea. I relaxed too much. The drink flowed freely, and I took more than was good for me. To put it vulgarly, I got disgustingly tight and had to be brought home."

"By whom, sir?"

"Fenwick. He doesn't take much. Stomach trouble."

"Is he your patient, doctor?"

"No. I've never examined or given him treatment, and I wasn't touting for patients, so never bothered him about it."

"Hm. Do you remember anything that happened on the way home?"

"Very, very vaguely. I seem to recollect Fenwick being about me somehow in the cloakroom at the club and in the taxi. We got into my sitting room and then I must have passed out, for the next I knew, Miss Latrobe was giving me something out of a glass. I was sprawling on the couch. I was damned ashamed of the exhibition afterwards... They got me to bed between them and I slept until morning."

"Miss Latrobe was on the premises, then?"

"Yes. She stayed late getting out the quarter's bills, which were very much behind-hand."

"What time would you get home, doctor?"

"About ten-thirty, Grace said, the following morning."

"Now, another question, doctor. Your poison cupboard: how many keys has it?"

"Two. I carry one on my keyring. The other's in my strong box at the bank. Can't be too careful, you know...or can you? I seem to have made a mess of things in spite of my precautions."

Preedy ran his hand through his hair in dazed fashion. "Do you carry your keyring wherever you go?"

"Positively everywhere. I put it on my bedside table at night, too."

"You took it to the dinner, of course?"

"Yes."

"Was your door key on the same ring?"

"Yes. Why?"

"Please answer the questions, doctor. They're most important. Who let you in when Fenwick brought you home, can you recollect?"

"No… Or…wait a minute. I don't remember getting in at all, but I call to mind a remark of Grace's the day after. She told me off for getting in such a state. Not for drinking, but for giving her a scare. We were in love, you see, and said what we liked to each other."

The doctor's voice trailed off despairingly again.

"Go on, sir. What did she say?"

"Oh, only that when Fenwick called her into the room and she saw me lying on the couch looking such a mess, she thought I'd had an accident and her heart almost stopped… Now her heart *has* stopped, hasn't it? Oh, my God!"

Littlejohn crossed to the sideboard, mixed a stiff peg of whisky for the doctor, and passed him the glass. Preedy looked up gratefully and drank.

"Nay, dammit man, mix yourself one, too. I'm not so inhospitable, even if I am at my wits' end."

"Just once again, sir," continued the detective as he sipped his drink. "Were your keys by your bedside when you wakened on the morning after the…ahem…the night before?"

"No. You see, they undressed me…or somebody did, and just left the stuff as it was in the pockets of my dinner suit. I found the keys where I'd left them, on the chain I wear fastened to the button of the trousers."

"Right. Lastly, when did you last check your poison register with stock?"

"I can't remember when I did it. Grace looked after that. But she was as methodical as clockwork. On the first of every month, at least, she did it herself."

"Borrowing your key, of course?"

"Yes. Now, blast it, you're not trying to implicate her, are you? I won't stand for it, I tell you, I won't stand for it!"

"Calm yourself, please, doctor. I wouldn't be drinking your whisky, I assure you, if I were on the track of you...or yours."

"I'm sorry. It's damned decent of you to put it that way. I've nothing more to say, except that whenever she dispensed medicines and wanted anything from the cabinet, she came to me for the key. I gave it her, and she always locked up and gave it back to me at once."

"Well, that's all for the present again, sir," said Littlejohn, rising and extending his hand, which the doctor took gratefully and shook heartily. "Will you show me where you were when you passed out, as you called it?"

Preedy opened a door out of the hall and showed the Inspector a large, well-furnished lounge.

"In here. There's the couch."

"And where was Miss Latrobe doing the accounts?"

"In the dining room. Across here."

He opened the door facing the lounge across the hall, revealing a small, snug room with formal dining furniture.

"It was cosier and homelier for her than in the dispensary."

"Where's that, doctor?"

"Here."

Preedy showed the way through the lounge again and to a small door leading thence to a well-ordered little place, with a plain desk, shelves of bottles, a sink, draining board and a white, locked poison cabinet.

"You'll think it's funny having a door leading from the lounge, but it isn't really. You see, I'm beginning to specialise in cardiac trouble and some of the local men are starting to send cases to me for second opinion. Then, I don't use the rank and file, panel patients' waiting room, but put on a bit of extra show. The consultant's cases wait in here. I had that door put in so that Miss Latrobe could slip in, take particulars, and bring them to my room, without going all the way round through the hall."

"Thank you, doctor. And now, I'm really going. By the way, did Miss Latrobe ever suffer from toothache?"

"What a funny question! No. Why? She'd very good teeth and looked well after them, too."

"Who was her dentist?"

"Bonamy, just down the Crescent."

"Not Fenwick, then?"

"Come to think of it, he did do a small filling for her a couple of months ago, when Bonamy was down with flu. I didn't encourage her... Fenwick's a decent chap, but he's not qualified. But she insisted, with his being a friend of ours and it being just for once."

"She's not had any recent dental trouble?"

"No. I'd have known, because I usually took a look round her mouth before she went to the dentist. Never touched her teeth otherwise, of course. But she seemed to like my doing a preliminary, well...you see how it was..."

"Quite, doctor. And now I'll go. Goodbye."

Littlejohn descended the steps of the doctor's house with the exhilarating feeling of having accomplished something worthwhile. He even whistled unconsciously a hit "plugged" by Sid Simmons on the one and only occasion on which the Inspector had heard him, *You're the Cause of my Nightmare, Baby*!"

15

CROMWELL'S PERFECT DAY

I t started to rain when Detective Sergeant Cromwell left
Scotland Yard, and it kept it up all day.

"There's a fellow here, Alan Fenwick. No. F-E-N-W-I-C-K.
"F" for Fanny. Got it? You might ring up the passport people and
ask where he was born. He's been abroad, so he'll have a passport. Then, go down to wherever is his birthplace and find out
as much as you can about him, his parents and his family
history. Keep it up till you reach the time when he removed to
Westcombe. All right? Go to it, old son!"

That's what Littlejohn had said over the long-distance telephone the night before.

The result of the passport enquiry was promising. Fenwick
had given Dimpsay, Norfolk, as his birthplace. That sounded
good to Cromwell. He liked Norfolk. The place abounded in
wild fowl of all kinds and Cromwell's major hobby was bird-
watching. He carried his field-glasses over his raincoat when he
turned up for duty the next morning.

"Grand weather for ducks this year be," said the bus
conductor as the detective descended into the town hall square
at Dimpsay. Soon his trouser bottoms were soaking, the rain

shot from his umbrella in torrents and even curved under it to patter on his bowler hat and drip from the end of his large nose.

The sky was like lead, everyone seemed to have taken cover, for there was not a soul about, and the only moving thing to be seen was a baker's van which passed perilously close to the melancholy Cromwell and covered him down the length of one side with a backwash of thin mud.

Cromwell was a very clean-mouthed officer, but in his present plight his past repressions caught him off his guard. Almost before he knew what he was saying he emitted a string of blistering oaths.

"...and it's just my blasted luck to land in a hell hole like this on a wild-goose chase on the only bloody wet day in a fort-night..." he ended up, and then seemed to realise what he had said. He stopped suddenly, looked over his shoulder as though seeking whoever had poured out such a stream of profanity and, realising that he himself had done it, blushed to the bottom of his back. His eye caught a sign facing him.

If the Est 1852 was intended to imply that Jeremiah had set up business in Dimpsay ninety years ago, thought Cromwell, his was evidently the place at which to call for local history. He hurriedly crossed the square and entered the dim, old-fashioned shop. There was apparently no one about, although a bell jangled to announce the intruder. Cromwell beat the counter with his clenched fist to attract attention.

"What is it?" said a voice and, turning, Cromwell saw the saddler sitting silent, a half-finished leather dog muzzle in his hand.

"I didn't see you," said the detective, for the man was squat-ting in the very window of his shop, which the rain had rendered opaque.

"It's too dark to see in the shop, so I moved my bench here," chirped the saddler, "and I was just sittin' quiet-like a-sizin' you up. What do you want?"

Cromwell's appearance must have belied any connection with horses, cats, dogs or budgerigars which, judging from the contents of the shop, were the four sources of Mr Jeremiah Shadlow's livelihood.

"My name's not Shadlow, nor Jeremiah either," said the workman in reply to Cromwell's specific enquiry. "He was my father-in-law, and he's been dead and gone these thirty years. Gabriel Baynes is my name, and I'm nearer eighty than seventy. Been here forty years…"

"The very man," replied Cromwell. "Glad to meet you, Mr Baynes."

"Same to you. Are you a Plymouth Brother?"

"No. Why?"

"Wondered if you were. Thought you were civil enough to be one of them. I'm one myself."

"Good for you," said Cromwell. It was all he could think of to say, for he didn't know the difference between a Plymouth Brother and a Plymouth Rock. He thought Baynes was naming his birthplace.

"Nice place Plymouth," added the Sergeant.

"Never bin there myself," came the reply.

Cromwell gave it up.

"And give me that umbrella," said Gabriel irritably. "I'll have to bail out with a bucket if you stand drippin' there much longer. And take off that wet raincoat, too, if you figure on stoppin' long."

Cromwell handed over the offending articles and Baynes removed them to the darkness behind.

The saddler was a tall, wiry fellow, with a shock of iron-grey hair, a long, wrinkled face, a bulbous nose and a heavy, grey moustache. His pale-blue eyes peered shrewdly through old-fashioned, steel-framed spectacles.

"You've come to talk and quiz, I can see it from your manner. Not interested in the contents o' the shop, but in me and what I've got to say about somethin', I'll be bound," he said.

"Right first time, sir," replied Cromwell. Whereat the saddler drew together two stools, offered one to his visitor and, taking up his knife, awl and thread, set to work.

"Well," he said. "What is it about?"

"Mr Baynes, I'm a detective, seeking information about people who left here years ago..."

"I knew it!" chuckled the saddler gleefully.

"How?"

"Served my time in London. At a place in Bond Street... Yes, Bond Street. And stayed there more than thirty years. And do you know how I got here? Answered a matrimonial advert, that's what I did. Daughter of saddler running own prosperous business in country town...that's what it said. And that's how I met and married Minnie Shadlow, best wife a man ever had. Lost her five years since and I'll soon be followin' her. Fed-up with being on my own. Now, if you was unwed and took my advice, you'd try your luck in the matrimonial adverts..."

"How did you know I was a detective?" interposed Cromwell, for he saw that unless he steered the conversation into his own channels, he'd be in for a whole day's, session of Shadlow-Baynes memoirs.

"Got to know the type in London. It's written all over you."

And as if to lighten the blow before which poor Cromwell wilted visibly, he got up and brewed tea from a kettle, which was boiling somewhere in the background.

"Now, let's get down to it," said the saddler, when at length they had settled to two large mugs of scalding liquor.

"Have you ever heard of anybody called Fenwick in these parts, Mr Baynes?" asked Cromwell, wondering if his tea would cool before he rose to go.

Baynes literally pounced on the theme, for he was one of those old men to whom the present is of little importance and who, as days pass, enjoy with increasing clarity the remembrance of times long gone.

"Fenwick? Yes. I remember a woman called Wilson, who changed her name to Fenwick. Must a' been almost forty years since. Just after I settled here. The reason I recollect her so well, was that she disappeared mysteriously. Did a moonlight flit with all her belongings."

"Is that all you know, Mr Baynes?"

"Give me a chance. I'm coming to it. She always was a bit of a mystery. Had a youngster and although she gave-out she was married, a lot of the women said she wasn't. How they knew, is more than I can tell, but some women seem to have a nose for such things."

"Yes, they do."

"It was quite a nine-days' wonder in the town when she vanished. But it got round that somebody'd been enquiring too much into her affairs; a solicitor chap had been here, and she must have taken fright and bolted. The women weren't half pleased with themselves. They said as it just proved what they'd said. Anyhow, it was all straight and above board. No murdering or kidnapping, I mean. Because Sam Edges, the removal man, dead and gone these twenty years, poor chap, took her stuff for her."

"Where did she go?"

"Ah! That would be tellin', mister. Anyhow, as it's all so long ago no harm'll be done. By the way, what are you wantin' all this for?"

"Private business. I don't even know myself, Mr Baynes. I was just told to get to know all I could about the Fenwicks," answered Cromwell truthfully.

"Well, I don't like workin' in the dark, mister. But I've taken a fancy to you and, if it'll do you a good turn, I'll tell you."

"Thank you, Mr Baynes. I'm more than grateful."

"Sam Edges, before he got the job, had to promise to tell

nobody where Mrs Wilson, or Fenwick, was going, and Sam was a man of his word. Didn't tell a soul till his dying day. But on the day that he moved her goods at night, Sam called here for a new harness we'd made for him and opening his wallet to put in the receipt, dropped a paper, which was a sort of account made out in advance so he could give it to Mrs Fenwick, or Wilson, when the job was done. Understand?"

"Yes."

Cromwell remained outwardly calm, but excitedly bent and unbent his toes in his large boots.

"On the bill it said somethin' like this: To moving household furniture, etc, from Dimpsay to Follington, and then the price, like. I remember the place, because it's in Essex, and I once went there. In fact, it was answering another matrimonial advert, which didn't suit me, but was a narrow and lucky escape, praise be. However, that's as may be. The paper wasn't in an envelope and Sam's writing being so big that it hit you right in the eye, I'd took it in before I realised I was readin' it. The name Mrs Wilson had been crossed out and Fenwick put instead. I asked Sam what it meant, and he said Mrs Wilson had changed her name for use in Follington. He didn't know why. Promised Sam on the spot, I did, to say nothing about it and till now, I've kept my word."

"Thank you very much, Mr Baynes. I'll respect the confidence. The information won't be broadcast, I can assure you. Follington, eh?"

"Yes. Fair stretch from here, as I guess you'll be off there now, if I know detectives."

"Do you know where the Fenwicks, or Wilsons, came from when they arrived here?"

"I wasn't here then myself. But my dear wife was. A native of the place, she was. I once heard her say that she believed Mrs Wilson — I call her that, as it was her name when here, though I've remembered them both on account of the circumstances being unusual — Mrs Wilson came from Hull. The baby was born here, you see, and her having to register the birth, gave the place she was born in as Hull. In those days, the registrar lived next door to this shop. It was a house then. The grocer who's there now, put a shop-front in it thirty or more years since, when he started business."

Cromwell wondered if everyone in Dimpsay was as aged, long-established and reminiscent as Mr Baynes.

"My dear wife, then a maid, of course, and the registrar's spinster daughter used to gossip a bit over the back fence, and that's where, if you ask me, the real facts about the illegitimacy of the child leaked out. Miss Parrott, the registrar's daughter, told my wife that Mrs Wilson, as she then called herself, was really *Miss* Wilson, and came from Hull. Mr Parrott's bin dead these twenty-five years, so it can't do harm to tell, although he might have lost his job through giving away private information if he'd been alive and registering now, mightn't he?"

"Yes, he might, Mr Baynes."

"I don't want to hurry you off, mister, but there's the 146 bus to Grantford Junction, and it goes in five minutes. You'll need to catch it for the train if you're going to Follington today. I don't know how you'll get there, but there's not another bus from here for two hours if you miss that one. It's still raining, so you'd better wrap up."

After heartily thanking Mr Baynes for his help and donning his mackintosh and bowler again, Cromwell raised his umbrella and hurried through the downpour to the ramshackle vehicle standing in the market square. He had an awful journey to Follington, arriving there at six in the evening with the rain still falling in torrents.

Follington was a fairly large market town, but the deluge of the day had swept the population indoors and washed the streets clean. The town centre was deserted, save for one country bumpkin, who was either keeping a tryst or thoroughly enjoying the rain, for he was wet through and grinning like a Cheshire cat.

Cromwell made for the nearest cafe, which was just on the point of closing, for its daily dose of rations was exhausted, but the two maiden ladies who kept the place were so filled with compassion at the sight of the traveller, soaked, melancholy and with the nasal thickness and rheumy eyes of one about to start a cold, that they lit the gas fire again and charitably served him from their own personal larder.

When the more business-like and talkative of these two good women had laid a repast consisting of Spam, pickles, prunes and cheese, before their guest, he invited her to take a cup of tea with him and explained the purpose of his visit, albeit he felt more like asking for a bed, a toddy and a hot-water bottle.

"Of course, I knew Mrs Fenwick," replied the elderly lady, the Miss Sophia Speakman of the firm of S & S Speakman, Pastrycooks, Est 1898, announced on the windows in letters of gold. "She attended our chapel and a good, hard-working woman she was, too. She died more than twenty years ago."

"She had a son, too, I understand."

"Yes, and a good mother she was. Worked her fingers to the bone for that lad. And a miserable end he came to in this town, I *must* say, although it was generally agreed that he was the injured party. He had to pack up and go, to avoid the scandal."

The senior Miss Speakman was portly, old-fashioned and good-humoured, and watching her as she sat before the fire, holding up her skirts to warm her calves and stroking the large black cat which had jumped in her lap, Cromwell thought how mellow she looked. Their conversation was disturbed by a telephone call concerning tomorrow's business, and meanwhile, her place was nervously taken by her younger sister who would never see sixty again. Very thin and very jumpy, and apparently totally dependent on Sophia, was Miss Selina. Most of her conversation consisted of verbatim renderings of her sister's opinions. "My sister says..." or by way of a change, "Whatever would my sister say?" occurred in almost every sentence, and Cromwell was relieved when the phone call ended and the human gramophone was replaced and scuttered off into the rear noisily to remove from one place to another what appeared to the miserable Cromwell to be about a thousand empty jam-jars.

"Yes, they came to our church," continued Miss Sophia. "The woman worked herself to death, eventually, for the boy. Gave him a good schooling and then, Mr Hardcastle, a dentist, who also attended the chapel, took him under his wing and trained him from errand-boy to partner in the business and, when he died, left him the practice. Not a very good one, I'm afraid, but a windfall for a boy like Alan. He was a sickly sort of lad, who kept very much to himself. In fact, he ought to have gone about with other boys, instead of always hanging on his mother's apron-strings. Filial love is admirable, but a boy can suffer from too much and become warped and introspective through it."

Miss Speakman had read articles on psychology in religious journals and knew all about it!

"What was the scandal you spoke of, Miss Speakman?" asked Cromwell, full of Spam and prunes and feeling a bit better.

"Oh, a girl set her cap at Alan and led him a dance. She was called Cherry, Dulcie Cherry — stage name! — and her mother looked after Fenwick's rooms and 'did' for Hardcastle before him, too. Dulcie evidently thought Alan a good catch and her mother encouraged her. It ended by Alan assaulting Mrs Cherry for something she'd said. There was nearly a court affair about it. Mrs Cherry, a common sort of woman, told all sorts of tales. Insinuated that Fenwick had seduced her daughter. But, as the girl was apparently no better than she should be, nobody bothered much about it. As regards the assault, however, that was more serious and, but for the police being uncommonly kind and considerate to Fenwick and sort of acting as peacemakers between the parties, goodness knows how it would have ended. I think the matter was settled out of court in some way, for Fenwick seems to have paid Mrs Cherry's doctor's bill and more for wounded pride. But it drove away his patients. Nobody's going to submit themselves for treatment to a dentist who half strangles people, even in temper."

"Quite right. Could you tell me, who of the police was in charge of the case, Miss Speakman? I might be able to get his angle too, if you remember who it was."

"Yes. I recollect him quite well. Sergeant Boumphrey, his name was. He left the town long ago and, I believe, has got on very well. I don't know where he is, actually, and I don't care, for he wasn't a fellow I greatly liked. Instinctively, I mean. I'd nothing really against him."

"Do you know where Fenwick eventually ended up, Miss Speakman?"

"Yes. Westcombe-on-Sea, I think the place is. One of our church members was there some time after his unfortunate affair here and met him on the promenade. He wasn't very glad to see her from what I can gather. Always a queer, introspective boy."

"Well, I've had an excellent meal, Miss Speakman, and a very illuminating talk with you. I'm really sorry to go. However, all good things come to an end. So, if you'll give me my bill, I'll be on my way."

"Two and eightpence, please, Mr..."

"Cromwell, madam. And thank you very much."

"Always be glad to see you again whenever you're in these parts," said Miss Speakman as they parted at the door of the shop.

"Goodbye. Always be glad to see you..." echoed Miss Selina. "My sister always says there's no friend like an old friend."

Cromwell found the doors of the railway station closed, and

seeking someone to ask about trains, found only the soaked yokel smiling in the rain which continued unabated.

"Any trains to Pikeley Junction from here?" asked Cromwell.

"Yes," smiled the youth, seemingly delighted at the fact.

"What time's the next, do you know?"

"It's gone. Last un that be, and all."

"Any buses?"

"Yes."

"How do they run, and where's the bus station?"

"Last one's gone."

"Good Heavens! I suppose I'll have to stay the night."

Cromwell's heart sank. The rain came down in sheets, and unlike his companion to whom it seemed a tonic, the sergeant felt like nothing on earth.

"Where's the best hotel here?"

"Stag. Over there."

"Can I get a room, do you think?"

"Aye, most times. But I heard say they was full-up."

Sure in his mind that the bumpkin was intent on depressing him to the stage of committing murder, or suicide, or both, Cromwell left him and there he remained smiling, the unsolved problem of this narrative.

They managed to fit in Cromwell at The Stag and gave him a good dinner. He afterwards telephoned his news to Littlejohn, a process which involved clearing a number of regulars from a small room which contained the only instrument, and which the landlord was persuaded temporarily to make private by a sight of Cromwell's impressive warrant card.

At the end of his long tale, Cromwell was heartily congratulated by Littlejohn. The cheery sound of his chief's voice at the other end of the line put heart into the sergeant.

"You've done jolly well, Cromwell. It might have taken days to collect what you've got in a few hours," said the Inspector.

"Oh, I was lucky," humbly replied Cromwell. "I struck the right people first bang off. Atishoo!!"

"Don't be modest, man. You've done good work. Did I hear a sneeze? Been getting your little feet wet?"

"Never stopped raidid all day. Bid wet through all the tibe. Just bissed the last trade to Ludud, too," choked Cromwell, now properly in the throes.

"Well, I won't keep you. Thanks a lot and let me have a written report when you're fit. Meanwhile, get a hot-water bottle in the bed and a good strong glass of rum and milk inside you. Goodbye, old chap."

Cromwell thought his chief's suggestion a good one. He ordered a double whisky to begin with, for he thought the landlord might take umbrage at the mention of milk. He felt no better for it, however. In fact, it cast him down considerably, so he braced himself to find the landlady and ask her for his hot-water bottle. She, good woman, took him in hand, mixed him a strong rum and milk and bade him drink it, as it would do him good.

"I feel heaps better already," said the detective to his gratified hostess after the mixture had disappeared. "I think I'll have another, just to make sure."

"You'd better be careful, hadn't you? You'll feel the effects of it when you get on your feet."

Cromwell felt fine. He insisted on repeating his order, after which he seemed to float upstairs to his room. There, as he took off his clothes, he began to sing *The Last Rose of Summer*. The guest in the room to the right was a commercial traveller, who had deliberately reached the state of bliss achieved accidentally by Cromwell. This man began to sing in harmony and for some time they trolled away merrily.

The occupant of the room to the left, however, was a colonial bishop making a tour of East Anglia and Essex on foot and, rudely awakened by ribald singing, he smote hard on the wall in protest... An indignant Victory V.

"You go to hell," replied the intoxicated detective.

Whereat the high clerical dignitary, who was a meek man, if impulsive, drew the bedclothes' over his head in horror, and later suffered a nightmare in which he figured as Dante in mild obedience to Cromwell's orders.

Kindly sleep drew a veil over the rest of that shocking affair. The bishop, leaning heavily on his ash crosier, left early the following morning, whilst Cromwell slept. It is as well they did not meet, for the exalted reverend gentleman was the uncle of an Assistant Commissioner of Scotland Yard!

LITTLEJOHN SUMS UP

Cromwell's excellent work in the Eastern Counties delighted Littlejohn and considerably clarified the problem which faced him. There were one or two gaps still to be filled-in in the jigsaw, which was gradually beginning to take shape, and these the Inspector began to investigate the first thing on the morning following his subordinate's report.

First, he telephoned to Scotland Yard for a brief history of the career of the Chief Constable of Westcombe. Boumphrey's name, suddenly appearing in the Follington information, started a train of thought and deductions which Littlejohn was eager to confirm.

Then, there was the news that Mrs Fenwick, or Wilson, had her origins in Hull, the city which, according to the meagre and uninformative file supplied by Boumphrey, had once harboured Sir Gideon Ware. The Inspector put through a call to the Hull police as well and enlisted their help in exploring past Wilson history.

Next remained Lady Ware. She had been too prostrate to see anyone since the death of her husband, but now Christopher

Swift had sent a message to say that she felt able to face the ordeal of police questioning.

The Ware home was some distance out of Westcombe, a graceful old house, surrounded by a park and fine trees. Swift conducted Littlejohn to Lady Ware, who received him in a cosy morning room. As much of the interior as Littlejohn saw, greatly impressed him. It was furnished in good taste. The pictures were excellent, the decorations in keeping, and the comforts chosen with care and sound sense. There was not a jarring or discordant note anywhere about the place.

The Inspector understood who had been behind Ware when he chose his home and fitted it out. Lady Ware was of a totally different type from her husband, and evidently came from a class far above the one whence he had sprung. She was well-bred and possessed of a resolute but gentle manner. Now, there was nothing of the distraught widow about her. She had mourned in secret awhile and then faced the world again. She had the future to meet and her responsibilities to fulfil. She had put self-pity away from her, and she received her visitor with calm fortitude.

"You will appreciate, Lady Ware, how distasteful it is to me to have to recall to you the tragic events of the past few days, but duty is duty," said Littlejohn after the preliminaries of getting to know each other had been overcome. "The next thing is to bring your late husband's murderer to justice and I'm responsible for it. I'll be as brief as I can."

"Don't hesitate to ask me anything, Inspector, regardless of how you might think it will affect me. The sooner the matter is closed, the better it will be. The formalities must be attended to, I agree, and I ask you to spare no effort in bringing the wretched criminal to book."

"Thank you, Lady Ware. First of all, do you connect anything during the days preceding the death of your husband with the cause of it? I mean, had he mentioned any threat, any incident, which might have led up to the crime?"

"Nothing whatever, Inspector. Let me say right away, that had there been anything, I would have learned of it. Sir Gideon was known as a hard man, a man of business, who insisted on his pound of flesh. There's no denying that, so why should I try? He was also said to be ruthless with his subordinates in exacting the utmost service from them. He was quarrelsome, too, I understand. All that I know and have gathered it from one source and another over a long life spent with him. Yet, never has he shown those qualities in his own home. I can truthfully say that during the thirty years I have been married to him, he has been an ideal husband and father. In that, I have been blessed."

She paused a moment, fixing her eyes ahead, as though gratefully remembering the past.

"That is why I say I would have known of anything which might have upset or threatened him. He told me everything, for he was incapable of bearing his troubles alone. I speak quite frankly about his personality. That, I take it, is the best way to help. And to try to withhold anything about him would be mere useless sentimentality. He was good to *me*. That I know. Outsiders didn't find him so pleasant. That *you* know, and you would doubt my sincerity if I tried to tell you otherwise."

"I can't say how grateful I am, Lady Ware, for your confidence…"

"But you're not here to listen to my views of Gideon's ways. There must be something more important than that. Ask your questions, however painful they may be."

"Then, with your permission, my lady, I will ask the most embarrassing one first. Does the name Mary Wilson convey anything to you?"

A spasm of pain crossed the face of Lady Ware and was gone.

"Yes, Inspector. She was a sweetheart of Sir Gideon's in his early days. That was in Hull. I have told you that he was in the habit of opening his heart to me. He was so built that he couldn't bear the burdens of conscience alone. He cast them on me if he could. In this case, he confessed to me after the birth of our son, that he had deserted a girl of the name you mention, and that he had left her carrying his child. He tried later to make amends but failed. He was unable to trace her, for she fled without leaving a clue behind her. Have *you* brought something to light, because if you have, I'd be grateful if you'd tell me? I regard myself under an obligation to his memory to do the right thing by her."

"She is dead, Lady Ware."

"And the child?"

"I have reason to believe that a son was born, but he vanished after her death."

"And you suspect...?"

"I can't say, Lady Ware. The idea has occurred to me. I am pursuing it. That's all I can truthfully tell you for the present."

"I see."

"Another matter, your Ladyship, and I must ask you to treat this with the utmost discretion. It's important, but very embarrassing to me. What were the relations between Sir Gideon and Mr Boumphrey the Chief Constable here?"

"Ah! I see you are very wide awake, Inspector." Lady Ware smiled knowingly at Littlejohn, and then recovering, nodded gravely.

"Yes. They were associated in several matters. Boumphrey was Inspector of Police at Battleford, a small east coast town in which we had a summer cottage years ago. In fact, he was instrumental in tracing some jewels of mine which were stolen at the time. When the post of Chief Constable became vacant here, Sir Gideon put forward Boumphrey's name, at Boumphrey's request, of course, and pressed it for all he was worth. And that, as you'll have guessed, meant that the job was already in Boumphrey's lap."

"And Sir Gideon cited the jewel robbery as his main example of Boumphrey's ability?"

"That and what he said he had learned and experienced of him in other directions during the times we were at Battleford."

"But that wasn't all there was to the story, Lady Ware?"

"No. The jewellery affair was only a side-line. Boumphrey knew about Mary Wilson. He came to Gideon one day at Battleford and told him that, in the course of his duties in some place or other, he had learned from a woman that Sir Gideon had, at one time, been her lover, and that an illegitimate son had been born as a result. My husband told me and asked me what he must do about it. We thought that nobody else knew, for Mary Wilson's father was long dead. He turned her out, I gather, when he learned of her disgrace, although she would never say who was the father of the child which was to come. Boumphrey was very close in the affair and said he'd been informed in confidence after a kindness shown to the woman. The thing amounted to blackmail, for we couldn't afford the scandal to get abroad. Gideon was a very prominent figure in many circles and, although such things happen in the best regulated families at times, he was very sensitive about it. He did his best for Boumphrey and I must say Boumphrey never seemed to take advantage of his information."

"Did Sir Gideon ever enlist Boumphrey's help in trying to trace this Mary Wilson, Lady Ware?"

"Oh, yes. The matter never really dropped. Previous to that, Sir Gideon had tried discreetly through solicitors to find her. In fact, they did find her and offered provisionally to arrange for the child's adoption. But the woman just fled again after refusing to consider it. Boumphrey tried, too, but didn't succeed."

"Was he established at Battleford when you took up residence there?"

"No. He came new to the place about six months after we bought the cottage."

"Well, I don't think I need trouble you further, Lady Ware. You have helped me greatly and have brought me considerably nearer my goal."

"I can't see how, Inspector. In turn, I'd like to thank you for your tact and consideration in the whole matter. I'm infinitely grateful."

With such expressions of mutual appreciation, the pair of them parted.

The enquiries concerning Boumphrey and the origins of Mary Wilson, in Hull, had been made from an outside telephone, lest Boumphrey should object to any raking into his own past history. The results which were awaiting Littlejohn when he asked for them would have been revealing had Lady Ware not already supplied the bulk of the information. The reports merely confirmed what she had said in each case.

Hazard was waiting for Littlejohn at the Grand Hotel when the Inspector arrived there.

"And where are we now, Littlejohn?" asked Hazard eagerly. "I'm quite in the dark. Are we nearing the winning-post or just running round in circles?"

"We're very warm, Hazard. And now, with a vote of thanks to you for your help and your patience, I'm going to outline what I've found out so far and, finally, tell you who I think killed Sir Gideon Ware. You know as well as I do, that there are only two likely suspects. The men who gave Ware injections on the day he died. Fenwick and Preedy. Which one is it?"

"Looks black for the doctor, I'd say. Motive is there. Opportunity, too. Then, his dispenser, who, having access to his poison cabinet and knowing his movements, must have known what happened. She might have threatened him with exposure, and been killed, too. Have you smashed his alibi?"

"Let's begin at the beginning, shall we?"

"Well…will it take long? It's lunch time, isn't it? What about something to eat here and then a talk over coffee?"

"Admirable. I'm sorry I didn't give a thought to food, although now you mention it, I'm damned hungry. This air gives one an appetite and no mistake. Let's eat, then."

After lunch, in a secluded corner of the lounge they resumed their conference.

"The whole business began in Hull about forty years ago," said Littlejohn when they had lit their cigars, the first they had smoked there at the Corporation's expense. "Ware was then a penniless bricklayer and was courting a girl called Mary Wilson. He seduced her, ran out on her, and left her to bear the brunt alone."

"Just like him!"

"Wait a bit! As the Hull police have told us, also Lady Ware, this girl was turned-out by her father and left the town. She next turned up at Dimpsay in Norfolk, where the child was born, a boy. There she settled for a time, a decent, respectable person, working hard to bring up the kid. Meanwhile, Ware had struck lucky and started his upward climb to fame and fortune…"

"Disgrace and misfortune, you mean."

"Have it as you like. Ware had never quite silenced his conscience about his treatment of the girl. He married, however, a very fine woman who had a big influence on him and whom he vastly respected and, I must conclude, loved very dearly. He told her of his escapade and treachery. She must have persuaded him to try to make amends, with the result that solicitors were sent to trace Mary Wilson. In some way or other, they caught up with her at Dimpsay, but she bolted before anything could be done, changing her name in the bargain. Thanks to Cromwell, we know she moved to Follington, in Essex."

"A bit of damned good detective work, that, if you ask me."

"Cromwell *is* damned good. You must meet him one day. You'll take to him right away. But this is the first surprise for you. Do you know what the new name of Mary Wilson was? Mary Fenwick!"

"Good Lord!"

"Yes. I thought that would astonish you, Hazard. Cromwell found out that Alan Fenwick was Mary Wilson's son, who became a dentist in Follington. Alan Fenwick is Gideon Ware's son."

"By Jove! That puts a new light on things, doesn't it?"

"It does, with a vengeance. You know what Fenwick is. A strange sort of chap. Inhibited and, if I may use that hackneyed term, one with an inferiority complex and a mind that plays merry hell with him all the time. Fenwick must have discovered who was his father. Perhaps his mother told him, or else he found it out himself. He made up his mind to make Ware pay for what his mother had suffered."

"But the fellow's been here for years. Why didn't he get on with the job?"

"Opportunity, for one thing, I think. He must have been pondering the perfect crime. As far as I can see, he never approached Ware and disclosed who he was, for if he had done, Lady Ware would surely have known. Now, in the light of our information look at the crime..."

"I say, Littlejohn, what made him decide to kill when he did?"

"First of all, Ware changed his dentist and tried Fenwick. Thus, he played right into Fenwick's hands. Secondly, and very important in the case of a lonely chap like Fenwick, Ware caused the death of his dog. Are you a dog lover, Hazard?"

"Yes. Our bullpup's one of the family."

"Well, then, remember Fenwick's best friend was his dog. He

was too stunned to realise what had happened at first when the dog died. He didn't even go and slang Ware for what he'd done. He just went home and started planning to kill him. He bought a book on poisons quite recently and must have been picking his dose. Then, along comes Ware. Fenwick does half a job to get him back in the surgery after he's made a few preparations. He studies his toxicology book and, when the patient arrives, gives him an injection of strychnine. But it won't do for Ware to die on Fenwick's hands. Now, one of the developments of modern dental anaesthetics is the use of adrenalin, which seals off a portion of the circulation from the main bloodstream for a time. Fenwick gives Ware a dose of adrenalin first, following it by the fatal shot of strychnine under cover of giving a local anaesthetic. The adrenalin slows up the action of the poison, and not until the effect of it wears off, does the strychnine begin to work. By that time, Ware's on his feet making a speech at his banquet."

"Ingenious!"

"Yes, but that's not all. At first, it looks as though Fenwick is in luck and someone else is going to take the rap for his crime. You see, Preedy, the doctor, has used a hypodermic on Ware the same day and could easily have done it. Furthermore, Fenwick hasn't any stock of strychnine, but Preedy has, and it's a fatal dose short on his records. Fenwick pinched that dose, I'm sure, when he took Preedy home drunk after the club dinner a few weeks before."

"Fenwick must have been a cold-blooded fish to try to frame his own pal."

"His pal who'd stolen the girl he fancied. Miss Latrobe's friend tells me that Fenwick was in love with Miss Latrobe, but that she turned him down for Preedy."

"So, he framed Preedy for Ware's crime and…why, he must have killed Grace Latrobe!"

"Yes, I think so. I don't actually say he was clever enough to frame Preedy. Circumstances just helped him. Preedy struck me as being patently honest, however, although he'd no love for Ware. His alibi, too, was clean-cut. But Fenwick, like these introverted types, had it worked out too pat. He'd planned to steal the poison after the dinner. So, to prevent himself having to drink too much, started a tale about being off alcohol on account of an ulcerated stomach. Yet, we see him eating lobsters at the Jolly Sailor. The thing just doesn't tally."

"You don't miss much, do you, Littlejohn?"

"It's our job to notice little things. But this is more important. When he got Preedy home blind-drunk, Miss Latrobe was there, working late getting out the doctor's bills. When the strychnine was missed and Preedy was suspect, she rallied to his aid. She remembered something that happened on the night of the dinner and faced Fenwick with it. I learned that before she went to the amusement park, Miss Latrobe visited Fenwick. She must have accused him of taking the strychnine and threatened to expose him. That put him properly in a jam. He'd got to kill her before she could talk. He followed her on his bike to the pleasure beach, saw her go in the House of Nonsense, and went in by the back exit. The place was dark, and he sneaked up on her and throttled her. Next, he hurried out, cycled off to the links and created what he thought was an alibi, by calling the attention of two players to the time and saying he was on his eighth hole. Don't you see, Preedy might easily have taken the blame there, too, and been suspected of killing Miss Latrobe to silence her about what she knew of *him*? But I've had my eye on Fenwick of late. He's been following me about. It's just the same thing as the criminal revisiting the scene of the crime. In this case, he's fascinated by the machinery which is slowly moving upon him. He wears a black slouch hat. I saw that hat one night from my bedroom in front of the hotel. It would be about two in the morning to be precise. Fenwick, wondering which was my room no doubt, and morbidly hanging round. He was trailing us when we went to the pictures the other night. I called your attention to it. He's met me a time or two in the hotel lounge. We saw him in the Winter Gardens and the Jolly Sailor. He was cashing a cheque at the bank the day I called to see Oxendale. It's not all coincidence, you know."

"The man must be mad…"

"Not mad, but just too clever by half. He thinks he's keeping up with us on the case."

"Incidentally, Littlejohn, one thing's puzzled me. Why didn't you get on to the medical report about the hypodermic injections right away? There was quite an amount of time wasted through our thinking he'd taken the strychnine at the banquet in food or something."

"That was Boumphrey's doing. He'd got the proper report, but said he hadn't, and gave me a word-of-mouth account, omitting the injection part."

"Whatever for? Although knowing Boumphrey as I do, I'm not surprised at anything."

"Well, prepare yourself for a real surprise now. Boumphrey was in the police force at Follington when Fenwick and his mother lived there. He must have discovered in some way that they were connected with Ware, for he blackmailed Ware into getting him the job here."

"I thought there was some jiggery-pokery about that appointment."

"He told Ware he didn't know the whereabouts of his son. But he must have known. He got Fenwick out of some trouble with a girl in Follington. He was most kind, I believe, and prevented a court case, by acting as intermediary between the parties. Cromwell saw the girl, name of Cherry, this morning and phoned me again. I think Boumphrey's reasons for intervening were to keep the affair out of the papers. He didn't want Ware to see anything about his illegitimate son in the press, although Fenwick, as a name, wasn't likely to excite Ware's curiosity. But things might have got out if the case was aired.

I'm prepared to bet that Ware must have found out just before he died that Fenwick was his son. You remember, Father Manfred said that Ware's dying words were 'My son!' Not the one with the RAF in Canada, but Fenwick!"

"Boumphrey mustn't have told Sir Gideon who Fenwick was. Perhaps keeping it up his sleeve as a trump card... At any rate, when he heard from the doctors that Ware had been poisoned, especially as it was by an injection of strychnine, he thought of Fenwick right away and must have held back the precise manner of death from me until he could cook up a tale. He also took some information from his private file on Ware before he lent it to me. That was probably about Fenwick's being Ware's son."

"What are you going to do...with Boumphrey, I mean?"

"I'm going for Fenwick first. You might see the Chief Constable and tell him. Then obtain a warrant and join me at Fenwick's house. I don't want to see Boumphrey yet, until I've spoken to Fenwick. You'll attend to that then, will you?"

"Yes...and talk of the devil. There's Fenwick now. Crossing the promenade apparently on his way home."

"I'll be there almost as soon as he is. You'll be sure and get the warrant meanwhile, Hazard?"

"Sure. I'll see you at the dentist's. Keep your eye on that syringe while you're there, Littlejohn!"

"Trust me, Hazard."

And Littlejohn disappeared through the revolving doors of the Grand Hotel on the track of his quarry.

17

THE DANCE OF DEATH

"He's seeing a patient," said the old lady at the door, as Littlejohn asked for Fenwick.

"I'll come in and wait," answered the detective, and put his words into effect by brushing past her.

As he entered, he observed that the door to the room opposite the surgery was open and, glancing in, saw on the mantelpiece an ancient, faded photograph in an old-fashioned frame.

"You can't go in there," quavered the attendant. "That's private. I've just been turning it out. The waiting room's here."

But Littlejohn took no heed. He was interested in the photograph. It was of a young woman, primly posed before a dropscene representing a luscious garden, and with a cardboard sundial by her side. The artistic fashion of a bygone age. The artist himself was announced in gold print beneath his handiwork and his address was in Hull.

The old woman was still by Littlejohn's elbow, trembling with anger as though afflicted with the palsy.

"I've cleaned this place out. It's private. You'll have to go to the other room..."

"Do you remember Sir Gideon Ware calling here the other day?"

The woman hesitated and then closed her little, thin mouth like a trap.

"Mr Fenwick told you not to tell he'd been here, didn't he?"

No answer. The woman remained dumb and immobile as one of those little wooden figures of peasant women bought by travellers as souvenirs in the Black Forest.

"I know all about it, so you may as well speak up."

"If you know all about it, why ask me?"

"Did Ware wait in here?"

"Yes. Being the Mayor, I put him in the best room. Mr Fenwick was cross about it when he found out. How was I to know?"

So, Ware had recognised Mary Wilson's photograph and, putting two and two together, had realised that Fenwick was his son.

"My son! My son!" he had said in dying to Father Manfred, trying to convey the name of his murderer. And nobody had understood.

"Things are very quiet in the surgery," said the Inspector to the woman, who had apparently made up her mind to hang around Littlejohn until he did as he was told.

"I don't know who's in. Mr Fenwick said he wasn't to be disturbed."

Littlejohn was out of the room in two strides and made for the surgery. The place was empty. No sign of a patient or of the dentist.

"Where is Mr Fenwick?"

"Don't ask me. Thought I heard the back door slam, but then I thought I'd imagined it."

Littlejohn made a quick search of the house but found no Fenwick.

He was preparing to ring up the police station and give the alarm, when the telephone bell rang.

"That you, Inspector Littlejohn? I thought I'd find you there. This is Fenwick…"

"Where are you?"

"Wouldn't you like to know? You chose a most unlucky place in which to give Hazard your confidences. The panelling there is hollow behind, and just covers an old doorway they blocked up because of the draught. I was sitting in the next room on the other side of the panel. Of course, you couldn't be expected to know the geography of the Grand Hotel, could you? I heard all you said and that you were coming for me, so made off."

"It's no use, Fenwick. You can't get away, you know…"

"Let me speak. I'm going to create an even bigger sensation than my late-lamented illegitimate father did when *he* died. So look out. You'll hear more of me. Sorry, I can't talk all this over with you. I like you, Littlejohn, and I've been in your company a lot of late, unseen, of course."

"Not so much unseen, Fenwick. I've seen you."

"You must have eyes at the back of your head, then. But you didn't see me in the coffee room today and that's all that matters. But even if I hadn't overheard you then, I knew it was all up. I could see you coming closer and closer, you devil…you honest-faced devil! Well, I must be off. Just wanted to say goodbye and good luck. By the way, all that stuff you told Hazard…or as much as I could hear of it, was damned good. You'll find it all confirmed in 'Memories from Beyond the Grave… Chateaubriand,' you know. Goodbye again."

The line went dead. Littlejohn was about to dial the exchange but realised that it was automatic. It would take hours to trace the call.

Just then the bell rang again. This time it was Hazard.

"I say, Littlejohn, I've just seen Fenwick. He was hurrying along the promenade like one in a dream and turned in at the

Winter Gardens. Thought I'd try to catch you but had to wait. Your line was engaged."

"Where are you?"

"Phone box near the Winter Gardens."

"Get some men and station them unobtrusively round the place. Fenwick's to be taken if he tries to get out. Then meet me at the main entrance. We'll have to search the place. I suppose it's teeming with people."

"Packed. There's a gala on."

"Damn the gala. Meet me there then."

"Memories from Beyond the Grave..." Of course! *Mémoires d'Outre-Tombe...* Littlejohn hurried out of the surgery and called the old woman again.

"Where does Mr Fenwick keep his books?"

"In the room you wouldn't clear out of. There's a locked case of them there. You can't go in again. I've cleaned it."

Littlejohn took no heed but sought the bookcase and forced it open. After a search among the titles he found the one he sought, turned over the leaves, nodded with satisfaction and, pocketing it, greatly to the anguish of the agitated woman at his side, hastened away to meet his colleague.

* * *

ALAN FENWICK HURRIED along the promenade intent on his purpose. Passers-by paid little heed to his eager, feverish appearance, for they were absorbed in their own pleasure-seeking and the hundred and one other devices provided by enterprising Westcombe. Only an eccentric and aged philosopher who had not long to live and knew it, observed the look in Fenwick's eyes and said to his companion, "That young man's looking on death." Whereat, the person addressed said in his mind, "The old chap's more loony than ever. We'll soon have to put him away."

The day was hot and sunny, and the beach was full of sunbathers. The Beach Mission was just beginning its afternoon session with a hymn and Mr Gaukroger, muffled in an overcoat in spite of the hot weather, was bawling the words of the first verse to a huge crowd.

"Two pills in the morning; two after lunch; and three when you're getting in bed for the night, and goodbye to your kidney complaints. I don't ask a guinea a box. Sixpence is my price. Lady over there..." yelled the professor of herbs on the next pitch.

Nearby was a Punch and Judy show. The incoherent, twittering voices of the dolls, the busy thrashing of Punch's stick, the yells of delight from the young audience.

The Mission opened out in full blast and drowned all else, like the great breakers of an incoming tide.

> *"Yes, we'll gather at the river,*
> *The beautiful, the beautiful river.*
> *Gather with the saints at the river,*
> *That flows by the throne of God."*

Fenwick stopped for a minute to take it all in with the look of one who says farewell to life and laughter for the last time.

WINTER GARDENS
Westcombe.
GALA DAY.
MASKED BALL.
Sid Simmons.

The words caught his eye and he turned in at the main entrance. The masked dancing was held in the afternoons as a wartime measure, for children, in particular, and many adults would not turn out to watch the proceedings after dark. The dancers themselves, of course, would be there if the heavens were falling!

At the door of the ballroom two girls were selling cardboard masks. Within, Sid Simmons and his Ten Hot Dogs were already hard at it. Fenwick bought a disguise consisting of a grotesque painted face, with two slits for eyes, a pathetic long nose, turned up at the point, and a heavy crêpe moustache. Fixing this by elastics over his ears he entered.

The floor was packed. The dance itself consisted of a shuffling step, contrived to enable you to thrust your partner into the thin gaps between the sliding couples and repeat the performance indefinitely. The tune was a mere tattoo played by the piano, a drummer performing on what seemed to be the products of a salvage drive, and the double-bass executing what the initiated term "slapping and picking" his gut. Sid Simmons and the others were resting in preparation for the next big hit, the Slap Bang.

All round the room were seated flirting couples who preferred dalliance to dancing, and single girls waiting for partners. Nobody stood on ceremony and you just picked up one of them if she took your fancy and agreed to dance with you. Four MCs in evening dress and with their own ideas concerning propriety, kept the couples moving and, now and then, admonished some libertine or other with gestures reminiscent of those used by boxing or football referees.

Under present conditions it was impossible to choose a partner by her looks, for the featureless masks of the girls reduced them all to facial uniformity. You might go for ears, hair, or as much of figure, legs or poise as you could see in that packed throng, but you must take the consequences for your behaviour when the time for unmasking arrived.

Iris Clarke, a munition worker on holiday, was sitting waiting for something to turn up in the way of partners. She had arrived at the gala with a friend, taller and better proportioned than herself, but inferior in looks, who had forthwith been whisked-off by a forward young man, who had simply said "Have a go?" and borne her away. Iris didn't much care, for she had the consolation of having a fiancé with the Eighth Army and was conscious of her superiority when the ordeal of unmasking had to be faced. She was rather astonished, however, at the figure which now stood, bowing before her, asking for the next dance.

The man under the mask was obviously of a superior type, for he put forward his suit with a grace and consideration usually unknown on that dance floor. The disguise, too, gave him a pathetic, suppliant air, like that of a broken-hearted clown, and the sensitive tip of the monstrous nose looked like the pathetic head of some lost insect rearing itself anxiously to take its bearings. The well-kept hands, the cut of the clothes, too, told their own tale. "Evidently a gent," thought the girl, and rose in acceptance, just as the three instrumentalists ceased their capers. This did not deter Iris and her partner, however, for, with a blast of trumpets, Sid Simmons and all ten of his men, struck up the next number.

The Slap Bang was the hit of the season in Westcombe that year. It was reminiscent of an Apache dance, only ten times more sadistic, and to a wild cacophony of jungle music, the participants knocked each other about in good-humoured abandon.

The tune started on the drums and then the rest joined in like unleashed madmen. Sid Simmons, especially, shone in an exhibition of trumpeting which earned him fame and envy among those expert in such things, but caused the ignorant to doubt his sanity.

Slap Bang! They slapped hands first, then fended each other off, turned back to back and butted each other in reverse, first with the buttocks, then with the shoulder-blades. Then, face to face again, fling your partner at arm's length, perform a solo convulsion from head to foot, like a dog shaking himself after a swim. Next, drag your partner back to your embrace with a thud. The movements were repeated with growing frenzy, until the whole room became a surging mass of thrashing, milling, contorted humanity. Some more advanced exponents got down on their haunches, slap-banging around the knees of the rest, whilst one highly expert couple performed complicated back to back assaults on each other sitting on the floor, until the MC admonished them. As the dance progressed and the music increased in wildness, many of the performers openly surrendered themselves to the sensual delights of knocking each other about. The drummer of the band, completely absorbed in his work, trembling with ecstasy, his hair all over his face and his eyes wild, became possessed of demoniacal energy and speed and whipped the whole room into a wild orgy, MCs and all.

At first, Iris and her partner sedately performed the routine movements and steps of the dance, but as the fury increased, they too became absorbed in the ritual. They had soon reached the stage when, as their heaving, panting bodies met in a formal embrace, they longed to remain so and kiss in swooning delight. Their masks remained impassive as the faces of corpses, but they did not need looks to convey their emotions. There were many more around them who felt the same, but Sid Simmons and his Hot Dogs gave them no respite. Like slave drivers, they flogged their tortured victims along with relentless trumpets, saxophones and percussion.

Suddenly, Iris's partner became like one demented. It was as though, having held himself in check for as long as flesh and blood could bear, he had kicked over the traces and surrendered himself to madness. He tore himself from the girl, sagged jerkily at the knees, groaned, sank to the floor and lay there, arching himself at full length in horrible spasms of agony, as though stimulated by a strong electric current. The most ardent slap-bangers felt prim compared with the new performance now going on and edged away from the man. Meanwhile, Iris stood dumbfounded, looking down in horror at the exhibition. Then, the partner at her feet lay still a moment, only to resume his contortions with increasing violence. The girl sensing something wrong, screamed wildly, two MCs rushed to the spot, seized the frenzied performer by the scruff of his neck and bore him limply struggling from the hall. Littlejohn and Hazard, who had just arrived, followed them into the ante-room.

Fenwick, his mask removed and lying like a carefree part of himself, a pathetic, questioning look still on its eyeless face, was now calm and breathing his last. He raised his hand, with infinite effort showed Littlejohn a hypodermic puncture in his gum at the front and then was seized with another horrible convulsion. He died on the way to hospital, just as his father had done and from the same cause.

In the gallery of the Winter Gardens, the Chairman of the Watch Committee, an elderly man, and physically long past taking his pleasures on the floor below, albeit he would gladly have done so had his old limbs obeyed his instincts, swore horribly that he would see that no more disgusting exhibitions, such as the one on which he was now gazing with jealous and resentful fascination, were ever given in Westcombe.

18

BOUMPHREY GETS BUSY

As soon as the news of Fenwick's death was brought to him, the Chief Constable of Westcombe grew alarmingly busy. He did not wait for Littlejohn and Hazard to return in person from the hospital to which they had accompanied Fenwick, but rushed off to the dentist's surgery right away, accompanied by two constables.

"We must get to the bottom of this at once," he said, his eyes prominent with the lust of the chase and when he arrived at his destination, he set about frenziedly going through the papers of the dead murderer. In his eagerness, he even forced open drawers, went through wardrobes and searched articles of furniture for possible sources of information which might throw light on Fenwick's life and guilt. He was frantically reading through a pile of diaries and private memoranda, which he had found in the dentist's desk, when Littlejohn arrived.

"You'll not find it, Mr Boumphrey," said the Inspector without more ado.

"What do you mean, find it?" asked Boumphrey, hot and sweating from his feelings and his efforts.

"Fenwick's diary, or autobiography, or whatever you care to call it. I've got it here in my pocket."

"You've got it! And on whose authority have you impounded the dead man's papers?"

"My own."

"Well, give whatever you've got to me, at once."

"No."

"What?!"

Boumphrey's complexion assumed a dark purple hue and splashes of livid colouring appeared on his forehead and cheeks like bloody nebulae in a night sky.

He held out his flabby hand, which trembled with his rage, like a palsied beggar asking for alms.

"Give it to me and no insubordination!"

"Send your men out of the room. I want a word with you about it," said Littlejohn. The laughter which usually lurked somewhere in Littlejohn's blue eyes, had vanished. Boumphrey avoided meeting his gaze.

"Get out," said the Chief Constable to his men, who were so astonished at the turn of events, that they made their exit at the double, like bad boys fleeing from the wrath of a teacher.

"Now," said Littlejohn, "Let's be seated and talk this thing over. Before I hand over the evidence I've got, I shall need an explanation from you, Mr Boumphrey, concerning your conduct in this case. I've no authority to demand one, but I must warn you, that unless one is forthcoming at once, I shall turn it over to Scotland Yard and you'll have to answer for it to the Home Office."

"What the hell do you mean?" thundered Boumphrey, who had made a half-hearted attempt to pull himself together and was sitting glowering in the chair at Fenwick's desk.

"I mean this. That throughout this case you've been in possession of information which you have not seen fit to disclose to me. In fact, your attitude has, at times, been obstructive."

"By God, I'll make you sit up for this insolence, Littlejohn," thundered Boumphrey, rising to his feet and looking like a wild bull about to take a crazy turn round a bullring.

Littlejohn cut him short.

"Perhaps you'll explain, Mr Boumphrey, exactly why, in the first place, you didn't disclose that Sir Gideon Ware had been killed by a hypodermic injection of poison. Instead, you led me to believe that he'd taken it with food or something at the banquet. It was not until I heard the precise cause of death from the doctor that you corrected the impression..."

"I've already explained that it was an oversight!"

"I disagree. Mr Boumphrey, you've a reputation for being a very efficient official. You don't expect me to believe that by an oversight, as you call it, you would cause the considerable delay due to giving wrong information to the Scotland Yard officer you'd called in yourself?"

"Believe it or not. It's all the same to me."

"I don't believe it, Mr Boumphrey. I believe you misled me for your own ends. You wished to divert my suspicions from a certain quarter in which you were interested... No, let me finish. You had impulsively called in Scotland Yard because, in your ambition, you feared making enemies among the people you'd have to question in the case. But later, and just before my arrival, medical evidence pointed to either a doctor or a dentist having committed the crime. Your mind turned to a dentist and for a very good reason. That dentist was Alan Fenwick... Sir Gideon Ware's illegitimate son!"

Boumphrey collapsed in a chair again. None of the fight had left him, but the shock of realising that Littlejohn had probed his motives dealt him a temporary knockout. He soon recovered.

"What's all this nonsense?" he bluffed. "If you think you'll discredit me by fabricating a tall tale, Littlejohn, you're very much mistaken. I've thought all along you were trying to get all the kudos in this case for yourself. Let me tell you, that a full report of your conduct will go to the proper quarter. And now, get out."

Littlejohn was calmly smoking his pipe. He was sitting in the dental chair, which he had swivelled round to face Boumphrey. He looked very comfortable, like a patient about to take gas.

"I know all about your past relations with Alan Fenwick, Boumphrey," he said quietly, "So it's no use your trying to bluff it out."

"What do you know?"

"Your connection with smoothing-over Fenwick's trouble with the Cherry women. You were a sergeant in the Follington police then. You deliberately hushed up what was a criminal offence, Boumphrey, and you did it to prevent full details of the causes of it and the parties to the case leaking out in the press. The reason being that you didn't want Ware to chance across the name and location of his bastard son…"

"It's a lie…a damned lie," roared Boumphrey, but the effort was without conviction.

"Listen. I know all about your appointment to the Inspectorship of the Battleford Police. You got in touch with Ware and secured his recommendation. Then, when your predecessor left Westcombe, you followed as Chief Constable. He was your backer throughout, Boumphrey, and I suggest the reason for that was that you'd got a hold over him. You knew about his illegitimate son and, although you took good care not to confess to knowing who or where the son was, you made the most of your knowledge of Ware's past and blackmailed him into supporting you. Ware was in for public honours. It would never have done for it to become known that he had a son on the wrong side of the blanket. You knew all the time that Fenwick, Ware's son, was in Westcombe and you'd a good idea that he hated Ware enough to kill him. You deliberately tried to lead me off his track, because you knew that if Fenwick was arrested, he'd probably spill the beans about you. Furthermore, you deliberately removed all information from your private file on Ware which might lead me to Fenwick. You pressed for the arrest of Preedy, prematurely, in the hope that a red herring might be dragged..."

"I wouldn't have let him go to trial..." interjected the wretched Boumphrey. His pompous façade had crumbled under Littlejohn's relentless battering and he now slumped, a pathetic figure, like a sack of sawdust, in his chair.

"You'd, at least, some conscience left, had you, Boumphrey? I give you the credit for that, in spite of your history in this case. Now, are you going to give me a fuller explanation, or must I make a special report for the Home Office?"

Boumphrey looked round the room helplessly. A man seeing all the fruits of his hopes fading away before his eyes and ruin staring him in the face.

"I was in love with Mrs Fenwick when I was in Follington years ago," he said quite simply, and immediately Littlejohn felt a deep compassion for him.

"You'll have to tell me more than that, you know, Boumphrey."

"There's not much to it, Littlejohn. I might as well be candid. Like most policemen in towns I was friendly with below-stairs folk in Follington in the old days. I used to call in the course of patrols and have a chat with butlers and cooks and such like and among others I met Mrs Fenwick. She was a daily-help, quiet, neat, proud and reserved and she'd a son who was the apple of her eye. That was Alan."

Boumphrey sighed and stared ahead of him like a man in a dream. It was as if the past were unfolding before him like a cinema picture.

"I took a fancy to the woman. Hard work had left its marks on her and a lot of other trouble, as I discovered later, but she was good-looking and decent and would have made anyone a good wife. She seemed a cut above the average servant. I suppose that was because she'd tried to raise herself to keep-up with her boy, who went to the local grammar school. She was a religious woman, too. Thrifty, she was, and a good housewife. What more could a man want? I was on the look-out for a wife, and Mary Fenwick seemed as good a one as I could find…"

Boumphrey glanced awkwardly at Littlejohn.

"…besides I was in love with her. Don't ask me why. I don't know myself. Who does know why we fall in love?"

Littlejohn looked kindly at Boumphrey. He was seeing a new man, a human being beneath the veneer of officious bombast which had hitherto obscured the real Chief Constable.

"She was a bit of a mystery, though. I'd no idea who she was, really, or where she came from. I didn't know who her husband had been. All I learned was that she'd given out she was a widow and that even the members of the same church had no information about her past. Her life and conduct were exemplary and that's all anyone knew. I made up my mind, before making any advances, to find out what I wanted. I had to be sure there wasn't a husband still alive, hadn't I? You see that, don't you?"

"Certainly, I do."

"It was a hell of a job, I'll tell you. Nobody seemed to know where she'd come from to Follington. However, one day, quite by accident, something was said about Mrs Fenwick in the police station, and a remark was passed about her being a bit of a mystery woman. I wasn't in the conversation, but I naturally pricked up my ears. And then, one of the constables quite innocently mentioned that he'd been on night duty when her belongings arrived. He merely said it, I guess, to show that she was so mysterious as to arrive there by night. I took him aside after and pretended to be jocular with him. 'I bet your powers of

observation didn't reach to finding out who the carrier was and
whence he came,' I said, quite excited inside me. 'You're wrong
there, sir,' he said, sure that I was testing his powers for promotion. 'Although it's so long ago, I recollect the carrier's name was
Edges and he came all the way from Dimpsay, in Norfolk.' Well,
it ended by my going to Dimpsay on my next day off. There, I
found that Mrs Fenwick had been known as Mary Wilson. The
rest was easy. I saw the registrar of births, who was sure that the
kid was illegitimate, and he said she'd given her birthplace as
Hull. I went to Hull and, with the help of the police there, soon
got a tale. The kid *was* born out of wedlock and the father was
Gideon Ware. I didn't much care. So long as the woman hadn't a
husband and would confide her troubles truthfully to me — and
I could test her honesty there, couldn't I? — so long as she
trusted me, I didn't mind. I determined if she'd have me, I'd take
her and the boy and settle down with them as my own. Well…
instead, she died."

Boumphrey cast a pathetic look at Littlejohn, who, in turn,
wondered what would have become of Fenwick and
Boumphrey if it had come off. Probably both would have been
happy by this.

"There's not much more to tell. Instead of getting married, I
set about making a career. I went and saw Ware, disclosed that I
knew about his purple past and, whilst assuring him I wouldn't
say a word to discredit him, promised to try and trace his son if
I could. Meanwhile, unknown to him, I'd kept a kindly eye on
Alan for his mother's sake. I never told him why…never even
made a friend of him. Just kept an eye on him. I got him out of
the Cherry mess because of his mother…or rather her memory.
He packed up and went to Westcombe. I knew why. Ware got
me the job at Battleford and then this one here. I met Fenwick,
who recognised me, but we didn't have much to do with one
another. This job was too much for me. I wasn't the class for
Chief Constable. The town was corrupt, thanks mainly to Ware.

It was as good as my job was worth to meddle... Then, Ware was murdered. You know the rest. I did my best to shield Alan. But I'd called you in, you see, and do what I might, you were too good for me. I'm beat. Better report it and I'll face the music."

Littlejohn removed his pipe. Then, he slowly rose to his feet, crossed to Boumphrey and offered him his hand.

"I believe you, Boumphrey," he said. The Chief Constable gratefully took the Inspector's hand in both his own, wrung it and then sobbed harshly.

Littlejohn felt like fleeing, for the situation was intensely painful.

"You'll have to resign, you know, Boumphrey. But it's better that way than getting the sack after an enquiry. Fenwick's diary is bound to contain references to you. I can't suppress that, even if I omit mention of our differences in my report. I'll put as strong a case as I can for leniency in the right quarters, but you understand, I can't withhold evidence, can I?"

"No, Littlejohn. I'll resign. There are plenty of jobs I can do these days and, if I'm given a chance, by God, I'll make good."

The embarrassing interview thus ended and shortly afterwards, Boumphrey left Westcombe. A retired army man became Chief Constable and Hazard, who was persuaded from leaving for Manchester, took on the job of Superintendent of Police. 'The incorruptible' soon cleaned up the local corruption.

The following recently appeared in the daily press:

The George Medal was recently awarded posthumously to Stephen Boumphrey, Air Raid Officer of an East Coast town, for conspicuous gallantry during an air raid. He was responsible for rescuing fourteen people entombed in a bombed building. Tunnelling to their aid, he cheered and comforted them until they could be released. He was crushed by a fall of masonry just as he had freed the last victim.

Boumphrey, who until recently was Chief Constable of Westcombe, asked to be released for service in a bombed area, where he felt he could be of more use. Before his death in hospital, he was informed that he had been recommended for decoration and asked that any token of such honour might be handed to the police at Follington as a memorial of happy days spent in the force there.

Thus Stephen Boumphrey atoned in full measure, pressed down, and overflowing.

1 9

THINGS PAST – I

(A journal, found by Littlejohn, interleaved in Chateaubriand's
"Mémoires d'Outre-Tombe".)

Whenever I read such exquisite works as the one in whose pages I am concealing this manuscript, I always feel moved to write about myself and my sufferings.

I might, given the right time, publisher and press, produce a masterpiece, a best-seller, for I have the material of which such things are made stored in my memory. Probably the goddess of luck, who has always turned her back on me, would play me a dirty trick again!

Inspired by the great works of others, I would often rush hot-foot to my desk to write, my brain teeming with unborn thoughts and a great eagerness to translate them into the written word. But when I took up pen and paper, I found myself struggling for that facile, flowing expression, which is a joy to the reader and the consummation of the artist's work. I was like a dumb man whose tongue cannot shape the treasures of his glittering brain into forms which will delight all who hear, or a woman whom the pains of false labour continually torture, yet from whom the ecstasies of creation are forever withheld.

Time and again, I have begun and time and again lain down my pen in utter despair after feverishly covering half-a-dozen pages with matter which, when I have read it afterwards, has filled me with disgust. As though a gramophone record of the most exquisite singer rendering the loveliest of songs were played by a rusty needle on the titubant turntable of a machine whose speeds were constantly changing.

Could I only have broken down the barrier between thought and its expression, that mental lock-gate which dammed up the waters of my mind and let flow forth the surging flood of my heart, I would have known the happy joys of relief. But no device would bring this about. Stimulants, tonics, drugs, were of no avail. Fasting was equally ineffective in tapping the hidden springs, as were the bottles of whisky I emptied or the cocaine I sniffed in my desperation.

Now — irony of ironies — when my time is short and justice knocks at the door, my brain seethes with inspiration, the once dried-up wells are bubbling to overflowing, and my hands can hardly move fast enough over the keys to anchor my thoughts on paper before they are gone, like migrant birds which die in foreign lands.

Nay, I do not need to think in words. An automatic liaison has been established between my unconscious and the tips of the fingers which manipulate my typewriter. My body, like that of a medium, translates thoughts from an unseen world of the spirit, into ordered letters of the alphabet without any conscious sorting into speech.

I could go on like this for ever, but Nemesis, in the form of one Littlejohn, is almost on the doorstep. Yet another of the ghastly jokes of fate!

Autobiography suits me. If truth were told, it suits everyone.

We can never know anybody but ourselves and that but dimly, like a dark room with dirty windows viewed from without. In the case of the second or third person, the glass of the windows is opaque. We cannot even guess what goes on behind it but discern only the vagueness of shadows moving to and fro inside. We cannot know whether the words of our dearest friend contain truth or falsehood. Even the kisses of the beloved in the orgasm of passion may be to her those of another, held in the heart, whilst the poor dupe in her arms merely provides the stimulus of the flesh and the stage-setting of the event.

Well do I know that distant look, that almost forcible ejection from paradise which brings one back to the dull reality of the world, to the realisation that some other, some unattainable holds the stage in the soul of the loved one and that one's self is the mere lifeless puppet capering forlornly outside, receiving nothing!

But I digress. My own tragic life began before I was born. Foolish thought, you will say. But do not most parents of a first-born, even before he has taken the shape of man and is yet a mere amoeba, a dog, an ape in the slowly unfolding course of evolution, begin to prepare the silver spoon for his arriving, to plan the road which they dream he will take and which fate so often diverts into the wilderness? And is he not, at least, granted the full span of the dreamless, effortless rest in the heart of his mother's body until the allotted time for his awakening and birth into the world?

Such things were not for me. I was conceived in dark corners, fashioned in agony and bewilderment, and finally rejected in torment. For I am an illegitimate child, born after seven months with a physical endowment which was for years the despair of all who knew me and the one who loved me, and with a wounded spirit which has been my private hell since first I knew the truth.

I am choosing my words like one who has a whole lifetime in

197

which to select and ponder! At any time now there will be a ring on the doorbell which will sound my knell. Then I shall fling away in disgust the life which was forced on me. This is no time for washing for the fine gold of my thoughts and expressions. I was born in Dimpsay, Norfolk, early this century, two months before my time. Not considering that my mother had enough trouble, the fates gave her another in advance of schedule!

I can still remember my mother as though she were alive today and in the next room, waiting for me to finish my work and to make my malted milk before I retire. Her name was Mary Fenwick. I thought her a widow and it was not until after her death that I found she had never married at all and that I bore her maiden name, or rather, the name she had assumed. That was a blow from which I never recovered. Not that I blamed my dear mother. She was the saint to whom I owe all that is best in me... But more of that tale later.

Physical weakness may naturally be expected in one cast into the world with two months of preparations not completed. I gather that I was a puny, howling baby, half-dead more than a dozen times, yet clinging to life as though it were something worth keeping. Would that they had left me to perish, or, in a fit of rage, smothered my puling until there wasn't breath in me any longer. I was seven when I was fit to go to school, by which time, thanks to my mother's efforts, I could read, write and figure better than most at my age. I never took to games; I disliked my schoolmates as much as they disliked me. They used to call "Pansy" after me and "Mother's darling," but I grew accustomed to it. At any rate, I could beat them in class and kept away from them outside. Once they caught me alone and knocked me about until I was sick. After that, I was sent to the High School where it was every bit as bad. But why go on...

By this time, we were living in Follington, Essex, where my mother took me as a baby.

I could not have hoped for anything but the life of a member of the unskilled working-class, for my mother was compelled to keep the pair of us by toiling every hour of the waking day and night. She could, with justification, have turned me out to earn my living as soon as the law would allow me to leave school. When not 'obliging' the so-called better-class ladies of the town by assisting them to keep their hands out of slop buckets and away from scrubbing-brushes, she took in laundry and sewing at home.

At night, she made our clothes and those of quite a number of the women of the church we attended.

Sustained by a scholarship, I managed to finish my education at the local High School. I was not in those days greatly concerned in how the family budget was balanced. Like a fledgling in the nest, I opened my mouth widely and plaintively and swallowed all, regardless of how it arrived.

One day, I suffered the first of a series of emotional shocks which since then have occurred like volcanic eruptions in my life, with periods of apparent quiescence between each.

We were granted an indefinite holiday through an outbreak of scarlet fever in the school and, going home at an unusual hour in the middle of the morning, I passed a large house, the steps of which I was horrified to see my mother cleaning with a bucket of dirty water and a scrubbing brush.

I cannot analyse the sensations of shame and degradation which flowed over me in hot waves as I first perceived her. Thank God, I did not feel ashamed of *her*. Rather did I wish the *cause* of it all would materialise in order that I might assail it with my fists and boots.

She was kneeling on the bottom step, like a suppliant grovelling for life or food before some arrogant Ruler or Dives who stonily averted his face. When, in later years, I stood before the picture of Monmouth crawling, pleading for his life before James II, the memory of that moment returned, filling my eyes with the bitter tears of hopeless despair. For my mother was then long dead and there was nothing to be done about it.

I remember standing speechless beside her, knowing not what to say or do, but aware that I loved her past telling, until she turned her head and saw me. Her hair had fallen over her face, beads of sweat stood on her brow and upper lip, and a long scar of soot stretched like a brand from her mouth to her cheekbone. She turned pale at my thus discovering her, and anxiously enquired what I did there at that unaccustomed time. With one hand she pushed the bucket and its fetid contents from her, as though attempting to conceal it from me, and with the other brushed away the fallen wisps of hair.

I can still see her hands, the skin of the fingers in folds through long immersion in water, the looseness of her knuckles and finger joints lined with grime. I would have kissed them had I had the grace to do so. As it was, I ran home and threw myself on the bed in a turmoil of despair. I had witnessed sacrilege like the violation of a holy place, the trampling underfoot of sacred relics, the feeding of the Host to swine.

Thenceforth, I realised that during my absence, my mother led a hidden life of humiliating and menial toil for my sake, yet hastening to meet me, clean, sweet and cheerful when I returned at night. This was the beginning of my constant enquiry into the past which she had hitherto kept concealed from me. I asked about my father. Who and what was he? What had he looked like? Why had we no pictures of him? When did he die, and how? My mother was a religious woman and such an inquisition must have sorely tried her, for lying was abhorrent to her. She must have been an astute diplomat, for there comes back to me no recollection of any unsatisfactory answer, no memory of any reply which was of a nature only to stimulate further questions. She died with her secret undisclosed.

Meanwhile, nothing destroyed our happy train of domestic associations. As I grew older and the sap of life rose within me, I felt that indefinable unrest, that sad seeking for the unattainable which in youth is torture, but, recollected in later years, one of its dearest memories, but I singled out no other woman for its object. I was not to be found at night parading the High Street, philandering up and down the 'Cakewalk,' as it was called locally, casting longing eyes, making swaggering gestures or uttering those sibilant whistles, shouts or spurious, almost hysterical laughs which constituted the mating-calls of the young males of Follington and, I suppose, everywhere else. In Westcombe, of course, the overtures of such rough wooing are not essential, for under the influence of sea air and the sense of abandon known as "the holiday feeling," the preliminaries are flung to the winds and the partners in the game hurl themselves upon each other almost at sight.

Too late I realised that my mother had denied herself the bare essentials of life for my sake. Like the legendary pelican, she had fed her offspring on her own blood. I do not recollect her ever taking a holiday away from Follington. Sometimes, in summer, we would ramble out to the salt marshes to the east of the town and there, among the things of nature and under summer skies draped with vast white clouds of ever-changing shapes and speeds, the burden of years would seem to fall from her, and she would become young again. She even sang now and then the old songs and hymns she was fond of.

Last week, more than twenty years later, hearing Gaukroger and his Beach Mission bleating one of those hymns, I was so overcome that I sat behind one of the sham rocks which Gideon Ware made of cheap cement for the greater glory and decoration of Westcombe and wept in a spasm of overwhelming grief. After which, returning to my surgery to keep an appointment, I so mishandled a triple extraction, that the patient rose from the chair in pain and struck me in the face with his fist in uncontrolled rage before he left the house, spitting blood and pieces of jawbone.

The discovery of my mother's secret activities wrought a revolution in my life and outlook. I was fourteen at the time and had but vaguely thought of a career. Engine-driver, controlling a great locomotive; cinema manager in evening dress at the door of his picture palace every night; parson holding huge audiences spellbound like my mother's hero, Charles Haddon Spurgeon; these all had their day and passed by. The one which remained longest in my heart was the doctor. I once saw a local practitioner thrust his way through a huge, milling throng round a street accident and with deft skill, render help and healing before the awestruck crowd. I decided that was the job for me. I confided this ambition to my mother, who smiled and sighed. I might as well have wished for the moon.

As it was, she consulted Mr Hardcastle. He was a deacon of our church. A huge, black-bearded man who ran a dental practice in Follington. I think he would have married my mother had he been able, for he admired her greatly and always treated her with the greatest tenderness, which filled me with the jealous pangs of one who sniffs out a supplanter. But his wife was still alive and hopelessly insane in a mental home.

Hardcastle was an unqualified practitioner. That is, if you regard experience as no qualification and intricate book-learning as the Open Sesame to success and recognition. He could not call himself a dental-surgeon and the orthodox described him as a false-teeth maker. The blue lamp over his door had DENTIST strung round its circumference like strangely shaped continents splashed on a planet. He earned a respectable living by extracting poor folk's teeth at sixpence a time; cocaine or gas, a shilling extra and guaranteed painless. He had spent some years in America and served as mechanic to some good and up to date dentists. He made excellent dentures, which never betrayed themselves or their wearers, and executed fillings better than any man I ever met. To this giant I became apprenticed at the age of fifteen, for whatever decency was in me, revolted against my being longer dependent on my mother's humiliation.

"That's a sensible boy. There's a son worthy of his mother," boomed Mr Hardcastle in that voice which was almost as effective as his laughing gas in paralysing his patients. He had proved the financial impossibility of my ever acquiring a medical education and he had offered me a job as his errand, page and bellboy. I had agreed. "I'll teach you all I know. But you'll have to be patient, young man. You'll have to be patient."

When I was eighteen and making teeth as skilfully as my master, my mother died. My conversion from a liability to an asset in her finances had eased her burdens considerably, but the past had gnawn too viciously in her vitals and she began to fail in health. When nothing short of an operation would save her, she went valiantly to the Infirmary, keeping the severity of her condition from me, promising to be back speedily. They brought her back, dead. I remember calling with the undertaker to claim the body from the keeper of the Infirmary mortuary, who spat a stream of tobacco juice on the courtyard, handed me my mother's spectacles and the hymn-book she had taken with her to cheer her in convalescence, and said, "It's in there; ready for you." I was the man who had called for the "returned empties." In vain did my companion try to excuse the formality of the proceedings which had dulled the sensibilities of the tobacco-chewer. I made the precincts ring with my laughter and was hustled off the premises like a child who has suddenly revealed his whooping cough in a crowded gathering.

At first, her loss to me was mainly felt in loneliness, as when the familiar, almost unheard tick of a clock suddenly ceases, leaving a strange void and by the absence of its undertone alters all other sounds. She was dead and true realisation did not, at first, penetrate my understanding. Only weeks later, when I went again, alone, to the salt marshes, saw the bank on which we had so often sat eating our egg sandwiches and, finally and most poignant of all, found where she had lost it three months before, now tarnished and bedraggled, a little silver medallion on a blue ribbon which I had once bought her on her birthday ("St Bartholomew protect you and keep you from Sickness," it said) and the loss of which she did not discover until we reached home, did the full horror of the awful parting dawn on me. It fell like a hammer blow, sharp and overwhelming. I sank on the bank and wept, tearing the turf with my nails in impotent agony.

Mr Hardcastle took me to live with him and eventually made me his mechanic. It was due to him that I managed to scrape on the dental register without professional qualifications of the orthodox kind. He was, for as long as I knew him, my dear friend and benefactor. He died tragically before his time. His wife, whom he faithfully visited every Saturday for more than twenty years and whose long confinement cost him almost all he earned, persisted in regarding him as unfaithful to her, an unfounded obsession which, I gather, she contracted even when of sound mind. On one of these visits, having managed to conceal a table knife on her person, she plunged it in his chest with frenzied accusations, and killed him on the spot. Thus ended his long martyrdom, borne with fortitude. I inherited his practice and then occurred two incidents which set in motion the train of events which led to my undoing.

I was only twenty when Hardcastle died. The suddenness of events threw everything awry. In fact, he had no known next-of-kin except his mad wife, and I had to administer his estate with a solicitor who had been his fellow deacon at the chapel.

There was little in the estate of my old friend except life policies which ensured the maintenance for the rest of her life of the wife who had killed him. By his will, he left his practice to me unconditionally. I was overwhelmed by this generous gift. It was the first piece of real luck I ever had.

In the small deed-box he kept at the bank, Mr Hardcastle

had placed a sealed envelope addressed to me in my mother's handwriting, to be opened when I reached the age of twenty-one. I did not violate its contents at once, for I had some months to go before reaching the specified age. But my curiosity grew day by day. I argued with myself against this impatience whilst constantly fingering the envelope like a drunkard who, having signed the pledge, wrestles with his conscience with a bottle full of whisky on the table before him.

Finally, in a fit of impulsive resentment against my conflicting feelings which nagged me day and night like the exposed nerve of a rotten tooth, I broke the seal and read the contents of the packet.

Would that I had, then and there, thrown it unread into the fire, for it laid the train which led to my present sorry plight.

There were four sides of paper torn from the cheap, lined writing tablet, which my mother used to use because she could not write straight from one side to the other without the help of the ruling, and because she could never afford good notepaper. It pained me to imagine her setting it all down in her laboured hand, her head on one side, her pen scratching, her hand moving slowly with many dips in the penny bottle of ink I remembered so well from days gone.

The letter began by saying that by the time I read it, my mother would be dead. It ended by giving me her love and blessing. In between occurred the following paragraph which struck me like a thunderbolt.

"... I have done my best to conceal your origins because I was afraid that the knowledge of them would make you feel at a disadvantage with others who you had to fight against in the world. Now you are established in a good job, I feel it is only right to tell you that you are illegitimate. Your father is still alive when I write this, but I think it better not to tell you who he is, because that would do no good. You would perhaps hate him and seeing that once in my lifetime I refused to give you up to him when he would have taken you, there is no point in opening the question again. I had to leave the place where we had settled to stop him from finding us. He was not worthy of you and I was afraid if he took you, he would not bring you up to be the son I dreamed you would become and, thank God, you *have* become.

"All I will say is that he deserted me before you were born and after that, although he approached me to make amends by offers of money and to adopt you, through a firm of solicitors (for he was married to somebody else by then), I refused. Do not blame me, my son. I felt then as I do now, that I could not touch his money and my pride rather preferred drudgery than his charity..."

Enclosed in the envelope was my birth certificate and a bank draft for £500 dated seventeen years before! Covering the draft was a letter from a firm of solicitors saying they had been instructed by a client to forward the enclosed draft and should she care to allow the same client to adopt her son, the necessary arrangements could be made. I discovered, too, that after her so-called disgrace, my mother had changed her name from Wilson to Fenwick, which had been her mother's maiden name.

The news paralysed me! Bastard, by-blow, I called myself, preferring to flagellate myself with unpleasant-sounding words used by the vulgar rather than the milder politeness's of 'illegitimate' or 'natural'. Born on the wrong side of the blanket. I worked no more that day, but fled to the marshes, there to gnash my teeth and cry aloud at this further dirty trick of fate.

For, you must understand, I had begun to fancy myself socially! In later life, I grew accustomed to the bar-sinister and realised that many another under its shadow had found it no drawback to a useful, even famous life. At the time of the blow, however, when I needed all my powers, it seemed to brand me with the stigma of inferiority and obsessed me so much that had I borne the mark of it on my brow, I could not have suffered more. I had hoped for a socially good marriage and one day saw myself as the husband of one of the group of lovely girls which every Saturday afternoon titupped along on horseback past my surgery from the nearby riding school. They were daughters of the well-to-do of the town and I had set myself the task of raising myself to their level.

Now I felt flung down among the drabs and outcasts. Had Mr Hardcastle been alive, I might have found comfort in his sympathy and restoring counsel. But he was dead and there was nobody to whom I could turn. I alternately reproached my mother for her stubborn pride, her humility, her lack of consideration for me, and cursed and called down vengeance on the head of the man who had caused all the misfortunes of my mother and myself. I alternated in an unhinged and maudlin sentimentality and uncontrolled rage. I even meditated putting an end to my existence by an overdose of my own laughing gas but got drunk instead.

At length, the mental ferment into which my mother's letter had thrown me, died down, leaving a hard core of resolution. In spite of her silence and precautions, I determined to find my father and make him pay for his treachery and the life of agony he had inflicted on my mother and to which he had condemned me.

Among my mother's belongings was a faded photograph taken before my birth and presumably before she met her seducer. It bore the name of a photographer in Hull. I hastened to Yorkshire, neglecting my business and everything else under the lash of my resolve. The firm mentioned on the picture had become defunct years ago, they told me. I searched the out of date voters' lists in the city library, for the name of my mother's family. There were scores of voters bearing that surname. Without stopping even to eat, I tramped here and there seeking a clue. It rained hard as I rushed hither and thither and I must have been a sorry sight as I presented myself at various houses, where I was invariably received with great civility in spite of my disreputable appearance.

Six names on my list had vanished altogether. The seventh hit the mark! In the house already occupied for twelve years by a family called Joyfull, if you please, the previous tenant had been one William Wilson, captain of a river barge.

"You want to ask Mrs Bates in th'end house," said Mrs Joyfull, an enormous, good-natured woman, who looked as though she would have great difficulty in getting through the doorway of the dwelling where I found her. "She's lived in this street for fifty years and'll keep on doin', too, till they carry 'er out feet-first or her house comes from together."

Mrs Bates knew all about it. A little, wiry one of uncertain age, but very old and wearing a snow-white apron or "brat," as she called it.

"Yes, Will Wilson lived at Number 14 till he died. A sad man, he was, after he'd turned his daughter out of doors. A stern, unbendin' sort, 'e was... And 'er, poor thing, left in the lurch by a man who was courtin' her, and her own father quotin' the Bible to prove how the way of transgressors was hard. So the girl went off somewhere and nobody never saw 'er agen. Old Wilson was sorry when it was too late..."

"Who was the man?" I almost screamed, hardly able to contain myself.

Mrs Bates regarded me suspiciously and her mouth tightened.

"What d'you want to know for?"

"I'm a solicitor trying to trace Miss Wilson," I improvised on the spot, rather cleverly I thought. "There's money for her."

"What does it matter then who *he* was? He'll want none o' thy brass, I can tell you," she replied. "He's made his fortune, and no mistake. Guess that's why he left 'er in the lurch when he found out she were in the fambly way, poor lass. Didn't want no dockside girl for 'is wife...aimed higher nor that..."

"His name…?" I asked chokingly, like poor Punchinello.

I could have wrung her neck in my anguish, but whilst seething inwardly, I managed to be patient. I almost feared that the unkind fates might strike her dead or bear her off, like Elijah, in a heavenly chariot before her secret was out.

"Ware, his name was. Gideon Ware. Now he's *Sir* Gideon Ware and much good may it do him… Why! Whatever's the matter, mister?"

My search successful, my goaded body protested against the spirit which had driven it, without food or drink, through pouring rain, throughout the length and breadth of Hull and I fell fainting across the beautifully clean doorstep of old Mrs Bates.

20

THINGS PAST – II

N ever in my life have I sailed calm seas for long at once. It is as though my very presence is a challenge to the elements or fates, which, for some fortunate ones, leave the waters untroubled for great stretches of life. There has never been any respite for me. Perhaps that is why I contemplate the deeds I have done without a qualm.

I had just nicely accustomed myself to being my own master and a professional man, and was beginning to aspire hopefully towards those higher social spheres in which I intended to move and from which I would choose my wife. Then the whole of my plans were thrown into a turmoil by Dulcie Cherry!

Dulcie Cherry! The name is enough! Where she got it from heaven only knows. In moments of ironical humour I used to call her Dulcinea del Toboso to dazzle her with my learning. She retorted by somehow discovering the origin of the name and, apparently having read Sancho Panza's description of the wench, took it as an amorous compliment and grew coy with me. How she would roll her eyes at me and simper! For she had fine eyes. In fact, she was too fine altogether for my liking. A lovely figure and lush bosom, the latter frequently displayed by gaping blouses or tight jumpers. Her face was pretty and shapely, and her black hair crowned the lot very fittingly. A perfect Carmen! Except that she was stupid. I can't bear stupid people. It spoils the loveliest women for me, just as other men might recoil from ill-kept fingernails, thick ankles, dingy teeth, or a nervous tick. A very Venus herself is repulsive under such disadvantages. Murders have been committed for less.

Dulcie — I shudder as I write the name — Dulcie was the daughter of the woman who "obliged" by cleaning my quarters and answering the doorbell. Mrs Cherry herself was a large, flat-faced, shuffling woman, who had quarters in the basement. Her underground habits gave her features an etiolated look from want of fresh air and light. Her complexion, pitted by some past disease, was powdered to hide the scars and reminded one of the cratered surface of the moon. Her one ambition was to see her lovely daughter settled for life and she was prepared to go to any lengths to achieve it. As it was bound to do, her glassy eye soon fell on me.

I began to find Dulcie about the house more, ostensibly relieving her dropsical mother. The girl worked in a local shop, and as soon as her day's work was done, appeared at the surgery, quite without my consent. She made a dead set at me right away. Her cheeks grew flushed in my presence, her eyes sparkled, her lips became moist and inviting, and her hips undulated voluptuously as she came and went before my eyes. I was the chosen victim and hers was the ritual dance.

How it might have ended I don't know, for in spite of her silly style, her tactics were such as caused the blood to beat in my ears out of sheer desire. I could never have loved her. The competition of the riding school was still too great, but her flesh drew me like a magnet and the one false step between me and destruction might easily have been taken had not Mrs Cherry, in her anxiety, sprung the trap too soon.

She had latterly resorted to mothering me in a most

revolting fashion. She gave me advice about my health, fussily attended to my comforts, told me how the shop keepers cheated me, and spoke her mind concerning my physical and moral welfare. I wanted a nice little wife, she said. Not content with that, she followed up with a bolder card, like a fanatical whist player, who, intent on sweeping the board, plays aces and kings with reckless abandon, forgetting that the trumps of her adversaries are not exhausted.

"My Dulcie's fond of you," she said confidentially one day, in a burst of effrontery inspired by the gin bottle, to which she resorted in times of emergency. And with that, she almost took me by the throat and wrung a proposal from me on the spot.

The pupils of the riding school cantered by as she spoke, and I recoiled speechless, my thoughts in confusion.

She must have sensed my repulsion and all my objections in a brief intuitive flash for, from being a wheedling, fawning match-maker, she suddenly turned into a tiger, defending this time, instead of peddling, her young.

"And why not?" she yelled. "My girl's as good as you any day. And better. Come to that, I wouldn't *allow* her to marry a common shrimp like you. Son of a charwoman and no better than she should be..."

She got no farther. I had her by the throat, choking the life out of her. A red mist engulfed me. I thought only of the insult to my mother.

Mrs Cherry's windpipe was too lost in fat to be closed. She contrived to yell the house down in spite of my efforts. Two waiting patients rushed in and tore us asunder.

It ended in being what looked like a first-class local scandal. And then a strange thing happened. Instead of making a full-dress court affair of it, the police acted as intermediaries between the parties and hushed up the whole business. I gracelessly begged the pardon of Mrs Cherry, paid up the suggested damages for injuries to throat, nerves and pride, and then packed up and left the accursed place for good. Who would patronise a dentist who'd just missed an indictment for attempted murder? Besides, whenever the girls from the riding school met me after that, they stared, put their heads together, whispered and laughed.

"There's that appohling dentist," I overheard one of them say. "Traved to strengle his miftruss."

"Appohling! Ameyzing! Fezzinating! Fentestic! Gawstly! Too, too praceless!" replied her equestrian friends in the language they assumed was cultured, and which at length revolted me so much that I was glad to leave them behind for good.

But here I go, singing my swansong, polishing my periods, airing my new gift of words, as though I had all the time of eternity at my disposal.

Let me now say a word about the strange attitude of the police. The man in charge of the case was one Sergeant Boumphrey. For some reason — later to become clear — he adopted the role of mediator and settled the matter out of court.

I left Follington with little money with which to bless myself, thanks to the abominable Cherries who seemed to know just how much I could afford to pay and wrung it all from me. The practice was worth nothing, for was I not a quack?

There was only one place for me to choose. Westcombe. Sir Gideon Ware, the one who had wronged my mother and imposed on me a life of miserable bastardy, was there. I could not have gone elsewhere, for that evil man drew me as a magnet attracts steel. I would keep him under my eye. The town was growing as a resort and perhaps I could build up a practice in it from scratch. Besides, I'd make Ware pay.

Time presses. I must abandon style and summarise a bit.

I made a good start in Westcombe and soon had enough patients to earn a living. Meanwhile, Sergeant Boumphrey, my benefactor at Follington, turned up here as Chief Constable. Obviously, he had blackmailed Ware into getting him the appointment and, probably, my history was involved in it. I never got to the bottom of it, for I never cultivated Boumphrey's acquaintance. A pompous upstart! But one more reason for caution.

I got on speaking terms with Ware in time, but he never guessed my identity till the last. We first met at the golf club, which I joined for the sake of business. He often insulted me, for my game suffered as soon as I came up against him or played as his partner on those chance occasions when they drew us together in competitions. He once called me a piddling little runt!

It was as much as I could do not to tell him I was a chip off the old block!

I pondered my revenge but deferred it again and again. I could do nothing else but postpone it, for he flourished and was powerful. Short of killing him, there was nothing for it but to bide my time and hope. The drawback of my illegitimacy weighed relentlessly upon me, for I knew no decent girl would want me. At the thought of thus remaining like a hungry waif for ever looking in the cookshop window yet unable to feast on the good things within, I grew like a heavily charged infernal machine, merely requiring the ultimate spark to the fuse to complete its destructive work.

The fire came with the death of my dog.

When Ware thrashed my setter and caused her, in panic, to run under a passing car, it sealed his doom. I said nothing when they told me. I was too stunned, for she was better than any human friend I ever had. Those who love dogs will understand. No doubt, everyone who knew thought me a coward. But I planned more than a public brawl. I would shoot Ware and myself.

Then, suddenly, two surprising things happened. Ware became my patient, and I fell in love with Grace Latrobe.

Ware must have had some idea of making amends for the

dog, for he made an appointment for my professional attentions. When he did this, I bought a book on poisons. I would change the weapons!

As for Grace, I met her through Preedy, a local doctor, who took to me for the reason that we were both starting practices from nothing. One night, in a burst of confidence after a few drinks at the Winter Gardens, Grace sentimentally confessed that she'd never had a father. Illegitimate, too! She suddenly became the key which would unlock the torture chamber of my soul, capable of freeing me from all the pent-up passion, hatred and inferiority there. I took the first chance of telling her I loved her. She discouraged my pleading. I implored almost in tears for just a word or a sign of hope. She confessed that she loved Preedy and had promised to marry him when her divorce came through.

Chronologically the events were:

Death of dog.
Ware made appointment.
Proposed to Grace Latrobe; turned down.
My mind reacted like clockwork:
(a) Kill Ware.
(b) By poison.
(c) Try to secure poison from Preedy, who had a public grievance against Ware, to whom his father's suicide was said to be due. As my successful rival, Preedy should unwittingly cooperate in the destruction of Ware and, if I could manage it, he'd swing for it and leave Grace to me.

My luck took a temporary turn for the better.

Just before Ware was due to keep his appointment, Preedy and I went to the annual dinner at the Roosters' Club. We'd almost drunk ourselves under the table there in past years. To protect myself from a recurrence of this, I went off alcohol altogether, pleading an ulcerated stomach. I saw Preedy home and before handing him over, helpless, to Grace, who was there doing his book-keeping, I stole four grains of strychnine from his stock, helping myself to his keys. In his condition, he didn't know a thing about it.

A few days later, Ware arrived for treatment. I'd thought out a plan. Ware had assisted in it, because when he made the appointment over the phone, he had said I wasn't to tell anyone he was coming. "You're not getting a free advertisement out of me," he said. "So don't broadcast it that you're my dentist. No testimonials till you've proved your worth." That suited me. So much the worse for him.

I planned to suggest a local anaesthetic on the strength of the threat that the job was near the nerve and would hurt. Then, I'd give him adrenalin first, followed by a dose of strychnine, which would kill him later. Where the poison took him didn't matter to me, so long as he was far enough away from Oxford Crescent. Maybe they'd think it was a seizure or a heart attack. In any case, nobody would suspect me. It appears I was too sanguine. The police are clever these days.

When I'd got Ware in the chair and persuaded him to have an injection, I turned coward. Yes, I funked it! I just couldn't give the injection, my hand seemed to lose contact with my brain, my head whirled, and I couldn't go on.

"I'll have to kill the nerve, sir," I managed to say. "I'll put in an arsenic dressing, and perhaps you can call the day after tomorrow again…"

"Damn you, you bungling little duffer," said Ware in his usual blustering fashion. "I've too much on, then. I've a luncheon at one, and at eleven I've to call on Dr Preedy for an injection for these confounded colds I get every autumn."

I pricked up my ears. An injection by Preedy! My very chance. Right into my hands! It was as much as I could do not to *beg* of Ware to come as I'd suggested.

"If you come after you've seen the doctor, I won't take ten minutes," I lied.

"Very well," said Ware. "And see you don't. I'll be here."

All my nervousness vanished. I almost leapt for joy. I took a stiff dose of bromide to steady my nerves just before the appointment and when Ware was next in the chair, I calmly set about my task.

I took out the temporary filling with which I had stuffed his canine tooth. I suggested a slight local anaesthetic again. I injected the adrenalin. As I drew the strychnine into the barrel of the syringe, I felt as light as air. I wanted to shout aloud in triumph. All the time Ware kept his eyes fixed on me as though puzzled about something. I drove the plunger home in the gum. I'd done it! Hastily I stopped the hole in the tooth. He'd be past worrying about his teeth by the time that canine began to ache!

As soon as he had left the room, my nerve cracked. I wished I hadn't done it. I felt sorry for him... But there was another patient being ushered in. An extraction, and he asked for a local anaesthetic! I couldn't have given another injection to save my life. I managed to persuade him to have gas. A fellow called Dashwood, an auctioneer's tout, he was. How I got through it, I don't know. I fumbled the valves of the gas apparatus and didn't give the patient enough. I broke the tooth in the gum and, to end all, the fool recovered himself and rushed from the place howling and spitting blood. All I cared about was, had he seen Ware? No, he hadn't, said my housekeeper, because she'd put Ware in the dining room instead of the waiting room, on account of his being Mayor. I was pleased at first and then I could have screamed. My mother's photograph was in the room where Ware had been, he *must* have recognised it, for it was taken at the time he knew her. Had he guessed who I was? That probably accounted for the queer looks he kept giving me.

Well, the job was done. Ware died in a more spectacular fashion than I could ever have devised. And Preedy looked like being accused of the crime. I thought I was safe until Grace Latrobe called on me and said she knew that I'd stolen the strychnine the night I brought Preedy home drunk! She'd come in, she said, as I was tucking something in the pocket in which the doctor kept his keys. She said she wasn't going to let her lover suffer and would go to the police unless I went myself and at least confessed to taking the poison from Preedy's stock. I couldn't do that. She'd chosen Preedy and would have to suffer. I watched her go home from the upper window of my house. I changed into my golf clothes, took out my clubs and my bike, and was ready to follow her when she came out again. If she spotted me, well, I was just off for a game.

Strangely enough, Grace went to the amusement park. Why, I can't for the life of me guess. I cycled behind her, saw her enter, parked my cycle and clubs behind one of the shows and followed her. I lost her a time or two but found her again. I'd learned to know her hair anywhere. Here, I could get very senti-mental, but there is no time for self-pity now. I saw her go into the House of Nonsense.

I'd parked my bike behind the House of Nonsense and knew there was a back entrance. I went through the little door and eventually found myself in a room full of eccentric mirrors. My own image, pulled about like a piece of tortured India-rubber, confronted me and seemed to reflect my anguished spirit. I hid behind a pillar until Grace arrived. Then I followed her into the darkest room and strangled her, pushing her through a door which led from the place down a chute into the open air. This done, I hurried back. I saw that I was weeping as I again passed those nightmare mirrors. The convex glasses threw back a hideous distortion at which I almost screamed. Around me, the shouts of flappers in the midst of all the Nonsense drowned every sound but their own. I rushed into the open air, stole away on my cycle, rode across the beach to the links and, hiding the machine in a ditch, began to play golf, stopping the first pair of players I met and asking them the time to give myself an alibi. I thought I was safe. I felt *more* safe when first I met Littlejohn!

Littlejohn has neither the sleuth-like appearance of the traditional criminologist, nor the crushing relentlessness of the official detectives of fiction. He looks more like a country gentleman and moves with slow, purposeful ease, as though he's all day to do the job in yet is taking every step with his goal well in mind. A well-groomed, clear-eyed, well-built man of middle age, with a fresh complexion and a close-clipped moustache. I felt my scheme might be proof against him, especially if, as I suspected, Boumphrey would not put all his cards on the table, lest it be discovered how the Chief Constable's path had crossed my own, and his blackmailing of Ware should come to light. Whilst Boumphrey had never, I am sure, disclosed my identity to Sir Gideon, he had nevertheless held me as a trump card to further his plans.

I first met Littlejohn in the long bar of the Winter Gardens, where, for some reason, the efficient and incorruptible Inspector Hazard had led him. I had heard that Boumphrey had called in Scotland Yard right away, and I was on the look-out for their man, for it was to be *Rex v Fenwick* henceforth, and if Littlejohn got the wrong man, Preedy, as I'd planned, Rex had lost, although nobody but I would know it.

At first, seeing him good-humouredly drinking beer at the bar, I thought I was as safe as houses against Littlejohn. I spoke to him and Hazard. I followed him to the Grand Hotel in the darkness, I heard him bidding his wife goodnight, for I was in the next telephone box, and I saw him drink a nightcap of cocoa. Cocoa! I suddenly realised that I was up against someone unusual. I stayed for long outside the hotel, wondering which was his room and what he was doing. As I prepared to depart, a cigarette end fell at my feet like a spent rocket, and I wondered if Littlejohn himself had been watching me from above and had thrown down the gauge in that fashion.

I couldn't work, and I neglected my practice. I followed the Inspector at a distance fascinated by his technique. I kept hovering round him unseen, like a moth which is compelled instinctively to wheel round and round the flame in which it finally perishes. Or, more correctly, I was like the quarry hunted by hounds which, somehow, in the tangle of trails, has got behind, instead of in front of its pursuers.

Littlejohn astonished me one night by even going to the cinema, where I sat behind him and Hazard, trying to overhear their conversation and, for my pains, getting a lot of information about Manchester, of all places, where it seems, Littlejohn started his career and Hazard was shortly being transferred. Nothing was said of the crime I had so skilfully engineered. I would have liked to hear their professional opinion of it.

But later, when Littlejohn called on me, I knew I wasn't as safe as I had imagined. I had already become alarmed by the results of cautiously trailing him round the town, where he seemed interested in a number of local bigwigs and a trio of clergymen. I wanted particularly to know what Father Manfred had told him and resorted to a cunning subterfuge to get the priest to talk.

I had learned that the Catholic priest had been with my father when he died. I was anxious to know whether or not anything had been said at the death. That was a day full of emotion for me. On the one hand, I had to deal with Grace Latrobe; on the other, I *must* know my father's last words.

I pretended to be visiting the church to view the alterations. There, I met Father Manfred and, feigning interest in the dead benefactor of the place, I turned the conversation skilfully to the death of Ware.

"Did he die reconciled to the Church?" I asked Manfred, my mouth dry with anguish and the blood racing through my veins like a boiling torrent.

"Yes," came the answer. "And like David, mourning Absalom, he died with the words 'My son! My son!' on his lips."

And with that, the crafty Jesuit fixed me with his steely, relentless eyes, which seem to bore right into your soul.

Had Ware, I wondered, named his murderer in confession to the priest before his death? If in confession, I was safe, for Manfred's lips would be sealed. Otherwise...

After the inquest on Grace, I began to feel a return of confidence. Littlejohn had kept out of my way, although, unseen, I had hung on his heels every minute I could spare. At night, I followed my man to the Jolly Sailor. There, pretending to eat a meal, which I took from the serving-table and set around me to make it appear that I'd been there some time (fool that I was, I dispelled the myth that I suffered from stomach trouble by choosing lobster in my haste!). I felt that the end had truly come when the idiotic Dashwood started boasting about the mess I'd made of his face. And he *had* met Ware on his way out!

The bolt was shot! I hastened to confess to Littlejohn that Ware had been with me just before the banquet, pretending that I'd not known the police were interested in the dead man's movements and that I had suddenly thought myself guilty of not helping the law with what I knew. The man almost treated my information with levity! Said he'd call to see me about it tomorrow! But I knew in my bones that there would be no letting-up by that cocoa-drinking bulldog. I was truly in the soup but hoped the motive wouldn't come to light.

Next morning, I received the promised visit. He was very efficient in his questioning and kept me to the point, refusing every bait I held out in an effort to find precisely where he was in the course of investigation. He asked for details of the filling I performed on Ware's tooth and brought up the matter of my dog, too. I thought when he went that I'd acquitted myself satisfactorily and had made no slips.

My satisfaction was short-lived. On going to the waiting

room I noticed that the book on Toxicology had been moved. Fool! Why the hell had I left it there and, above all, why hadn't I locked the case securely? I was getting over-confident and had better take care. I took out the book and turned it over and over. Had he suspected anything? I was soon to know.

Hardly had I closed the bookcase and, full of agitation, commenced to make an awful job of a patient's tooth, when Littlejohn was back. He'd discovered in some way or other, that Grace had visited me on the day of her death. I was thoroughly taken aback and scared, although I don't think I showed it. I made excuses and said she'd wanted a tooth filling. I even pretended to consult a card on the file concerning the precise nature of the work. I thought I'd got away with it again, for he seemed satisfied and then, just as he was at the door, he turned and pitched me a body-line ball. He asked me for an alibi on the afternoon of Grace's death! I recited the piece I'd already rehearsed, and he went away, convinced or not, I had no idea.

I was too excited to work anymore that day. I packed off my patient and set about finding out what Littlejohn had been up to. I called on Mottershead, the bookseller, who as soon as I arrived, unwittingly knocked me for six by saying that if I wanted to sell my *Forensic Medicine*, he knew a gent who'd buy it from me for a profit. Yes, the chap had been in a short time ago, asking who'd recently purchased the book. And to complete the terror, a group of old idlers in the gardens greeted me as I passed with the gleeful comment that a fellow had been tracing Grace's movements on the day of her death and they'd told him they had seen her going in my place about noon. How pleased the doddering old fools seemed about it all, staring accusingly with their rheumy lizard's eyes and sucking their toothless gums! I called them a pack of gossiping old dotards and left them with something to talk about for days to come.

In a turmoil of fear, I hurried to the golf links. I wanted to be sure that Littlejohn hadn't deduced anything about my movements at the time of Grace's death. He was there when I arrived! And walking across the fairway, almost retracing my steps from the links to the House of Nonsense! Dashwood, the idiot, almost laid him low with a golf ball. Would that he had! An unseen spectator, I cowered behind a gorse bush on the sixth hole and, I confess, I sweat blood and actually retched with excited fear as I saw what was going on.

What next? I almost feared to follow Littlejohn and Hazard, yet I was now as closely bound to Littlejohn as a *Doppelgänger*, an unseen wraith, until the case ended either with my release or my doom.

A rift appeared in the clouds. The police called on Preedy. Maybe Littlejohn wasn't satisfied about the doctor after all and couldn't make a case against me, so was after Preedy and would bring my schemes to success after all.

All night, I have been writing this account and asking myself what the next step will be...

* * *

ANOTHER DAY, and this time a barren one. I have tried to think what I would do if I were Littlejohn. My brain seems utterly devoid of power and arid of ideas. Wait. Yes. I know what I'd do. Why haven't I thought of it before? Why, I'd try to unearth the past life of my quarry and find out his connection with Ware. I will ring up some old ragbags of spinsters in Follington, who were once friends of my mother. Nothing happens in that town without their long ears hearing it, or their prying eyes spotting it round the lace curtains.

* * *

YES, yes... Oh God! ...yes, yes. Someone has been in Follington, a lawyer or somebody, enquiring about my mother and me. I am lost. I feel like rushing out, button-holing Littlejohn, and asking him to fill in the gaps in my knowledge. Have the doctors discovered the puncture I made in Ware's gum? How went it with Preedy? Has he told them anything which threw light on the theft of strychnine?

Why bother? I am weary of the suspense. My brain is failing as I write. I have had frightful headaches lately. The intense brainstorms which gripped me when I killed Ware and Grace have taken too much vital force from me. Changing for dinner on the night I went to the Jolly Sailor, I grew so mentally limp that a kind of amnesia seized me temporarily and I put on my pyjamas instead of my dinner clothes! Comic enough for a farce, were it not so tragic for me. I have made some awful mistakes in the surgery, too.

Would that I had never set foot in Westcombe or seen its accursed sea! For, I suppose Westcombe owes its evil growth to the sea, which has raised Ware to fortune, too. Like Xerxes, I would fain scourge the waves for the evils they have wrought to me... What am I talking about?

I have had my moments of elation of late, however. I have set the town, nay the whole country, talking about what I've done. Oh, the care with which I planned the crimes; the perfect timing; the dramatic climax of each; the relentless finale! They all give me the pride of an artist whose work sets the public agog and who experiences the satisfaction of self-expression perfectly achieved.

All spoiled by Littlejohn! The whole scheme wrecked, the edifice sent crashing down and I, like Samson, destroyed by the ruins of it, all passion spent. Yes, all passion spent. My mother, to whom I owe all that has been worthwhile in my wretched existence and the only friend I ever could trust. Dead! Gideon Ware, her seducer, my father and the cause of the burdens my mother bore in life and which she bequeathed to me. Dead! Grace Latrobe, who could have made up to me for all the miseries of the past in a future bright with hope. Dead! Mr Hardcastle, my benefactor and friend, who left me his practice and Mrs Cherry. Dead! Thumb, first finger, second, third…and who's the fourth? Yes. Alan Fenwick. Rattle the earth on his coffin. Alan Fenwick. Dead! What more have I to live for? I shall take the way I gave my father. A reparation. Like Smerdyakov in Dostoyevsky's *Crime and Punishment*, having brought vengeance on my mother's betrayer, I can now die. My purpose is accomplished. Since my birth I have been fated for this, driven about like an outcast, a dog on a chain, whining at the free curs who pass him by, who sniff and ignore his howling.

Littlejohn will be sure to call for me tomorrow. I've calculated it all out. A little time to collect his evidence and set his thoughts in order. Then, a warrant and… "Alan Fenwick, I arrest you…" He will not fail me.

Tomorrow he'll call for the last time. At least, I'll get a good-night's sleep before it happens. I shall use morphia tonight. Not a fatal dose, however, for I've planned something better than that…

* * *

LITTLEJOHN IS COMING. He is crossing the square, and he's actually smoking his pipe! At the back of that man's life is the good woman he rings up to bid goodnight when he's away from her. Lucky, happy man…

He's keeping his tryst with me. The syringe.

Adrenalin first. A good dose, as before.

Now the strychnine left over from my lamented father's performance.

I've done it. In the bottom gum.

As Littlejohn strikes the door knocker at the front, I shall go out by the back. To the Winter Gardens, there to die in the arms of a girl, my Solveig, to the music of the dreadful Sid Simmons.

And just before I commence the dance of death, I'll telephone my adversary to let him in at the final curtain.

My pen flows along inspired. I could write for ever. My thoughts take shape in a way which could surely produce a masterpiece.

But I am like the artist to whom inspiration comes as the daylight is fading. He seizes his palette and brushes...but it is already night. Endless night for me...

LITTLEJOHN GOES HOME

M rs Littlejohn removed her spectacles, rubbed her eyes and yawned. She had just finished reading the strange autobiographical document left behind by Fenwick. Her husband was in the habit of bringing home to her many of the queer things he encountered in the course of duty. He enjoyed her comments on them and liked to feel that she shared in his work, even in retrospect.

Littlejohn himself was enjoying his favourite meal of rarebit made in accordance with an ancient recipe bequeathed by Mrs Littlejohn's Grandmother Uprichard. It contained among other things, chopped onions, small supplies of which had arrived in Hampstead that day, and cheese accumulated from the detective's rations unclaimed during his stay at the Grand. Propped against the sugar bowl was a detective story which Littlejohn had bought on Westcombe station and in which he was so engrossed, that he almost believed that the mirage created by the eloquent author was real and he saw himself moving in a new and elegant Scotland Yard far different from the vast building which contained his own shabby quarters.

"This poor chap didn't stand much chance, did he? With his

fixation on the mother who seemed to have completely monop-
olised him, his *idée fixe* concerning his illegitimacy, and his
persecution mania, he was bound to come to grief," said Mrs
Littlejohn turning over the pages of Chateaubriand's *Mémoires*
in which the confessions were interleaved.

"Eh?" said her husband looking over his glasses and marking
his place with his finger. "Beg pardon."

"Fenwick was a terrible introvert. Lived in a tortured world
of his own, didn't he?"

"Oh, yes, yes," said Littlejohn. He always gave his wife the
credit for being right on matters of psychology, for she was a
member of a university extension class conducted by the
refugee psychoanalyst, Professor Bloch of Vienna. "I think he
went mad in the end. Kept following me about and wondering if
I were on his track. All the same, the confession is a bit pathetic,
isn't it?"

"Very sad, Tom. And his choice of book, too.
Chateaubriand's very morbid and introspective, isn't he? ...
Fenwick seemed to admire you, you know. And he envied you,
too."

"I'm not surprised, Letty, after he found I'd got you."

Mrs Littlejohn blushed and began to scan the pages of
Chateaubriand's book. Meanwhile, her husband continued his
meal, spreading on his toast liberal portions of honey supplied
by his friend, the Rev Ethelred Claplady, the enthusiastic
apiarist, whose parish the Inspector had once cleansed of
another mad murderer.

Mrs Littlejohn began to clear away the dishes and to wash
them in the kitchenette. Her husband lighted his pipe, settled in
his armchair, took up his book again and switched on the
wireless.

"Evenin' folks. This is Sid Simmons and His Hot Dogs
broadcastin' to you from the Winter Gardens, Westcombe. Our
first number's a cute arrangement of a waltz by Brahms and

Mick's goin' to sing you the words, 'I've got a Hornet in my Cornet, Baby,' … Okay boys. Give 'em the works…"

It all came out before Littlejohn realised what was happening. He rose to his feet like one stung, and hastily fumbling for the switch, turned off the set.

"I think I'll help you with the washing up, Letty," he said.

Stripping off his jacket he assumed his official apron.

The Case
of the
Famished
Parson

GEORGE BELLAIRS

THE TOWER ROOM

Wednesday, September 4th. The Cape Mervin Hotel was as quiet as the grave. Everybody was "in" and the night-porter was reading in his cubby-hole under the stairs.

A little hunchbacked fellow was Fennick, with long arms, spindleshanks accentuated by tight, narrow-fitting trousers—somebody's cast-offs—and big feet. Some disease had robbed him of all his hair. He didn't need to shave and when he showed himself in public, he wore a wig. The latter was now lying on a chair, as though Fennick had scalped himself for relief.

The plainwood table was littered with papers and periodicals left behind by guests and rescued by the porter from the salvage dump. He spent a lot of his time reading and never remembered what he had read.

Two or three dailies, some illustrated weeklies of the cheaper variety, and a copy of Old Moore's Almanac. A sporting paper and a partly completed football pool form...

Fennick was reading "What the Stars have in Store." He was breathing hard and one side of his face was contorted with concentration. He gathered that the omens were favourable.

Venus and Jupiter in good aspect. Success in love affairs and a promising career...He felt better for it.

Outside the tide was out. The boats in the river were aground. The light in the tower at the end of the break-water changed from white to red and back at minute intervals. The wind blew up the gravel drive leading from the quayside to the hotel and tossed bits of paper and dead leaves about. Down below on the road to the breakwater you could see the coke glowing in a brazier and the silhouette of a watchman's cabin nearby.

The clock on the Jubilee Tower on the promenade across the river struck midnight. At this signal the grandfather clocks in the public rooms and hall began to chime all at once in appalling discord, like a peal of bells being 'fired.' The owner of the hotel was keen on antiques and bric-a-brac and meticulously oiled and regulated all his clocks himself.

Then, in mockery of the ponderous timepieces, a clock somewhere else cuckooed a dozen times. The under-manager, who had a sense of humour, kept it in his office, set to operate just after the heavy ones. Most people laughed at it. So far, the proprietor hadn't seen the point.

Fennick stirred himself, blinked his hairless eyelids, laid aside the oracle, stroked his naked head as though soothing it after absorbing so much of the future, and rose to lock the main door. Then he entered the bar.

The barmaid and cocktail-shaker had been gone almost an hour. Used glasses stood around waiting to be washed first thing in the morning. The night-porter took a tankard from a hook and emptied all the dregs from the glasses into it. Beer, stout, gin, whisky, vermouth... A good pint of it... One hand behind his back, he drank without stopping, his prominent Adam's-apple and dewlaps agitating, until it was all gone. Then he wiped his mouth on the back of his hand, sighed with satisfaction, selected and lighted the largest cigarette-end from one of the many ash-trays scattered about and went off to his next job.

It was the rule that Fennick collected all shoes, chalked their room-numbers on their soles and carried them to the basement for cleaning. But he had ways of his own. He took a large newspaper and his box of cleaning materials and silently dealt with the footwear, one by one, as it stood outside the doors of the bedrooms, spreading the paper to protect the carpet.

Fennick started for the first floor. Rooms 1, 2, 3, 4 and 5, with the best views over the river and bay. His gait was jaunty, for he had had a few beers before finally fuddling himself with the dregs from the bar. He hummed a tune to himself.

> *Don't send my boy to prizzen,*
> *It's the first crime wot he's done...*

He tottered up the main staircase with his cleaning-box and stopped at the first door.

Number 1 was a single room. Once it had been double, but the need for more bathrooms had split it in two. Outside, on the mat, a pair of substantial handmade black shoes. Fennick glided his two brushes and polishing-cloth over them with hasty approval. They belonged to Judge Tennant, of the High Court. He came every year at this time for a fishing holiday. He tipped meticulously. Neither too much not too little. Yet you didn't mind. You felt justice had been done when you got it.

Fennick had been sitting on his haunches. Now and then he cocked an ear to make sure that nobody was stirring. He moved like a crab to Number 2 gently dragging his tackle along with him.

This was the best room, with a private bath. Let to a millionaire, they said. It was a double, and in the register the occupants had gone down as Mr and Mrs Cuhady. All the staff, from the head waiter down to the handyman who raked the gravel round the hotel and washed down the cars, knew it was a lie. The head waiter was an expert on that sort of thing. With thirty years' experience in a dining-room you can soon size-up a situation.

That was how they knew about the honeymoon couple in Number 3, too. Outside their door was a pair of new men's brogues and some new brown suede ladies' shoes. "The Bride's travelling costume consisted of ... with brown suede shoes..." Fennick knew all about it from reading his papers in the small hours.

There were five pairs of women's shoes outside Number 2. Brown leather, blue suede, black and red tops, light patent leather, and a pair with silk uppers. All expensive ones.

Five pairs in a day! Fennick snarled and showed a nasty gap where he had lost four teeth. Just like her! He cleaned the brown, the black-and-red and the patent uppers with the same brushes for spite. The blue suede he ignored altogether. And he spat contemptuously on the silk ones and wiped them with a dirty cloth.

Mr Cuhady seemed to have forgotten his shoes altogether. That was a great relief! He was very particular about them. Lovely hand-made ones and the colour of old mahogany. And you had to do them properly, or he played merry hell. Mr Cuhady had blood-pressure and "Mrs" Cuhady didn't seem to be doing it any good. The magnate was snoring his head off. There was no other sound in Number 2. Fennick bet himself that his partner was noiselessly rifling Cuhady's pocket-book...

He crawled along and dealt with the honeymoon shoes. They weren't too good. Probably they'd saved-up hard to have their first nights together at a posh hotel and would remember it all their lives. "Remember the Cape Mervin ... ?" Fennick, sentimental under his mixed load of drinks, spat on all four soles for good luck... He crept on.

Two pairs of brogues this time. Male and female. Good ones, too, and well cared for. Fennick handled them both with reverence. A right good job. For he had read a lot in his papers about one of the occupants of Room 4. An illustrated weekly had even interviewed him at Scotland Yard and printed his picture.

On the other side of the door were two beds, separated by a table on which stood a reading-lamp, a travelling-clock and two empty milk glasses. In one bed a good-looking, middle-aged woman was sitting-up, with a dressing-gown round her shoulders, reading a book about George Sand.

In the other a man was sleeping on his back. On his nose a pair of horn-rimmed spectacles; on the eiderdown a thriller had fallen from his limp hand. He wore striped silk pyjamas and his mouth was slightly open.

The woman rose, removed the man's glasses and book, drew the bedclothes over his arms, kissed him lightly on his thinning hair, and then climbed back into bed and resumed her reading. Inspector Littlejohn slept on...

Fennick had reached the last room of the block. Number 5 was the tower room. The front of the Cape Mervin Hotel was like a castle. A wing, a tower, the main block, a second tower, and then another wing. Number 5 was in the left-hand tower. And it was occupied at the time by the Bishop of Greyle and his wife.

As a rule there were two pairs here, too. Heavy, brown serviceable shoes for Mrs Bishop; boots, dusty, with solid, heavy soles and curled-up toes, for His Lordship. Tonight there was only one pair. Mrs Greyle's. Nobody properly knew the bishop's surname. He signed everything "JC Greyle" and they didn't like to ask his real name. Somebody thought it was Macintosh.

Fennick was so immersed in his speculations that he didn't see the door open. Suddenly looking up he found Mrs. Greyle standing there in a blue dressing-gown staring down at him.

The night-porter hastily placed his hand flat on the top of his head to cover his nakedness, for he'd forgotten his wig. He felt to have a substantial thatch of hair now, however, and every hair of his head seemed to rise.

"Have you seen my husband?" said Mrs Greyle, or Macintosh, or whatever it was. "He went out at eleven and hasn't returned."

Fennick writhed from his haunches to his knees and then to his feet, like a prizefighter who has been down.

"No, mum ... I don't usually do the boots this way, but I'm so late, see?"

"Wherever can he be ... ? So unusual..."

She had a net over her grey hair. Her face was white and drawn. It must have been a very pretty face years ago... Her hands trembled as she clutched her gown to her.

"Anything I can do, mum?"

"I can't see that there is. I don't know where he's gone. The telephone in our room rang at a quarter to eleven and he just said he had to go out and wouldn't be long. He didn't explain..."

"Oh, he'll be turnin' up. P'raps visitin' the sick, mum."

Fennick was eager to be off. The manager's quarters were just above and if he got roused and found out Fennick's little cleaning dodge, it would be, as the porter inwardly told himself, Napooh!

It was no different the following morning, when the hotel woke up. The bishop was still missing.

At nine o'clock things began to happen.

First, the millionaire sent for the manager and raised the roof.

His shoes were dirty. Last night he'd put them out as usual to be cleaned. This morning he had found them, not only uncleaned, but twice as dirty as he'd left them. In fact, muddy right up to the laces. He demanded an immediate personal interview with the proprietor. Somebody was going to get fired for it...

"Mrs" Cuhady, who liked to see other people being bullied

and pushed around, watched with growing pride and satisfaction the magnate's mounting blood-pressure...

At nine-fifteen they took the bishop's corpse to the town morgue in the ambulance. He had been found at the bottom of Bolter's Hole, with the tide lapping round his emaciated body and his head bashed in.

The first that most of the guests knew of something unusual was the appearance of the proprietor in the dining-room just after nine. This was extraordinary, for Mr Allain was a lazy man with a reputation for staying in bed until after ten.

Mr Allain, a tall fat man and usually imperturbable, appeared unshaven and looking distracted. After a few words with the head waiter, who pointed out a man eating an omelette at a table near the window, he waddled across the room.

They only got bacon once a week at the Cape Mervin and Littlejohn was tackling an omelette without enthusiasm. His wife was reading a letter from her sister at Melton Mowbray who had just had another child.

Mr Allain whispered to Littlejohn. All eyes in the room turned in their direction. Littlejohn emptied his mouth and could be seen mildly arguing. In response, Mr Allain, who was half French, clasped his hands in entreaty. So, Littlejohn, after a word to his wife, left the room with the proprietor...

"Something must have happened," said the guests one to another.

Join the
GEORGE BELLAIRS
READERS' CLUB

And get your next
George Bellairs Mystery free!

When you sign up, you'll receive:

1. A free classic Bellairs mystery, *Corpses in Enderby*;

2. Details of Bellairs' new publications and the opportunity to get copies in advance of publication; and,

3. The chance to win exclusive prizes in regular competitions.

Interested?

It takes less than a minute to join. Just go to

www.georgebellairs.com

to sign up, and your free eBook will be sent to you.

Made in United States
North Haven, CT
24 May 2022

19489523R00148